A REASON TO BELIEVE

A Reason To Believe

By Major Mitchell

Shalako Press
Oakdale, CA

A REASON TO BELIEVE

This is a work of fiction.
All characters and events portrayed in this book are fictional, and any
resemblance to real people is purely coincidental.

For information contact: Shalako Press
P.O. Box 371, Oakdale, CA 95361-0371
http://www.shalakopress.com

ISBN:978-0-9798898-3-7

Cover Artist: Jinger Heaston
Editor: Judith Mitchell

PRINTED IN THE UNITED STATES OF AMERICA

Dedication

We tip our Stetson to Kaila Mussell, the only lady to accomplish what my character in this book dreams of doing.

Acknowledgments

This book is a combined effort of many people. We would like to thank Kelly Phillips, Josie Costa, Melody Groves, The Oakdale Saddle Club, and the several other people who read the manuscript, caught the author's mistakes, and offered their input.

A big thanks to Sue Harbison for allowing our daughter, Debbi, to photograph her and Easy for our book cover.

Thanks to Easy's mom, Karen Lawrence, for allowing us to borrow Easy for our afternoon photo shoot.

Most of all, hugs and kisses to Major's wife and partner, Judy, whose editing and ideas always turns our scribbles into something readable.

A REASON TO BELIEVE

"Because the Saddle Club says you can't and they own the arena, that's why." Harold Swaim gave me a nod and grinned. "You ought to feel happy they're gonna let you ride at all." We were standing in the mud behind the announcer's booth arguing, as a continuous line of people began filling the rodeo grounds.

"Well why wouldn't they? I'm just as good as any of the guys," I snapped.

"That's debatable. I've seen you ride, and I'll admit you're not half-bad. But it doesn't make any difference how good you are. You're not a PRCA member and..."

"I'm a WPRCA member," I said, cutting him off.

"Maybe so. But you're still not a PRCA member, and the board says they're not gonna let you compete against the men riding saddle broncs, and that's final. What's more, they couldn't if they wanted to. It's against the rules. You know that as well as I do, Margie. You've been rodeoing since you were six or seven." He took a deep breath and exhaled slowly before continuing.

"Now, they're willing to let you ride exhibition, but your score won't be official, and you won't be going against the men."

"Ugh! That's not fair, Harold, and you know it! They're just scared I might beat some of their precious men!"

"It might not be fair, and I don't know whether or not they're thinking you might beat some of the men. You'd have to do some fancy riding to beat the likes of J. C., or Bobby Mote, or Terry Walker…"

"I can," I said, cutting him off.

"Maybe you can. That remains to be seen. The thing is you're getting your chance to prove it. You're just not getting scored or paid.

"Look, Margie," he added after a long minute, "Kaila Mussell's the only woman that's been able to do what you're asking, and she had to prove herself in Canada before coming to the U. S. The fact is, I don't know why you're so intent on riding saddle broncs. From what I hear, you've been doing pretty well riding bareback in the women's circuit. Why not be content with being one of best women?"

"Because I want to be the best, period. Why can't you see that," I said, tossing my arms in the air.

"You're already one of the best, knuckle-head! You're the one who can't understand it."

"I'm one of the best *women riders*, Mr. Swaim. You said so yourself. I don't want to be just another *woman rider*, or even the best *woman rider*. I want to be the best rider period, and that includes everybody…even men."

"Okay, you little spitfire, I get your drift. Now, you've got your chance to show how good you are right here in Oakdale, in front of people you grew up with. Go out there and prove it."

"Alright, I think I will," I said with a grin. "It took them long enough to make up their minds. What horse are they going to let me have?"

Harold dug his fingers inside his shirt pocket before handing me a slip of paper. "You drew Irish."

"Irish?"

"Yeah, Irish. Don't tell me you've got a problem with that also."

"No…well, yeah. He's one of the *C & M* horses, and I work at the *C & M*, remember? I knew Mable had struck a deal with The Flying U to use her animals in their rodeos, but I didn't think they'd be using them here in Oakdale."

"Well, they are…several of them, including that bull of hers. What's the problem?"

"I know that horse, Harold."

"That ought to make it easy for you to look good," he said with a chuckle.

"Yeah, and everybody will be saying exactly that. How about seeing if I can't trade with someone? Maybe even get a chance to ride Crescent?"

"Crescent?" He burst into a belly-splitting laugh.

"Yes, Crescent. He's one of the best, isn't he?"

"He's one of the meanest, I grant you that. He's stomped a mud hole through half the riders on the circuit. No, Barry drew Crescent. You get Irish."

"Barry? Give me a break," I yelled. "He'll never be able to stay with Crescent. Besides, he'll contaminate a good horse! Put him on Irish and let me have Crescent."

"Nope," Harold shook his head, "you know how it works, Margie. You're lucky to be riding in the first place, and you'll ride Irish, or not at all. You should've been here when the board held the drawing, if you wanted to argue."

"Well, I couldn't help it, so I'm arguing now. I protest."

"You're too late. The names of the riders and their horses have been given to the judges. You can lodge a written protest, but it won't change a thing. You're still riding exhibition, and you drew Irish."

"But I've been begging for a chance to ride with the guys for years, and when I get my chance, they give me is a glorified barrel-racer to compete on."

"Irish is far from being a barrel-racer, and I personally think he's too much of a horse for you to be on."

"Ah! I can't believe you said that!" I gave him my *go to blazes* glare and he grinned.

"Look," he said with a chuckle, "I don't have any say in which horse any rider gets. I wish I did. Just be happy they're letting you ride with the men, even if it is an exhibition. They could be insisting you go back to the women's circuit, or barrel-race with Marline."

"This wouldn't have anything to do with you being scared I might show Barry up, would it?"

"You know better'n that." Harold's smile vanished. "I'm the one reason they even considered your request in the first place. You being a girl, or breaking your engagement to my son, doesn't even figure into the situation. I kind of hoped you would be grateful I stuck my neck out, even though I think it's a blamed fool idea." He spun on his heel and stormed toward the arena.

"Sorry, I didn't mean it," I yelled, but he either didn't hear, or was too angry to care. Harold Swaim was one of the nicest men ever, and I've often wished I could switch places with Barry. Barry would fit right in with my old man. They could sit around drinking beer and talking crap all they wanted. And I knew I'd make Harold a better daughter, than Barry did a son.

But drawing a horse that Mable Burris had raised from a colt was in keeping with the way my day had started. It began by my having a big argument with Mom and Dad over something so stupid, I couldn't remember why it started. But I remember slamming the door and screaming I hoped they both died and burned in hell. Then it rained.

Now, as a rule, I like a little California rain, because it's rare and never lasts too long. But mud and bronc-busting don't mix well, and fighting with my parents meant they were not going to watch me ride, let alone let me use the truck, or give me a lift to the Oakdale Saddle Club Arena. It also meant I had to walk two miles carrying my grip. Then, wouldn't you know it? This shower turned into a gully-washer, and didn't quit until I had reached the parking lot. While my hat had kept my head dry, I had to wade through mud toward the corrals, late and soaked to my skin, with about an inch of mud adding to the weight of my boots.

"What's the matter? Don't think you can handle Irish?" I jumped as Barry Swaim swatted me on the butt.

"What…? You…" I took a swing at him, but he laughed and danced easily out of my reach. "Where the hell'd you come from?"

"I was cleaning the horse trailer and heard you arguing with the old fart. You actually think he had something to do with me drawing Crescent, don't you? Fat chance. He doesn't even like me. Besides, I'm a better rider and stand more of a chance staying with Crescent than you ever would. My name's in the top twenty, while you're not even listed. No one even knows who Marjorie Green is, unless they happen to live around here."

"The only reason I'm not listed is because I'm a girl!"

"Well, you're that alright." He snorted. "But you're also a lousy bronc-buster who hasn't won anything all year."

"I've stayed my eight seconds riding the women's circuit more times than you have."

"I guess so, since I've never ridden the women's circuit." He laughed. "But my grandmother could hang on the nags you guys ride."

"Kiss my…." I caught myself as Marline Dickerson appeared with two small children in tow. They stopped beside the trailer Barry had been cleaning and stared as Barry continued.

"Drop your pants, and I just might." He ducked away laughing as I took another swing. I watched him push past Marline and the kids, before kicking a bale of straw.

"Oh, Jesus!" I said, hopping on one foot. I had no more than plopped down on the bale, thinking I might have broken my toe, when the little towheaded boy pulled away from Marline and dove into my lap.

"Mommie! Mommie!" he yelled, wrapping both arms around my neck.

"That's not Mommie. Silly!" The girl began tugging at the boy, but her efforts only started him crying as he clung to my neck. Marline stood gawking like she'd been struck with a stupid-stick.

"It's okay," I said, and wrapped my arms around the boy. The girl stopped her tugging as a hunk of a dark-haired man

13

appeared behind Marline and stopped to stare. He gawked like Marline for a long minute then smiled, and Christ Almighty, he was the prettiest man I'd ever seen.

"Donnie thinks she's Mommie, Daddy," the little girl said, taking one of the man's hands.

Figures, I felt my heart sink. The good ones are always married. In fact, most of the good men I'd known were not only married, but old enough to be my father. Men like Harold Swaim and Chuck Burris. Chuck's the *C* in the *C & M Stables*, where I work. Anyway, for a fleeting second, I thought I'd like meeting the incredible hunk with dark-brown hair and million-dollar smile. But it was plain as the mud on my size seven Durangos, that *Daddy* had a wife somewhere. She was probably waiting for him that very minute somewhere in the stands. It didn't take long for me to picture her as some bitchy bleach-blond, with makeup thick enough to plow a cornfield in. The hunk was more than likely tending their kids, because she didn't want to mess up her forty-dollar manicure.

"I'm sorry," the hunk said, scooping the boy into his arms. "Come on son, let's leave the lady alone." He took a couple of steps backward as his face flushed. "Sorry," he repeated.

"No problem." I shrugged and grabbed a stick laying near the bale to scrape my boots with. When I glanced up, he was still staring.

"You want something?" I felt my own face flush and turned back to the Durangos.

"Ah, no," he said, clearing his throat.

"The way you're staring, I thought maybe you wanted to say something."

"No."

I glanced up again as he shook his head and backed away. Marline suddenly came out of whatever daze she'd been in.

"Oh, I'm sorry," she giggled, "Margie, I'd like you to meet our new pastor, Reverend Gardner. Pastor Gardner, this is my best friend ever, Marjorie Green."

"Pleased to meet you, Marjorie," he said, extending a hand for me to shake. "Mind if I call you Margie?"

"No," I said, wiping my palm against my jeans before standing to take his hand. "It's better than what most people call me."

"You'll have to excuse Donnie. You do look something like his mother." He shifted the boy in his arms and smiled.

"No problem. I thought it was kinda cute myself. You've got a real pretty family, Reverend," I said, and touched the boy's nose with my finger.

"Don...Donald Ray Gardner, but I'd rather you call me Don."

"Okay, Don," I said with a nod. It was all I could do to keep from laughing. Reverend Donald Ray Gardner had a son named Donnie? Yeah, right. The boy's name was more than likely Donald Ray, the same as his father's. If his parents had their way, he would probably grow up to be Reverend Donald Ray Gardner the second. Made me wonder which one had stuck the boy with that title. The Reverend, or his snooty wife?

"I'm Caroline." I felt a small hand tugging on mine.

"Well, Carol, I'm pleased to meet you." I squatted to stare into her face. She had crystal blue eyes and small freckles across her nose. Her hair was the same color as her brother's, only slightly lighter than my own, which made me think I might be wrong about their mother. She was probably the genuine article, instead of a bottle-blond, seeing as their dad had dark hair.

"You can call me Margie."

"Okay." She clung to my hand as I stood.

"Margie comes to church with me once in awhile, when I can talk her into it," Marline was saying.

"Well, perhaps between both of us, we can talk her into coming more often."

"Maybe, but don't count on it. I work most Sundays and sleep as late as I can on the others."

"What were you and Barry arguing about," Marline said.

"Mainly, because he snuck up from behind and swatted

me on the butt. But what really got me ticked-off, was his needling that I drew Irish, while he got Crescent."

"There's nothing wrong with Irish. He's a pretty horse. I love him," Marline said, with a shrug.

"Yeah, that's just the problem. We both know Irish, and see him nearly every day. He's Mable's horse. I groom, feed and exercise him. He loves me, Marline. He ain't gonna buck when I climb on his back."

"Excuse me," Reverend Gardner said with a laugh. "Did I hear you say *buck*?"

"Yeah, why?"

"Why would you want your horse to buck?"

I stared at him a long minute before Marline did the explaining.

"Margie doesn't barrel-race like I do, Pastor. She rides broncs."

"You what?" It only took a second for him to burst out laughing, and I felt the blood rush to my head.

"I ride broncs. You got a problem with that?"

"No, no. It's just that…," he looked me up and down, "you're so small and pretty. I just thought…"

"You just naturally thought I would be *Barrel-Racing*, is that it? Or, maybe *Mutton-Bustin'*, or competing in the *Boot-Scramble* with the children? How about *Rodeo Queen*? Would that fit the image?" I was trying hard to sound offended, but watching him squirm caused a grin to creep across my face.

"Margie," Marline warned.

"No, it's just that…I don't know what I thought. It took me by surprise. It seems like such a dangerous sport, I didn't think many girls would be interested in it. Especially ones like you."

"Like me? What about me?"

"Nothing. You're not going to let me out of this one, are you?" He laughed. "Just let me say, I'm sorry."

"You ought to apologize to Marline also. Barrel-racing is dangerous. Girls get hurt all the time, and for your information, the Rodeo Queen is a barrel-racer."

"Okay, I give up. I surrender." He held one hand high in the air. "I have been chastised ladies, and you have my respect. I wish you both success."

"There's no doubt Marline will win. She's real good, and she's riding Buster. But there isn't much use in my even climbing into the chute. They're not going to give me a score, because I'm a girl, and the PRCA doesn't really like girls competing against men."

"I'm sorry, what is the PRCA," he asked.

"The Professional Rodeo Cowboy's Association. Anyway, I doubt that Irish will even buck when I climb on his back," I said with a shrug.

"Well, look on the bright side," he said, giving me a million-dollar grin. "If your horse doesn't buck as hard as the rest, there's less chance of you getting hurt."

"I did it again, didn't I?" he added after a long minute.

"Don't pay any attention to him, Carol," I said, holding the girl's cheeks in my palms. "Girls can do anything boys can, and most of the time, do it better. I'm going to prove to your dad, and everyone else, I can ride as good as any of man. Just watch me."

Chapter 2

"Aw, too bad," PRCA Rodeo Announcer Chad Nicholson's voice crackled over the loudspeaker. Casey Evans was covered with mud as he limped toward the gate. His ride had lasted only six seconds. He cast an angry glance toward the horse bucking around the arena and kicking mud against the Fireside Dodge sign decorating one of the chutes. "Folks, give Casey a big round of applause. It'll be the only pay he will receive today."

The sun was peeking through the clouds and the stands were three-fourths filled. The line of those waiting to get in extended into the parking lot. Bad weather had never put a damper on the true cowboy spirit. Gloria Rodriguez, this year's reigning queen, claimed that several thousand people had lined the streets during this morning's downpour to watch the parade. Now they were here, willing to brave the wet seats and watch their favorite sport, knowing there was a chance of more rain.

"Gonna be a slow arena today, ain't it," I said, as I leaned into the railing to watch. There were only four more riders before my number, and I was hoping to prepare myself for whatever might happen once the gate flew open.

"Slow ain't the word for it," Chuck Burris said, giving me a sideways glance. "Dangerous is more like it. Watch ol' Terry here," he added, as the Budweiser chute flew open. A black and brown mustang named *Paper Tiger* burst into the arena, snorting, kicking and bucking like a demon. Texas Terry Walker rocked in the saddle and spurred, looking like a true champion. Then, four seconds into his ride the mustang slipped

18

and tossed him head-over-teakettle into the mud. The horse never actually went down, but the unexpected move had caused Terry to be thrown.

"See that," Chuck said.

"Yeah, so?"

"Well, ya better learn, girl. This ain't gonna be no ordinary ride. You've gotta expect the unexpected."

"Now, how do I do that? How am I gonna expect something, if I don't expect it?"

"You just gotta...that's all. Now, come on. Only three more before you're up." He tossed his cigarette into the mud as Chad's voice boomed over the loudspeaker.

"Turn your attention toward the Fireside Dodge gate, folks, because you're about to see one of Oakdale's local, home-grown boys. Now, I'm kinda partial to this cowboy, because he happens to be the son of our good friend, Harold Swaim. I was over visiting the Swaims a couple of nights ago, and I'll tell you what, Harold's wife, Betty, can cook some of the best fried chicken you'll ever sink your teeth into. Let's just hope her cooking has caused her son to grow up big and strong, because he's drawn one of the orneriest, meanest critters to ever throw a cowboy inside any arena. And here he is folks, Barry Swaim, riding Crescent."

"Wait," I grabbed Chuck's arm as the gate flew open, "I wanna watch this."

Crescent only made two bucking jumps toward the center of the arena before going into the crescent shape that had given him his name. He leaped some four feet into the air with his back arched toward the sky, dislodging Barry from the saddle, then turned toward the left as he came down. Barry met the saddle crossways, with feet pointing toward the stands, and head toward the judges as Crescent gave another giant buck. Barry looked like he'd been propelled from a cannon as he sailed through the air, flapping his arms. He landed in the mud with a splat, near where we were standing.

"Aw, too bad. Folks, give Barry a round of applause. It's the only pay he'll be getting today," Chad said.

There were as many people laughing as were clapping, and Barry didn't like it any as he stumbled to retrieve his hat. But it *was* funny, with him looking like a chicken trying to fly. He gave the crowd an angry glare before leaving.

"That's the horse you wanted to ride?"

"Yeah," I said, giving a sideways glance toward Reverend Gardner. He and his children were seated in the stands next to where Chuck and I had been standing. "I'll draw him one of these days. Just wait and see."

"Good Lord!" he said with a laugh.

"I will." My comment only made him laugh harder. "You got a problem, or what?"

"No," he composed himself, slightly, "I'll come visit and pray with you in the hospital."

I took an angry puff off the Camel that had burned itself to the filter and tossed it into the mud. I gave him one last glare before heading toward the Western Warehouse chute.

The next two riders did much better. Bobby Mote from Redmond, Oregon, scored an eighty-one on a mare called *Painted Lady*, and J. C. Selvester from Red Bluff completed his ride for a score of seventy. The knot inside my stomach lessened as I watched J. C.'s score on the Skoal scoreboard. I grabbed the top railing, then I paused as Chuck hooked a strap to one of the stirrups.

"Wait a minute. What the heck is this thing?" I let go of the railing and tugged at the stirrup.

"That's the hobbles." He ran the strap under Irish's belly and hooked it onto the right stirrup, holding both stirrups in place at the horse's side.

"Yeah, I know they're hobbles. Take 'em off."

"I can't. The board insisted on you using stirrup-hobbles during the ride," Chuck said.

"I don't care what they said. You know how dangerous those things are? I won't be able to rock, and Irish will shake me to pieces. I won't even be able to spur like I'm supposed to."

"Yeah, I know all that," Chuck nodded, "and believe me, it wasn't my idea. I argued some myself, but they think it will be safer, and they said either you use the hobbles, or you don't ride. What's it gonna be? Better make up your mind right quick. They're waiting on you."

"Oh, alright," I said, and climbed up on the railing to stare down at Irish's back. He was a beautiful coal-black mustang, with more muscle per square inch than most horses dream of having. There was no doubt he could be dangerous. An animal like that could kill a grown man in a matter of seconds, if he had a mind to. *Okay, Margie, you got what you asked for. You've ridden him before at the stables. Quit shaking, climb on and take charge.*

My only complaint about riding Irish was, I knew him too well. He'd become like a pet to me, if you can imagine having a thousand-pound man-hating pet. But as I was saying, Irish might have been supplied by The Flying U Rodeo Company, but he belonged to Chuck's wife, Mable, and I worked at their ranch. I washed and groomed Irish. I exercised and gave him treats. I had used him as a practice horse, and ridden him more times than I could count. He would come running to the edge of his corral to greet me when I arrived at the stables. The last time I'd ridden him at the C&M, he didn't even buck, and that was my biggest worry. A horse that doesn't buck well can hurt your score as bad as being thrown. I mentioned his not bucking the day it happened, and Chuck reminded me that I'd left the flank strap off. That's the fleece-lined strip that hangs loose around the horse's flank, causing him to buck. Of course it was on this day, and there was no doubt in my mind he would throw the first man who got onto his back. There was also the possibility he might kick my brains out. You can't really know how an animal is going to react, until they do whatever it is they are going to do. There was also the wet arena to contend with.

Irish glance toward me and snorted, then gave a friendly nod as I climbed into the saddle and wrapped the braided cotton rope rein tightly around my gloved hand.

"Aw, come on, don't be like that. Can't you even get into the spirit," I said, patting his neck. He bobbed his head up and down and snorted.

"Yeah, that's talking. Let's have some fun!" I jammed my hat down tight and readied myself. If this were a real ride, the judges would be judging Irish the same as they would me. A rider can stay in the saddle all day and not score a single point, if the horse doesn't perform. But there's a million ways you can have a good horse and not score. Of course, none of that really mattered, since they insisted on my using hobbled stirrups, and I wouldn't be receiving a real score.

Normally, they judge a rider on how well he sits the horse. He's got to keep both feet in the stirrups at all times, and begin the ride with his spurs above the bronc's shoulders in order to give the horse the advantage when the chute opens. Then, the rider's got to synchronize his spurring to the animal's bucking in order to receive a high score.

The best riders start spurring with their feet way up on the bronc's shoulders, then sweep to the back of the saddle as the horse bucks. Then, they have to snap their feet back to the horse's neck a split second before the animal's front hooves hit the ground. Believe me, it isn't easy, and you can get disqualified for any number of reasons, like touching the animal or equipment with your free hand, or if either foot slips out of the stirrup, or if you drop the rope, or even if you fail to have your feet in the proper *mark out* position when the gate opens. It's even harder for me, being a short-legged girl, because I have trouble raking all the way to the cantle during the bucking.

I could see Marline's brother, Gary, watching as I positioned myself in the saddle. He had his six-foot-four frame propped against the railing next to some giggly blond with red lipstick, hip-hugger shorts and a cropped top. She latched onto his arm as several other tennis-shoed, hip-hugging, cropped-top cowgirls joined them. I had my doubts that any of them knew a cotton-picking thing about horses or the rodeo. The only thing they cared about knowing was Gary. My mind snapped back to what I was doing as the loudspeaker crackled.

"Okay, folks. Up next out of the Western Warehouse chute is a lovely young lady who is a local favorite, Miss Marjorie Green. That's right men, she's single, pretty, and a real cowgirl, who works for the C&M Stables out of Oakdale. She's been making quite a name for herself on the Women's Circuit, but that hasn't seemed to satisfy her. She's been begging quite some time now, for a chance to compete with the men riding saddle broncs on the PRCA circuit like Kaila Mussell. Well, I reckon she batted those pretty blue eyes at the right person this time, 'cause she's finally getting her wish.

"Now this will be an exhibition ride, and her score won't actually be counted, but we'll all get to see how this young lady can handle herself. The only trouble is, she's drawn one of the biggest, meanest, critters in the lot. It doesn't get any better'n that folks. And here she is, Marjorie Ann Green, on Irish."

"Ready," Chuck said. I gave a nod and the gate flew open.

Irish bolted from the chute with a snort, then shot into the air and came down stiff-legged. My teeth clacked as pain shot down my spine, making me believe I'd just shrunk an inch. Somehow, between the friendly snort and nod inside the stall, and the opening of the gate, Irish had gotten into the rodeo spirit. I had no idea if it was the roar of the crowd or my little pep talk, but I suddenly found myself on top of a thousand pound beast, acting as though he wanted to kill me. I reminded myself it was what I'd wanted…sort of.

"Yeah!" I screamed and waved my left arm in rhythm with Irish's bucking. Let me tell you something about bronc riding. You don't hear the crowd, and mostly you don't see a thing. Or, you'd better not see anything, except the neck and head of the horse you're riding. That's something I'd learned the hard way. You take one glance anywhere else, and that's the way you're headed. I must've gotten thrown ten or twenty times before Chuck taught me that simple rule. Forget everything else and watch your own horse. And I was doing just that, until Irish lost his footing.

Chuck said later that Irish had leaped into the air, looking pretty much like Crescent, before his front legs went out from under him. All I knew was, the horse let out a loud grunt as he fell across my right leg. I can remember getting punched by bigger girls in high school and kicked in the ribs by more than one animal, but I don't recall anything hurting as much as my leg being crunched between the muddy arena and saddle. I guess the only good thing was that Irish didn't break or tear a thing. I almost wish he had, because he jumped up scared, and ran across the arena kicking and snorting like he'd just been released out of the chute, with my foot caught in the stirrup, being held firm by the stupid hobbles. The pain from the initial jolt felt like he had ripped my leg off from the knee down. Then, he spun to the left, dragging me under his belly with his rear hooves sweeping past my face. He turned again, causing me to roll and twist my leg. Everything went blank as the pain hit me. I came to while they were placing me on the stretcher. Chuck and Mable were staring down at me, and the arena was hushed. I could see people standing as the paramedics strapped and buckled me in.

"Where's my hat?" I don't know why I said it, but Chuck burst out laughing.

"Here's you're danged hat. It's all covered with mud, and Irish stomped it flat."

He was right. My beautiful eighty-dollar Stetson was flatter than a pauper's wallet. I took it anyway and waved in the air as they carried me toward the ambulance.

"It looks as though she's going to be fine, folks. Give her a round of applause," Chad Nicholson said over the loudspeaker.

"I don't believe it," Mable said as the crowd clapped and whistled. "You ought to be in Hollywood."

I didn't know about that, but the crowd seemed to enjoy my little show. The fact was, I didn't win any ribbons or buckles that day. But I did win the hearts of the crowd, and *Marjorie Green's ride* was all they would be talking about for months, even though Barry Swaim had taken fourth place by giving an almost perfect ride the following day. And I was certain everyone knew, including Barry Swaim and that hunk of a preacher, that I was good enough to ride in the same arena with the rest.

Chapter 3

"Hello, I'm Don Gardner, Marline's pastor. I happened to be at the rodeo and saw the horse fall on your daughter. All the hospital would tell me was that she had been released. How she is doing?"

His voice caused me to scoot to sit up from where I had been lying on the sofa. I almost fell to the floor as I struggled to reach the remote on the coffee table.

"Oh, pleased to meet you, Reverend. Are these your children," Mama asked, pulling the door wide open. My click caused the TV to go blank as Shania Twain twisted across the screen singing *so you're Brad Pitt...that don't impress me much...* The several crushed Camel butts in the ashtray were enough black marks against me. I didn't think I needed Shania's help convincing him I was a sinner.

"Yes, this is Caroline...and this is Donnie. Say hello to Mrs. Green." A high-pitched "hi" floated through the open door, and Mama burst out laughing.

"Oh, they are so sweet. Please come in. Margie's right inside on the sofa." She motioned with all the grace of a queen, while inviting them into our shabby house. That was one thing I could say about Mama. She was blind to how much money someone did or did not have, or where they lived. Everyone was the same to her, including us.

"It's so good of you to come and visit her. I think my husband is in the back yard. Please make yourselves at home, and I'll see if I can find him. I'll only be a minute."

Mama scurried through the kitchen, allowing the back door to bang shut, as she yelled "Harvey! Harvey, come here. We have company." I couldn't hear what he said, but it was one of his "I'm busy, don't bother me" growls.

I stared at the man standing at the opposite end of the sofa, and my stomach flipped. He was too pretty to be a preacher. I would have bet my spurs and saddle that half the women in his congregation sinned every Sunday, just watching him and thinking things they shouldn't.

"Be careful, kids!" He tried vainly to catch his son as he rushed to greet me. "Margie got hurt, and has a bad owie."

"I guess that's one way of putting it." I nodded with a laugh. I put an arm around Donnie and pulled him up onto the sofa while Carol sat primly on the coffee table, watching.

"You can sit with me too. It's okay, as long as you don't bang my leg," I said, and she joined her brother without saying a word.

"So, how is your leg," the reverend said, taking his daughter's place at the coffee table.

"They x-rayed me from one end to the other, and said nothing's broken. I tore the heck out of my right knee, but outside of a few bruises and scrapes down my backside, I'm okay. The doctor said I'd be using crutches and a cane for awhile."

"You feel much pain?" He leaned closer.

"I did at first…but not now." I fumbled until I was able to reach the bottle of pills on the floor. "I've got these, and they're strong enough to make me forget most anything."

He glanced at the label and raised his eyebrows.

"Yeah, I guess so. Be careful." He put the bottle on the table and smiled. "You gave us all quite a scare out there today."

"Really? You too, Reverend?"

"Yes, me too. And please drop the *Reverend*, will you?"

"Okay, how about *Pastor Don*," I said with a giggle. Everything in the room seemed to be floating.

"If you must," he said, rolling his eyes.

The back door slammed shut and Mama dragged my

reluctant father into the room and presented him like a king.
"Reverend, this is my husband, Harvey."

"Pleased to meet you, Mr. Green." He stood to offer his
hand. The old man held up a huge paw that was caked with mud
from working in the yard, and grunted his greeting.

"We just happened to be at the rodeo with Marline
Dickerson's family, and saw Margie's spill. We came by to see
how she was doing. I would have gone to the hospital,
except...we had no idea which hospital, or where they had taken
her. It took us quite awhile just finding the right one to call."

"That's quite alright, Reverend. She wasn't in the
hospital very long as it was. They X-rayed her from head to foot.
The doctor didn't seem to think there was anything seriously
wrong, and surprised me by sending her home. They didn't even
keep her over night," Mama said.

"Spent half the day sitting down there," Dad said with a
scowl.

"She's your daughter, Harvey," Mama scolded. "You
should be willing to sit as long as it takes."

"I know who's daughter she is. And I'd sit a whole year,
if necessary. That is, if she had cancer, or was busted-up in a
car-wreck. But she did this to herself. Going out there, riding
bucking horses, trying to get herself killed like a danged fool.
Next time," he raised his voice, "she'll break her stupid neck.
Then, we'll be having to bury her." He turned to glare at Pastor
Don.

"You're a man of the cloth. Maybe you can talk some
sense into her. I sure can't. Never have been able to. Get more
out of talking to that dog out back, than I do talking to her."

"Well," Pastor Don cleared his throat, "I'll do my best. I
must admit, it was a little scary watching her get bounced
around like that. Then, when the horse fell and drug her around
the arena..."

Mama gasped and held her hand over her heart, staring at
me.

"You didn't know about that?"
Mama shook her head.

"Well, Marline's mother, Mrs. Dickerson, screamed when that happened. I don't think I'll be hearing out of my left ear for awhile. Anyway, I'm glad she didn't get hurt more seriously, and will be okay."

"These your kids," Dad said.

"Yes, they are. Donnie and Carol."

"Cute. Keep 'em away from Margie and rodeos." He turned to Mama. "I think I'll go wash up. Why don't you make us some coffee?"

"Yes, that's an excellent idea. Care to follow me to the kitchen, Reverend? We can get better acquainted."

"Certainly." He followed Mama into the kitchen talking as Dad disappeared into the bathroom, leaving me alone with the kids.

"Well," I said, looking from one tiny face to the other, "I didn't know I was such a bad influence. Do you think I'm a bad person?" They both shook their heads. "I didn't think so. I mean, I cuss every once-in-awhile. I smoke a little. But I don't drink anything stronger than beer, and not much of that. And I don't mess around with guys, if you know what I mean." Caroline giggled as I leaned my forehead against hers to stare her in the eye.

"I always thought I was kinda okay. Maybe...just a little."

~   ~   ~

Dad returned looking more like the welder he was than a gardener. Mama had chosen herself a good-looking man, but there certainly was no way you could've passed him off as a banker or lawyer. His huge meaty hands where attached to arms bigger around than my legs, and his bulging chest always seemed to tug at the buttons on his shirt, no matter what size you bought. His unruly shock of brown hair was flecked with gray, and always seemed to hang over his bushy eyebrows. The only thing that ruined his looks, in my opinion, was his constant scowl.

Mama brought in milk and cookies for the kids, and coffee for everyone else. I listened as Pastor Don talked about the difficulty of getting settled in a new community, while trying to learn the wants and needs of a congregation. The pills were really kicking in, and I started floating like everything else inside the room. I could hear their words, but nothing seemed to register. That is, until Mama asked the one question I'd been dying to ask, but didn't know how.

"So, tell me, Reverend. Where is Mrs. Gardner? Is she home unpacking?"

"No, my wife passed away a year ago," he said, staring into his cup.

I quit playing with Caroline's hair and stared at Mama, who said, "Oh, I'm sorry."

"Thank you." He looked up with a weak smile. "But there wasn't much anyone could have done. She wasn't feeling well and went to the doctor. The test came back saying she had cancer of the lymph glands. They did all they could, but she died almost eight months to the day. So," he looked lovingly at his children, "it's just us now. But, we do okay. Huh, Carol?" The little girl nodded, and he quickly turned the conversation to lighter things.

I started floating again, and it turned out to be more of a visit between the pastor and Mama, than with me. I don't remember saying much, especially after hearing about his wife, and Dad just sat, drinking coffee, and grunting when spoken to. He was still sitting in his chair long after Pastor Don and the kids had left, staring at me, sipping his coffee.

"What? Do I have a bugger hanging from my nose, or something?"

"No, just thinking."

"About what? The way you're staring makes me feel like I've done something. But all I've done is lay here with an ice pack on my knee."

"Oh, nothing," he said, getting out of his chair. "Just watching you with those two kids, the way you were playing and hugging on them. I've never seen you do that before."

29

"They're cute. Both of them."

"Yeah, I'll grant you that." He nodded. "But they also look enough like you to be your own."

He went into the kitchen to pour himself another cup, and I looked at Mama, who raised her eyebrows and cocked her head with a grin.

"You know, I didn't realize it at the time, but he's right."

Chapter 4

"I don't know. I'll have to see you with them again."

"When will that ever happen? Like I'm going to call your pastor and invite him over for coffee. Ow! Careful that spot's tender," I said, as Marline applied antibiotic cream to the scrapes on my back.

"Hold still. I wouldn't be having to do this, if you would have decided to do something sane, like barrel-racing. But no-o-o-o. You've got to ride broncs, and just not any bronc, either. Margie won't ride bareback, like the rest of the women. Margie has to ride saddle broncs, like a man. What's next? Bull riding? Or how about bulldogging? Would that suit you? There," she added with a slap on my good butt cheek, "you can get dressed."

I pulled one of Mama's loose nightgowns over my head as Marline went to the bathroom to wash her hands.

"Besides, I don't know why not," she yelled over the running water.

"Why not what," I yelled back.

"Invite the pastor over for coffee." She leaned against the door drying her hands on a towel. "Pastors are just people like the rest of us."

"Ah, I don't think so," I said with a laugh. I took a couple of shuffling steps toward the living room on my crutches, and stopped to study her. "Look at me, Marline. I mean, have you ever known me to do anything the right way? Anything simple? Something like...just going to get a hamburger?"

31

"No, you made a big deal out of everything we did in high school. You almost got kicked out a dozen times I can think of. Nearly got me expelled twice. But, so what?"

"That's my point. He's a man of God. A holy man. And, and...I'm Marjorie Green." I held my palms up, trying to compare the two.

"We're talking about having a cup of coffee, not seducing the man, or getting married," she said with a laugh.

"I suppose you're right," I said with a shrug, and continued toward the living room. "It doesn't seem right. Me, asking a preacher to come over."

"Wait! Am I missing something here?"

"No," I said, and eased myself onto the sofa. "I hate to ask, but could you grab the icepack out of the freezer for me?"

"Not until you tell me what's really going on." She glared down on me with her hands on her hips.

"Nothing. I need the icepack for my knee. It's starting to hurt."

"It's going to hurt a whole lot worse, if you don't tell me." She grabbed one of the heavy pillows from the back of the sofa and held it in a threatening fashion over my leg.

"Oh, God! Don't even joke like that. You've got no idea how it hurts."

"Tell me!" She raised it higher.

"Tell you what?"

"You know. About you and Pastor Don. Why are you suddenly interested in him and that church?"

"I just met the man. I don't even know what you're talking about. Now go get my icepack," I said, fumbling with the lid on my pill bottle.

"Okay, but you'd better fess-up and tell me everything when I get back."

"There's nothing to *fess-up*," I yelled as she left for the kitchen.

"What are you two arguing about," Mama said, entering the room with a load of clean laundry.

"I'm trying to get Margie to tell me how she really feels

about Pastor Don, and she keeps denying there's any sparks between them," Marline said. "Here's your icepack, dummy!" She tossed the pack at me.

"That's because there aren't any sparks. Idiot!" I slammed the pack hard against my knee and cringed in pain.

"See? God's already punishing you for your lies," Marline said with a grin.

"Well, I find him a rather attractive man, myself," Mama said as she folded the clothes and stacked them in neat piles in Dad's chair. She glanced up with a grin and added, "Don't you?"

"Maybe, but what do you think Dad would say, hearing you say something like that about some other man?"

"I'm sure he would agree with me, from a man's perspective, of course." She paused to stare in my direction. "I've never gotten angry at him for thinking Meg Ryan and Julia Roberts are pretty. They are...I'd have to be blind to think otherwise. Thinking someone's attractive doesn't mean you're having an affair."

"Yeah, but we're talking about a preacher, here. A man of God. Don't you think God's gonna get a little ticked-off? I don't wanna die of cancer, or something.

"Well, I'm sure glad you both think it's funny," I added as they laughed.

"God isn't going to give you cancer for thinking Reverend Gardner is an attractive man," Mama said as she shoved the folded clothes back into the basket. "I don't think he would have made the man that attractive, if he thought it was a sin for women to appreciate the way he looked."

"A very wise observation, Mrs. Green," Marline said.

"Thank you."

"Okay, what if I do think he's good looking? What does that prove," I said.

"Nothing, except that getting tossed from Irish hasn't caused you to lose your eyesight. What I want to know," Marline leaned close to my face, "is what you feel...what you really think about the man."

33

"I think he's possibly one of the most arrogant, pig-headed, chauvinistic men I have ever met."

"Marjorie Ann," Mama said with a short laugh. "How can you say such a thing?"

"Because it's true, Mama. You should've been there, when Marline introduced us. He gave me the once-over, and said I was too small and pretty to be riding broncs. He acted like I was crazy."

"Well," Mama laughed, "I happen to agree with him."

"So do I," Marline added "but that still doesn't answer my question. Maybe he's a little on the chauvinistic side. Most men I've met happen to be that way. Now, I'm going to ask this one more time, and you'd better tell the truth, or I'll whack you with the pillow. Does Margie kinda, sorta, like the preacher...just a little?"

"Do I think he's cute? Yeah. Am I having fantasies about the man? No...not really. I mean, I've thought about him a time or two. But not really.

"What," I added after Marline and Mama burst out laughing.

"Why don't you just admit you like the guy? God isn't going to strike you blind. Half the women in the church swoon every time he gets behind the pulpit," Marline said.

"And that's another thing," I said, pointing at her. "If I did like him...and I'm not saying I do...but if I did, I'd be competing against every church-going woman in Oakdale. Look at me, Marline. I'm me. I seldom go to church. I smoke and cuss. I even drink a beer now and then, when the old man's back is turned. Besides, he's got two kids. I don't know why he'd be interested in the likes of me, even if I did like him...which I'm not saying I do."

"I don't know either." Marline leaned over and kissed my forehead. "I've got to go. But, for your information," she paused at the door, "you'd only be competing against the women who attend our church, not the whole town. It might also interest you to know that he *did* say that he thought you were very pretty. He also asked me a ton of questions about you.

34

Actually hurt my feelings, if you want to know the truth. I've been kind of interested in him myself." She studied me for a long minute with the door cracked open.

"That little girl of his is having a birthday in a couple of weeks, on the twenty-second. I don't know, I thought maybe you'd like to buy her a card, and maybe a little gift. Bye." She waved with her fingers and closed the door.

"I have no idea why he would be interested in the likes of you either," Mama said with a grin.

She disappeared into her bedroom with the laundry, leaving me with my thoughts, and they were suddenly headed in a direction they shouldn't have been. The man had kids, and I was only nineteen. I didn't want a family, even if they did look like me. And I didn't care what Mama or Marline thought, but some of the things that were running through my head had to really make God angry. I didn't know what a pissed-off God might do, but I certainly didn't want to find out. I clicked the TV on, and flipped through the channels to MTV, thinking it might help me think of something else. The last thing I remembered before falling asleep was a half-nude Madonna twisting and turning across the screen.

Chapter 5

I wrapped the braided rope around my gloved hand as the loudspeaker crackled.

"Out of the Western Warehouse chute, Marjorie Ann Green, riding Irish."

I gave Chuck a nod and the gate flew open.

We bolted from the stall with the sound of a cowbell and a cheering crowd. The animal beneath me sent chunks of mud high in the air as he heaved and snorted like an angry demon. My spine, neck and head throbbed with each jolt as he leaped into the air, twisting. He hit the ground and exploded upward against my returning body, each buck exerting greater force. Then, without warning, he rolled to the right. I tried desperately to free myself as the horse took forever falling, but my boot that was jammed into the hobbled stirrup seemed glued in place. I pushed against the saddle with my free hand, but the hobbled stirrup sucked my body downward as the horse rolled to the right. Then, my head slammed into the mud. I couldn't move or breathe as the weight of the horse drove my leg deep into the hard-packed arena.

As quickly as he fell, Irish bolted upward again, and darted toward the opposite end of the arena, dragging me with him. Fire shot through my leg as I twisted and turned, passing under his belly. The breeze caused by his razor-sharp hooves brushing past my nose felt like the devil's breath.

I jerked upward in bed, gasping for breath. Beads of sweat mapped their way down my cheeks and my night-tee clung to my damp skin like I'd been dunked in a pool.

"Oh, God!" I buried my face in my palms and bent over in bed. It was the same dream that had repeated itself for the past three nights.

Chapter 6

Caroline Gardner's fourth birthday party consisted of a small gathering at *Mountain Mike's Pizza*, mostly of people from the church who had children her age. I got the impression, real quick-like, the choice had to do more with her father's appetite for pizza than a proper location for the party, although it happened to be adjacent to *Baskin-Robbins*, making it a little more convenient when it was time for cake and ice cream.

Mama had taken me shopping and we picked out a nice bunny-card with pink balloons. I also bought a red cowgirl hat against Mama's wishes, and had it wrapped in pink happy birthday paper. The hat brought a squeal of delight, and stayed on the birthday girl's head the entire afternoon. It also earned me a big hug and kiss, making me wish I had included a pair of matching boots. The look on the proud father's face, watching her giggle and bounce around the pizza parlor with the other kids, caused me to feel and think things that were better left alone. The trouble was, I couldn't quite shake the thoughts or feelings, no matter how I tried.

Chapter 7

"It's getting better. I've graduated to using a cane," I said with a grin. "I'll be back at work before you know it. That is, if you still want me."

"You don't have to ask," Mable laughed, "but not without a doctor's release. I don't want you doing anything that might make it worse."

"Well, he already said I could do whatever I wanted, just as long as it doesn't hurt."

"Which brings us back to what I said." She grinned and pointed a finger in my face. "Show me something in writing that tells me what you can, or cannot do, and I'll let you come back."

"Look," she added after a long minute. "It's only been a few weeks. Besides, I've got an insurance company that gets pretty sticky when it comes to letting injured employees come back early. There's no need in rushing things. You might wind up limping around like Chuck."

"Yeah, but I'm bored stiff being stuck in that house all day. You can only watch so much TV before your head starts hurting. I've even started listening to Dad's old George Jones records."

"Well, they ain't half-bad," Chuck said as he lit a cigarette. "Especially when you've just cracked open a fresh brew. Ol' George can sing you through a good case of the blues."

"Yes, or give them to you," Mable snorted.

"What Mable's trying to tell you, is that we kinda sort of

think of you like one of our own young-uns. And we don't want nothing bad happening to you. So, whenever the doc says it's okay with him for you to come back pestering us, then it's okay with us."

I nodded and hobbled my way toward Irish's stall. The magnificent animal poked his head over the railing and snorted his welcome, bobbing his head up and down.

"Well, good morning to you too." I rubbed his soft muzzle. "See what you did to me? I know you didn't mean it, but it hurts like heck."

He moved his soft lips across my cheek like a kiss.

"I know you're sorry," I dug the apple from my backpack, "and I love you too." He took it from my palm and crunched it between his large teeth.

"I dream about you a lot, you know. They're not nice dreams. You're kind of mean...but I know you're not really mean. Are you? Anyway, I won't be riding you any time soon. The doctor won't let me. Besides," I glanced over my shoulder to make sure Chuck and Mable weren't listening, "I don't know if I can. Don't tell anyone, okay? That's just our little secret."

Chapter 8

"What's with you two?" I stood in the kitchen doorway staring. Mom and Dad were seated at the table drinking coffee, dressed like they were going to a funeral.

"It's Sunday," Mama said over the rim of her cup.

"So?" I limped my way to the cupboard and grabbed a cup from the top shelf.

"So, we thought we'd go to church with Marline and her parents."

I dropped the cup. "Oh, crap!" I said, as it shattered against the formica counter.

"I'll get it," Mama said. "Just sit down, and I'll clean this up for you."

I eased into a chair across from Dad in my night-tee as Mama poured coffee into another cup and slid it in front of me.

"Better clean that language up, if you're gonna try branding a preacher," Dad grunted, and took a long sip from his mug.

"Huh? Who's trying to *brand* anyone, and what's all this dressing up for church? I can't remember seeing you guys dress up before, let alone go to church."

"Well, we used to dress up once in awhile, and went to church quite regularly when you were younger. But, I guess you've forgotten. We kind of got out of practice, but we thought it wouldn't hurt to start again." Mama smiled real big and sipped her coffee like a lady.

"Why? I mean I don't have anything against your going.

It's just…why?"

"We thought if our daughter was going to start sparking a preacher, we'd better find out a little more about him," Dad said.

"Will you stop saying that. I'm not *sparking* or *branding* anyone." I slammed my cup down, spilling some of its contents. "Sorry," I said and wiped at the spill with a paper napkin.

"Why don't you go with us, dear," Mama said.

"Huh, like this? I'm sure!" I tugged on the night-tee.

"We've got a few minutes before we have to leave. I'll lay your things out while you finish your coffee." She jumped up and was headed toward my bedroom before I could stop her.

"Ma!" I yelled. "I haven't had a shower or anything. You guys go without me."

"Nonsense," she poked her head back through the door, "I've seen you dress much quicker to go shopping. Finish your coffee while I get your things."

"She's not going to give up and let me stay home, is she?"

"Nope," Dad said, taking a healthy sip.

~   ~   ~

The old church had more people than I could remember from the last time I had gone with Marline. We were late, and they were already singing some of their danged funeral music by the time we entered the door. I eyed the crowd while Dad and Mom shook hands with the greeter and got a bulletin. There was no way we were going to find a place near the door and slip in unnoticed.

"There you are. Come on, I've been waiting for you," Gary Dickerson said in a hushed voice. "We've got places saved up front."

"Great!" I gritted my teeth and followed him down the middle aisle, until I thought he was going to take us right onto the platform. I was positive everyone was staring at our little parade, especially me, leaning against my cane like a wounded pirate in a blue dress. The place they had been saving was on the second row, right in the middle. And from the looks of things, they might've been the only vacant seats in the building. Gary waited until Mom and Dad had seated themselves next to Marline's parents, then slid in next to crop top, who was seated by his mother. Although she was dressed a whole lot better than I remembered from the rodeo, she was still showing plenty of skin. I slid in next to Gary with Marline on the aisle.

The funeral music had finished by the time we were seated, and I couldn't help feeling that everyone was staring at the back of my head. Then, I started feeling a little resentful that they hadn't picked a spot nearer the back of the building, especially if they had conspired with the old coots into shanghaiing me into coming. As close as we were seated, I had to tilt my head to see whoever it was coming to the microphone. Some guy with a large nose and receding hairline talked in a monotone voice, telling us the same things that were printed inside the bulletin, like no one in the church knew how to read. I took the mirror from my purse and checked my make-up. I heard him introduce the pastor and everyone applauded, so I snapped the mirror shut and dropped it back inside the purse. Reverend Donald Ray Gardner came to the microphone smiling, and stared down at me.

Well, okay. Maybe he didn't single me out of the hundred or so people that morning, but it sure felt like it. And he did admit later that he knew where I was seated, and was guilty of looking my way once in awhile. I leaned over and hissed in Marline's ear.

"Why can't you guys sit in the back of the building once in awhile?"

"Because we like it here," she whispered back.

"Well, it isn't gonna make you any closer to God. You could sit in the back, you know. God's not gonna strike you dead for it."

"He isn't going to strike you dead for sitting up front, either."

"Shhhh," came the voice of one of the older women

43

seated behind us.

I can't say as I actually heard much of what he was saying, except for his being happy to be in Oakdale, and how nice people were treating him. I kept wondering what he must think about me, his being a preacher and all. I knew I hadn't given him the best impression by smoking and cussing. And he had caught me drinking a beer on the front porch the other day when he dropped by unannounced. *Yeah, way to go, Margie. That's someone a preacher would want to be friends with.*

I snapped to attention when he mentioned our names, and said what a wonderful time he and his children were having getting to know us, and referred to as *close friends.* Then I kind of drifted off again as he opened his Bible and began his sermon. Not that he was boring or anything. In fact, I'd have to say he was a better speaker than what the people at that church were used to getting. But I kept wondering about him and those kids, and what their mother must have been like. Then, I started wondering why he had asked Marline a ton of questions about me, and what kind of an impression I'd been giving. Then the cell phone inside my purse started ringing.

Now, you've got to understand that it just doesn't ring with one of those little *beep-beep* signals. I had chosen a setting that caused it to play a different tune whenever someone called, and because of the noise at the stables, had the volume cranked up as high as possible. So, here we are in church, in the middle of a sermon, when my phone starts blaring *Dixie.*

"Shit!" I grabbed for the phone before I realized I had said it out loud. I glanced up at the man behind the pulpit, then toward Marline with my hand on the phone, which continued playing *Dixie.* They were both staring at me open-mouthed while Gary burst out laughing. Pretty soon, everyone was laughing, except me, and I simply pushed the off button to kill the power. Then, dropping the phone back into the purse, I sorta bent over and covered my face with both hands.

"Does she need to answer that?" I could hear his voice over the microphone.

"No, she turned it off. You may continue, Pastor,"

Marline said real loud.

"I don't know that I can," he said laughing. But he did, and from what I could hear, it was a very nice sermon, although I couldn't tell you much about it. I was too busy checking for the nearest exit.

I remained seated after the closing prayer, then slipped through one of the side exits while everyone was busy shaking hands and making small talk. I limped my way through the children's playground to the remote parking lot. The only thing was, Dad had chosen to lock our old junky truck for some reason, and I had to wait, nodding and smiling at those who passed on their way to their cars. I checked the message center on the phone to discover it was Chuck who had called. He left a message, saying he thought it might be good, seeing as I had given him a doctor's release, if I rode Comanche that afternoon to get in shape for the Sonora Rodeo.

It took Mom and Dad most of fifteen minutes to quit talking and come unlock the truck.

"I'm sorry," Mama said when I complained, "but we were actually looking for you. If you would have told us you where you were going, we would have been her much sooner."

We had gone some three or four blocks before I realized we were heading in a different direction than home.

"Where are we going?"

"Marline's parents invited us to have Sunday dinner with them. Didn't I tell you," Mama said.

"No, you didn't. Take me home."

"Home? Why?" Dad growled.

"Because Chuck called, and wants me to ride Comanche this afternoon. I've gotta start getting ready for Sonora."

"Okay, but you've got to eat anyway. I'll take you out there after we've eaten." He kept the truck going straight.

"I don't want to go to Marline's. I don't want to see anyone. I want to go home," I hissed through clenched teeth.

"Don't be silly," Mama said with a laugh. "They are expecting us. Besides, if you're worried about what happened this morning, don't be. Everyone laughed. No one is angry with you."

"You're not going to let me go home, are you?" I said after a long minute.

"Nope," Dad said, as he turned onto Marline's street.

"Shit!"

"I thought you had gotten that out of your system this morning," he said, pulling to a stop in front of their house. "Once might've been funny, but I don't think Mrs. Dickerson would like you saying it at her table. Come on, let's go eat." He patted me on the leg.

Chapter 9

"It's over with." I could hear Chuck's voice as I picked myself up out of the dust for the third time. It had taken Comanche exactly two seconds to throw me. Everyone, including Pastor Gardner, had come to watch the spectacle.

"Hold him for me, while I get back on," I said, dusting my jeans.

"Na, ain't no use."

"Come on, Chuck. I've got to get ready for the rodeo."

"You ain't gonna be riding in no rodeo. Don't you understand, girl? It's over. You can't ride no more." He grabbed his lasso and roped the bucking mustang in one lazy toss.

"Whadda ya mean, I'm not going to be riding anymore? I'm a pretty darned good rider. You said so yourself," I yelled.

"Used to be. Not anymore."

"Chuck's right, Margie," Mable said calmly. "You've lost it, and you'll only hurt yourself trying."

"Lost it? What are you talking about? I haven't lost a thing. Comanche just happened to throw me, that's all. I'll ride him. Here, I'll show you." I reached for the rope, but Chuck slapped his gnarled paw around my wrist with a glare.

"Na-uh. You done forked him three times, and bailed when he commenced to bucking. When a rider starts bailing, it's over. You know that same as me."

I glanced at Mable, and she gave me a slow nod. I couldn't stop my chin from quivering as I limped toward the gate. I knew they were right. I'd known it for some time. I hadn't

47

had a good night's sleep since the rodeo. Irish had come close to killing me, and I relived the incident every time I closed my eyes, and woke in a cold sweat.

"It's okay, honey," Mama said, placing a hand on my shoulder. "You'll find something else to do. Maybe you can start barrel racing again, like Marline."

I stopped beside the truck and shook my head. Then burst into tears. It was Pastor Don who took me home, after asking Mom and Dad to watch the kids for an hour or so. We stopped at McDonalds for cokes and talked. Then, he kissed me.

Chapter 10

"I'm sorry, I don't know what's wrong with me." I sniffled and tried holding it back, but a big, fat tear escaped and rolled down my left cheek. The rest followed like they had a mind of their own.

"Oh, God, I'm sorry." I buried my face in a paper napkin. We were sitting in his car parked inside the McDonald's parking lot, when I suddenly came apart at the seams.

"Go ahead, it'll make you feel better," he said, handing me several more napkins.

"I don't know what's the matter with me. I haven't cried in years," I said, dabbing my eyes.

"Maybe you should do it more often," he said, taking a long sip through his straw. "Everyone should cry once in awhile."

"You too?"

"Yeah," he grinned, "I've cried a lot this past year."

"Oh, I'd forgotten about your wife. I guess that was a dumb question. I'm sorry." I sniffled and dabbed at my eyes.

"No, it wasn't dumb, and there's no apology needed. You're upset because you're afraid that you've lost something that you have wanted very badly."

"Yeah," I said with a nod, and took a sip of coke. "Tell me about her."

"Who, Linda?"

"Yeah, if that was your wife's name."

He took his time poking his straw around the ice inside

his cup before answering.

"Well, there's not much to tell, actually. We met in junior high and liked each other instantly. We dated though high school, and became engaged before I went off to college. Then, about six months before graduation, we got married." He paused to laugh.

"Everyone, including our parents, thought she was pregnant. Mainly because she *did* get pregnant with Carol about a month after the wedding. But, I'll tell you just like I've told everyone else. Linda McCormack was a virgin the day we were married." He grinned and took another sip.

"That's beautiful," I said thoughtfully. "You must've loved her very much."

"I did."

"Were you happy?"

"Yeah," he nodded, "very happy. Oh, we had our little fights. She had a bad temper, and I'm probably the most stubborn man you'll ever meet. But, yes…we were extremely happy."

"And you miss her, don't you?"

"Yes, but let's get back to you. Rodeo, and riding horses means a lot to you, doesn't it?" He put his cup in the cup-holder and shifted to put his arm on the back of my seat.

"You'll never know how much."

"Why?"

"Why?"

He nodded.

"Well, I've never thought about it much. First of all, I love animals, especially horses. They're beautiful, and more intelligent than most people give them credit for and, I guess I have to say that when I can stay on a good bronc for eight seconds, I feel like somebody. It's like I'm as good as anybody else, and I've earned my spot. I suddenly belong there. I don't know if I'm making any sense, but that's the way I feel here," I patted my chest, "inside."

"You're making perfect sense." He smiled and my heart stopped as he toyed with a strand of my hair. "Tell me what

50

happened out there today."

"I don't really know. I kept getting thrown, and I don't know why. I know Comanche's a good horse, but I've ridden him before...several times. Chuck and Mable both said I was bailing...but I don't know if I was. I honestly don't know what happened. Maybe they're right, and that's what scares me the most. That I'm afraid, and I'll never be able to ride again."

"And you don't want to barrel race with Marline, or try another event more suited for women," he said, playing with the hair close to my ear. It was getting stuffy and hard to breathe inside the car.

"No, and that's just it. If I settle for something that every other girl is doing, even if I win, I'm just another girl. But if I can compete with the guys...and stay with them...win or lose, or even if they don't really score me...I'm noticed for what I am. Me. Marjorie Ann Green, bronc-buster."

"Well, oddly enough, I can understand all that," he said, and quit playing with my hair to lean against the driver's door. I had a sudden urge to grab his hand and shove it back into my hair.

"I don't really think there's anything wrong with you," he continued. "You're just hearing footsteps."

"I'm what?"

"You're hearing footsteps. It's an old football term. Look," he said, shifting to get closer. "I earned my way through school on a football scholarship. I was a pretty fair quarterback in high school, and was doing well in college. Until we met Oregon State. They had a linebacker they called *The Tank*. Tank was 320 pounds of pure meanness. We were ahead in the middle of the third quarter, and I was picking their defenses apart, and feeling pretty good about myself. Then, Tank broke through our line on a blitz that I failed to pick up. He blind-sided me, and actually put me out of the game. We went on to win, with our backup quarterback. But, I was still out of the game."

"Didn't you ever play again," I asked.

"Play? Oh, sure," he paused to empty his cup, "but I started hearing footsteps. I was afraid of being blindsided again, so I kept leaving the pocket and hurrying the passes, which meant I got knocked down nearly every play, and my passes missed most of the receivers. They finally had to bench me."

"Oh, so it was over for you too. You never got to play again."

"No, just the opposite." He suddenly had his hand back in my hair, caressing my neck close to my ear. I could hear my pulse pounding inside my head.

"What happened?"

"I happened to be watching the San Francisco Forty Niners the day Steve Young got hit so hard he crawled off the field. Then, two plays later, he ran back onto the field. His spirit inspired the team, and they went on to win. I suddenly realized that everybody, including great quarterbacks like Steve Young, get knocked down and hurt, and getting knocked down is part of the game.

"You see, The Tank didn't really hate me, and he wasn't trying to kill me. The Tank was only doing what linebackers are supposed to do ... knock quarterbacks down and break up plays. I realized that if I was going to play the game, I would have to be willing to get knocked down and hurt once in awhile. Once I got that settled in my mind, I was okay. I got my starting position back again."

"And being a bronc-buster means I've gotta be willing to get bucked off and hurt once in awhile," I said with a nod.

"Exactly. I'll admit, it frightened me something awful, seeing that horse drag you around the arena. But, I don't believe Irish hates you and was trying to kill you. He was only being a horse, and doing what he was trained to do. It's all part of the game, Margie. If you can settle that in your mind, you'll be okay. If not...hang up your spurs, girl."

I nodded, and that was when he slipped his hand to the back of my neck and pulled me close and kissed me. It wasn't a little peck on the lips or cheek, like I half expected. But then, I'd never been kissed by a preacher, so I didn't know what to expect. This was a full mouth-to-mouth kiss that hung on for awhile. He wasn't using his tongue, or trying to seduce me either. It was a good honest-to-god kiss between a man and woman that meant something. I had just slipped both arms around his neck to return the favor, when he pulled away.

"I'd better go rescue your mother. It's way past Donnie and Carol's naptime."

Chapter 11

"We're going fishing. What does it look like?" Dad stood in the living room holding his pole and tackle box. It had been two days since Don had kissed me at McDonalds, and we hadn't seen each other or really talked much since. I was getting lonely.

"Like you're going fishing. But you're going with Don?"

"Yeah," he growled with a nod. "Preachers like to fish too. If I'm not mistaken, their boss used to fish some. At least he hung around with guys who made their living that way."

"Well, yeah...I just never thought about it before. I mean, he's never mentioned fishing before. But he doesn't talk to me that much. When he comes over, he just asks how I'm feeling, then leaves me with his kids and goes off to talk to you and Mom. I have no idea what he likes to do...or what he doesn't like, for that matter."

"Ah-huh," he snorted. "You're jealous because he's being friendly with your parents."

"Am not!"

"Are so."

"I am not jealous!"

"What's going on in here," Mama said, drying her hands on a dish towel as she came from the kitchen.

"Your daughter is jealous because Pastor Don's going fishing with me."

"I am not! I just said I didn't know he liked to fish.

That's all. I don't know what he likes to do, because he's never told me. He's always talking to you guys while I watch the kids."

"I didn't think you minded watching Donnie and Carol, honey," Mama said.

"I don't. I like them both. I just think it would be nice if he talked to me once in awhile, instead of using me like a babysitting service. I mean…" I waved my hands in the air, "I don't know what I mean. And it doesn't matter."

"Sure it matters," Mama said, wrapping me in her arms.

"Yep, I was right," Dad said with a nod. "You owe me five bucks, Edith. She's got a crush on him."

"Ah…I do not!" I said, pushing Mama away. "I simply said it would be nice if he talked to me once in a while, instead of dumping his kids on me and running off with you guys."

"Following me into the kitchen to get a cup of coffee, or talking to your father while he works on the truck, is hardly running off or ignoring you," Mama said.

"What would you call it then?" I folded my arms across my chest.

"Being friendly."

"Yep, she's in love," Dad snorted.

"Am not!"

"Are so, and from what I understand, lying's still a sin."

"I might've said I *liked* him, but I never said I *loved* him," I hissed.

"Well, you do, and he's here. I've got to go." He leaned to kiss Mama. "Bye. See you girls later."

I watched through the window as he crawled inside the green Mustang and they pulled away from the curb.

"Where's the kids? He didn't leave them."

"Your father said something about Marline taking them to see the new Disney movie showing in Riverbank. I think I'll have a glass of iced tea. Can I get you something," Mama asked.

"No, nothing for me. Thanks." I felt my chin tremble as I stared at the empty street. My father had Donald Ray Gardner as a fishing partner. My mother had her iced tea and a Rush

Limbaugh program going in the kitchen. Marline had Carol and Donnie at a Disney movie. Mable and Chuck had their horses, and Margie had an empty street to stare at. I felt alone.

Chapter 12

"How's the knee?"

"Whadda you care?" I had been sitting on the front porch having a cigarette and playing with my dog, Hobo, when Barry Swaim parked his four-wheeler and proceeded to make himself at home.

"I care. Why do you think I came all the way over here?"

"*All the way over here?* Geeze, Barry! It's only two, maybe three miles from your house. It's not like you drove to Modesto, or Turlock. What did you really come over here for?"

"To see how you are doing. Really." He sat beside me on the steps and tossed the tennis ball for Hobo.

"I'm healing just fine. Thanks for asking."

"I heard about you bailing off Comanche last Sunday."

"So that's it!" I jumped up and backed away yelling. "You came over just to gloat in my face. You're such a freaking slug! God, I can't believe you!"

"No, no, that's not it." He tried to grab my arm, but I slapped his hand away.

"Why don't you just go away, Barry? You never did anything but hurt me when we were together."

"I'm sorry. That's all I wanted to say." He paused to give the ball another toss. "That was a nasty spill you took, and I kind of understand what you might be going through. It scared the crap out of me when you rolled under his hooves. I thought he might've kicked you in the face."

"He came real close," I said, and gave the ball a toss into

the far corner of the fence. Barry waited until Hobo had returned with the ball, and gave it another toss.

"Anyway, I just wanted you to know that I hope you come back. I know we fight a lot, and it's mostly my fault, but I kind of like watching you ride. I seem to do better when you look good. It's like I'm competing against you. I try harder."

"Really," I snorted. "Like I'm supposed to believe you, after all the things you've said about me."

"Well, yeah. I know I'm a jerk. But getting beat by Terry, or J. C., or some of the better riders is different. It's sort of expected. Kind of like when you compete in the women's circuit. Everyone expects you to win. Know what I mean?"

I nodded and he continued.

"Well, me getting beat by some of the guys is kind of expected. But getting beat by a girl…?" He glanced up and gave a crooked grin. "Knowing you're out there, even riding the women's circuit and racking up mega points, makes me a better rider."

"I think you mean that."

"I do."

"You know, Barry, that's the nicest thing you've ever said to me, even while we were dating. Thank you."

"You're welcome. I hear you and that preacher are getting pretty friendly."

"Maybe. I really like him, if that's what you mean. And I think he kind of likes me too."

"He does."

"How do you know?"

"Believe me, he does." Barry grinned. "He'll be good for you. Just remember to go slow. He's different, and you can't spur him, like you do the rest of us." He checked his watch and got up to brush his pants.

"Better get going. Got someone waiting."

"Is she pretty?"

"Yeah." He grinned.

"Thanks, Barry. For everything."

"You're welcome."

I watched him drive away before continuing my game with Hobo. Barry couldn't be trusted to stay away from other girls while we were dating, and he could be a real jerk at times. But I'd never known him to lie to me, not once, even when I had confronted him about the girls he was seeing behind my back. I paused with the tennis ball as Hobo bounced around, barking at my feet. *Believe me, he does* had to mean Donald Ray Gardner liked me more than just a little…maybe quite a bit. I gave the ball a toss.

I had no idea what Barry meant by *spurring* him around like I did other guys. Heck, I'd never treated Barry or anyone any different than I thought they needed. Barry was mistaken about that one. But, he wanted me back riding broncs, because he thought it made him a better rider. Well, when I went back, it would be because I wanted to win, and not because Barry or anyone else wanted me to.

Chapter 13

Marline had given me a ride home after work, and we were sitting in her truck with the motor running while I stared at the green Mustang parked in our driveway.

"Oooh, it looks like you've got company," she said.

"Yeah, I wonder what he wants," I said, cracking the door open.

"What the heck do you think he wants, stupid? He's here to see you."

"I know. I just didn't expect to see him today…not like this anyway. I'm all dirty," I said tugging at my shirt.

"He doesn't care. They say sweat's kind of sexy, anyway. Go on." She gave me a shove on the arm and laughed.

"Wanna come in," I said as I slid out of the bucket seat.

"No, he's not interested in my sweat, he's after yours. Now, go on and give him a big kiss for me. I've got to run. Bye," she said, as I closed the door. I watched the Ford F250 turn the corner before bounding up the steps like Chester on my stiff knee and opening the door.

"Margie!" Caroline squealed and ran to latch onto my legs. She was followed closely by her brother who, not finding a spot at the front, grabbed the back of my legs, calling me "Mommie!"

I had no idea what the adults had been laughing at, but seeing as Mama was seated beside him on the sofa with a couple of her picture albums opened, I knew it couldn't have been good.

"Hi," Don said, still chuckling.

"Oh, hello, Honey. How was your day," Mama asked.

"Fine," I said, stooping to hug and kiss both children. My sweat and grime didn't seem to bother them, as they threw their arms around my neck and clung on.

"Okay, just a minute. Let me hold your brother first. Then, when I sit down, you can climb into my lap too."

"Okay," Carol said as I scooped her brother into my arms. She clung to my shirttail as I made my way toward the sofa, giving my mother the evil eyeball.

"What are you showing him, Mama?"

"Oh, just some of your old pictures." She smiled sweetly.

"Yeah, I had a clue as to what they were. Which ones?" I stood near the edge of the sofa.

"Some taken when you and Marline were in high school. Here, come sit down. I'll move over," she said, scooting toward the opposite end. "I thought Pastor Don might want to know a little more about you girls."

"I don't think he really wants to know, Mama," I said, shaking my head.

"Sure I do. Here," he said patting the cushion, "there's plenty of room. Join us."

"Ah, I just got off work and I'm all stinky."

"You must not smell too bad, or my kids wouldn't keep hugging you." He smiled and turned toward Caroline.

"Do you think Margie is all stinky and yucky?"

"No," she giggled.

"See? Sit down." He patted the cushion and I slid onto the sofa next to him to eye the photo album.

"Oh my God, Mama! I can't believe you're showing him those pictures!" I reached for the album, but Don snatched it away.

"Come on, Donald!" I stretched, trying to catch the book, but he laughed and held it out of my reach. "You shouldn't be seeing those. I was in my pajamas. Give it to me!"

"No, I'm not finished. Besides, I thought you girls were

kind of cute in your pj's."

"Aagh! You're evil." I gritted my teeth at Mama as she laughed.

"You must have thought you looked fine the day those pictures were taken. You went to school dressed that way," she said.

"I was a kid back then, and we were acting silly." I glared as Don turned the page with another chuckle.

"That was only two years ago, and you were a senior," Mama corrected.

"And not only did you talk Marline into going along with your little scheme, you both got kicked out of school for showing up in your pajamas."

"Really? You got expelled?" Don looked at me as though the news had shocked him.

"Just for one day. We were back in class the next day, so it wasn't any big deal," I said with a shrug.

"It went on you record, and you were labeled as a trouble-maker," Mama said.

"It went on my high school attendance record, Mama. And big deal…I was always known as a trouble-maker way back in grammar school!"

"You were?" Don said shifting toward me. "Tell me about it."

"Mmm, there's really nothing to tell. Well, okay," I continued as Mama started laughing, "so I *did* get in a few fights…"

"With as many boys as she did girls," Mama said.

"Yeah, but only in grade school, and they deserved it. But when I got into trouble in high school, it was for doing crazy things," I said, playing with Caroline's hair.

"Crazy like what," Don asked.

"The pajamas," I said with a shrug.

"And turning the gopher snakes loose inside the biology class," Mama said.

"Well, they were unhappy being cooped up like that. Besides, it was as much Marline and the other girl's fault, but I was the one who got into trouble."

"Go on, I've got to hear this one," Don said.

"Everyone kept complaining how the snakes were unhappy, and how someone ought to set them free. So, I took them out of their cage..."

"How many snakes are we talking about," Don interrupted.

"Only three. Anyway, I was headed toward the door, when Marline and the girls started screaming and running around. Someone bumped me and knocked the snakes out of my hands. Then, the teacher comes in while I'm chasing snakes around the classroom, and everyone points at me. Whadda you think happened?"

"I'd give anything to have a picture of that," Don said laughing.

"Well, you can't have one, because there aren't any," I said, giving him a kiss on the cheek. "Say," I added with a shove against his shoulder. "Where do you get off saying Marline looks cute in her pajamas? You're not supposed to be thinking those things."

"Well, she does. But..." he kissed me back, "I think you're much cuter."

"Well...okay, I guess it's alright. But only if you think I'm better, and you're not allowed to look at those pictures of Marline ever again." I gave him a quick kiss on the cheek.

"Okay, but only if I get to keep this one." He grinned and removed one of me with bunny rabbit slippers, holding a teddy bear.

Chapter 14

"What is this place, anyway?" Don climbed out of the driver's seat and turned in a slow circle, taking in the scene.

I poked my head over the top of the car to say, "It's the Oakdale Cowboy Museum," then crawled into the back seat to unbuckle Donnie from his car seat.

"The music's coming from the H-B Saloon. They've got a real good restaurant inside called *Bachi's*. And that," I hoisted Donnie into my arms before pointing toward the left, "is the Hershey's Welcoming Center. They used to give tours of the chocolate factory, but stopped after those idiots flew the planes into the World Trade Center. Guess they figured it was safer that way. We'll take the kids inside when we're finished in the museum."

"Now, that looks like a copy of a Jewish temple," Don said, pointing toward the ornate building across the patio.

"The Almond Pavilion? Yeah, I hear the guy who built it claimed God wanted him to make it look like Solomon's Temple." I came around the car and stood beside him while I talked. "The place has changed owners several times since. They rent it out now, for weddings, banquets and parties. It's pretty fancy inside. You'd better help your daughter. She's having trouble with the seatbelt."

"Oh, yeah," he said, ducking into the backseat. "Sorry, Baby. Here, let me help you."

"And that's El Jardin," I pointed toward the Restaurant on the far corner, "with some of the best Mexican food you'll find anywhere. Of course, that's debatable, seeing as I haven't really found a bad Mexican restaurant in Oakdale. I plan on us stopping there for tacos before we leave. My treat." I gave him a big grin.

"Come on, there's someone I want you to meet." I grabbed his hand and headed up the brick walkway toward the museum. I opened the Executive Director's door without knocking.

"Christie, if you have time, I'd like you to meet my pastor, Reverend Gardner, and his children," I said.

"Sure, Margie, come in." She dropped the pen she was using and stood as we entered her tiny office. The walls were plastered with pictures and cowboy memorabilia, collected over the years from local ranchers and performers involved with the professional rodeo circuit.

"Hi, I'm Christie Camarillo." She came from behind her desk to shake Don's hand and give him a welcoming smile. "I've heard so much about you."

"Really? I hope it's been good," Don said with a grin.

"Are you kidding? The way these girls talk, I was beginning to think you might walk on water." She giggled and bent over to greet the children.

"Hi, I'm Christie. What's your name?"

"I'm Caroline Gardner, and this is my brother. I'm four years old," she held four fingers in Christie's face, "but he's only two."

"My, you are a big girl, aren't you? And what is your brother's name?"

"His name is Donnie, like my Daddy," she said, pointing toward Don.

"Donnie is a good name, just like Caroline," Christy said with a nod. "They're both very pretty names."

"Is the museum open, Christy?" I grinned, cocking my head toward Don. "I want to give this tenderfoot an education in western culture."

"Ah, no. I haven't unlocked the door yet. Let me get the key." She scampered back to her desk to retrieve a set of keys, then paused to eye me up and down. "You look different without your boots and jeans."

"Yeah, I guess I do. I thought I'd let Don and the kids see me in something else." I glanced down at my white Nikes and bare legs. I had slipped into a pair of white shorts and tank top, and pulled my hair into a ponytail, after asking him to pick me up earlier that afternoon.

"I haven't asked, but I hope he likes me this way."

"Don't bother asking. He does." Christy gave me a crooked grin. "Come on, I'll open the museum."

"So, tell me, Reverend, how do you like living in Oakdale," she said unlocking the door.

"I love it. I find the people friendly, and I believe it will be a good place to raise my family."

"Well, here we are." She pushed the door wide. "I'm sure Margie can give you a tour as well as I can. So take your time, and make sure the door is locked on your way out. If you'll excuse me, I'm expecting an important call."

"Thank you," Don said as she closed the door.

"Welcome to my world, Pastor. This will explain a few things about me and my friends," I said, giving him a quick peck on the cheek.

"Yes, but where do you start?" He stared at the walls lined with trophy cases and plastered with photos. The pathways were lined with saddles, bridles, and horseshoeing equipment.

"How about right here?" I pointed toward one group of saddles. "This one belonged to Wilford Brimley."

"The actor?'

"Yeah, he's also a real cowboy and owns a cattle ranch. And here's Harley May's trophy saddle he got in 1952 for steer wrestling. This one's the 1947 Champion Cowboy trophy saddle from El Paso, and here's another for the 1958 world champion cowboy.

"And, oh, oh," I said grabbing his arm, "here's what I wanted you to see." I pointed toward a group of pictures. "That's Emma 'Pee-Wee' Ott. She rode saddle broncs, just like I want to do. She was only five foot tall in her bare feet, but rode with some of the best cowboys in the business, like Slim Pickens and John Bowman."

"Un-huh," Don nodded as he pointed to another photo, "and there she is getting thrown, just like another girl I know."

"But the thing is, she could, and did ride with the best. She did exhibitions for Harry Rowell's Rodeos, and even did some trick riding. She also competed in flat rail racing, and beat the best.

"And she's not the only one. Jane Burnett rode for years also. They don't have any of Jane's pictures, but she traveled all over the United States, riding broncs, and even appeared in some movies with Gene Autry."

"And where are they now?" He slipped his hand around my waist as we moved slowly past the trophy cases.

"'Pee-Wee' is in her eighties and living in Modesto. I think Jane's close to the same age. She lives in Arizona and writes books. But don't you see," I said, turning to face him. "When they tell me it can't be done…that women can't ride saddle broncs as good as men…they're full of baloney. Those women did, and there's others, too."

"Oh, I can fully understand. I've done some crazy things in my life also. It's just that I don't want to see you hurt again. Besides, I don't quite get it. I mean, what kind of a thrill can you get by getting bucked off a horse," he said with a laugh.

"Okay, have you even been on a roller coaster? I mean, a real good one?"

"Yes, I have," he said with a nod. "I took my little sister to Six Flags several times, and we went on some pretty scary rides.

"Alright, now picture yourself on one of those rides. Remember what it felt like, when you were at the top, ready to drop?"

He nodded.

"Now, multiply that feeling several times, and you're close to what it's like being on a real good horse," I said.

"Mmmm, I don't know if I could handle that type of thrill. Besides, you're strapped into a roller coaster, and they don't buck you off." He stopped to study a photograph hanging near Pee-Wee Ott's picture. "Is she related to the lady who unlocked the door?"

I took a good look the photo. "Sharon Camarillo? Na, the Camarillos are all into rodeo, and several of them are champions. But I think Sharon's an ex-sister-in-law or something. She made it all the way to National Finals barrel-racing. Right now, she's a top rodeo sports commentator, and holds clinics, teaching barrel-racing. I've never been to one of her clinics, but Marline and Angela have, and say she's pretty good. I guess that's why they're so good.

"And there, my friend," I pointed toward some photographs on the opposite wall, "is Ben Johnson winning his calf-roping trophy. Next to him is Sig Mitzner winning his 1956 roping buckle.

"And here's some local heroes." I pointed toward the pictures and trophies as I talked. "Phil and Bertha Stadler were a brother-sister team of bronc riders. Ted Nuce won the 1985 World Bull Riding Championship. I'll have to introduce you to Ted one of these days. He's a real nice guy. And here's Trav Cadwell. He started riding in rodeos when he was ten years old. He's been in the winner's circle in Salinas, Pendelton, San Antonio and Pocatello. Trav won the California Steer Wrestling Championship in 1994 and in 2000, and also qualified for the nationals that same year."

"And Margie wants to see her pictures and buckles displayed here also," Don said with a nod.

"Yeah, that would be nice. Would it bother you that much, Reverend?"

"Only if Margie had to give her tours on crutches or from a wheelchair."

"Would you still like me if that happened," I said with a grin. My heart fluttered as he stared at me long and hard.

"You're having to think about that, aren't you? That maybe you don't like me at all? I can always tell when you're thinking about something, because you blink your eyes real fast," I said as he continued staring.

"No, I was just trying to picture you in a wheelchair, and how that might change things. I wouldn't want that to happen. Not that I would stop liking you, or want to take care of you. But I would hate for something like that to happen to you...to anybody."

"You didn't answer the question, Pastor. Would you like, or maybe love me if I were in a wheelchair?"

"Is this some sort of trap, or something?" He put both hands on my shoulders and chuckled. "I know we've been seeing each other fairly regularly for some weeks..."

"Two months," I corrected.

"Okay, months. But I don't remember ever saying I loved you."

"You haven't, but I'd like to know. Do you, or could you love this Margie," I swept my arm around the room, "rodeo and all? I'm just sort of curious, you know."

"Do I love you? I am extremely fond of you. You could possible say yes, I might be falling in love with you. As to my loving the rodeo version of Margie? I think *that* Margie would eventually give me ulcers...but I'd still love her." He leaned to give me a long, tender kiss, then jerked away at the sound of a loud crash.

"Hey, kids, what did you break? Don't touch anything!" he said running into the next room.

Both children were standing mummified, staring up at their father.

"They didn't break anything. It's just a branding iron," I said placing the iron back into the display. "Hey, know what? How about us going next door to see how they make chocolate candy?"

"Yeah!" they yelled in unison.

"Come on Daddy, let's give the kids a little treat."

He paused to point at the picture of "Pee-Wee" Ott getting bucked off a horse and said, "That, my friend, is pretty stupid."

"I'll bet if I tried hard enough, I could find some pictures of a quarterback getting knocked on his butt by a three-hundred-pound linebacker."

"Touche'." He bowed gracefully, before grabbing a coiled rope from Donnie's grasp. "Come on, let's get out of here before they really break something."

I slipped my arm around his waist as we walked toward the Hershey's Center. I'd gotten what I wanted. Now, it was time to give the kids something they wanted.

Chapter 15

"What? I don't even know what I did that's got you so pee-o'd. What'd I do that you think is so bad," I yelled toward the kitchen. It was exactly a week after I'd given Don a tour of the Cowboy Museum, and Mama was fuming.

"That little dance of yours in front of Pastor Don and his children," Mama said, coming back into the living room. "It was totally unacceptable, especially in front of a minister."

"What? I was imitating Ann Margaret and having a little fun. What's wrong with that?"

"There is no harm in having a little fun. But that dance you did was sexually arousing, and intended for him. Am I right?" She got real close and glared.

"Well, yeah…sort of. But Ann Margaret is sexy, Ma, and I was just doing what she did with Elvis in *Viva Las Vegas*," I said with a shrug.

"Pastor Gardner is not Elvis Presley. And, I don't care if you are dating him, that type of dancing in front of any man…especially a minister…is not appropriate." She spun back toward the kitchen, where she paused to point at me and add, "Especially coming from a daughter I raised to know better!"

"Well, Marline was dancing too! What about her," I yelled as she disappeared through the door.

"Yes, but Marline was not doing the same dance, or acting the way you did," she poked her head back through the opening, "now, was she?"

"No, she was doing Elvis' part."

"Oh, I don't even know why I try." She rolled her eyes toward the ceiling and returned to what she was doing in the kitchen. I could still hear her over the clanking and clattering of pans as she rummaged through the cupboards. "The fact is, you owe that man an apology!"

"Okay, okay! I'll apologize! Geeze, you started the whole thing," I said, flopping onto the sofa next to a stack of picture albums.

"What was that last comment, young lady?" She glared at me through the door opening.

"Nothing. Just talking to myself," I said.

"Okay, just keep those types of comments to yourself." She disappeared and I made a face before opening one of the albums. She *was* the one who had gotten me started, and the picture of me with pink hair, and Marline with green, had been the fuel.

It all started with Marline popping in unannounced while Don and the kids were spending a quiet afternoon in our living room. That was when Mama produced some of her picture collection for Don to look at.

"What in the world happened here?" He laughed and pointed toward one of the pages.

"You wouldn't believe me, if I told you, Pastor," Mama said with a crooked smile.

"Let me see," I said, looking over her shoulder. "Oh, geesh, Ma. We were in the eighth grade. I can't believe you're showing him that!"

"These girls were forever doing something weird to their hair. I'm surprised they have any left," Mama continued. "The reason for the short hair…"

"Short isn't the word for it," Don said, cutting her off. "They look like they're fresh out of Boot Camp. I'm sorry, go on. Why the short hair?"

"We wanted to look nice for the spring dance," Marline said.

"And you thought this looked nice," he said with a laugh.

"Let me explain how these two think," Mama said. "They wanted to have their hair done, and buy new dresses. Well, the dresses they picked out...the ones you see in the picture," Mama pointed, "happened to be quite expensive. So, Marline's mother and I decided they needed a lesson on the value of a dollar, and refused to pay for the dresses and perms both. So, these brilliant women decided to give themselves home permanents. Which would have been fine in itself, but, unbeknownst to their mothers, they decided to lighten their hair first. They bleached Marline's to a strawberry blond, and Margie's to platinum. Then, they turned right around and gave each other perms the same day. The results were startling!"

"Well, no one told us not to do it," Marline said.

"If you had read the directions, it says so right on the box," Mama said.

"Who reads all that stuff in the first place," I said.

"You two certainly didn't," Mama said.

"Okay, tell me what happened after they gave each other perms," Don said.

"Our hair got all crunchy and started breaking off," I said.

"You're kidding," he said, allowing his eyes to bounce from us to the picture and back again.

"I'm afraid not," Mama said. "Every time you ran a brush or comb through their hair, you came up with handfuls of sticky hair. I called Mrs. Dickerson, and we ran the girls to a beauty salon. But there wasn't anything they could do, except give them crew cuts. They cried something fierce, before Margie came up with the idea of tinting their hair like punk-rockers."

"Well hey, it worked! We were the hit of the dance," Marline said.

"I'll bet you never tried anything like that again. Did you," Don said.

"No, not home perms, anyway," I said. "You get me the natural way."

"Oh, I wouldn't be too quick with that statement, if I

were you," Mama said turning the page. "Take a look at this one."

"Oh, wow!" he said, staring at the album. The page was covered with pictures of us at a Halloween party. Marline had cut her hair and dressed like Elvis, and I had mine tinted red, and went as Ann Margaret. "That's really you two?"

"Yeah," I said leaning over Don's shoulder. "That was two years ago, during our senior year. Pretty good, huh?"

"Good? It's great."

"That's not all," Marline said, crowding in to point at several photos. "Here we are winning for the best costumes, and this one is where we performed a couple of songs from *Viva Las Vegas* on stage with the band. We actually did our own singing."

"Yeah, everyone got a bang out of it, even if Marline sings higher than Elvis," I said.

"I would liked to have seen you two on stage," Don said with a laugh.

"Hey, let's do it!" Marline said.

"Huh? Where?" I said glancing around the room.

"Right here in the living room. Come on, we can do it." She grabbed the coffee table and pulled it toward the wall.

"What about music?"

"Get one of your records. Come on, it'll be fun!" Marline pulled me toward the bedroom before pausing, and motioned for Don to follow.

"Come here, Pastor. You've got to see this. You won't believe her room."

"No, Marline…I haven't cleaned it, and it's a mess!" I hissed.

"It's always a mess. Come here, Pastor," she said swinging the door wide. He stared a long minute at the walls covered with the Elvis memorabilia I had collected over the years.

"Whoa," he said, pushing past us and into the room. "I had no idea you were into Elvis. I expected to see cowboys and rodeo on your walls."

"Well, I've got that too, but it's mostly in the trophy case in the living room," I said. "But I've got a few of my buckles and pictures on top of the dresser. Come on, you've seen enough of my room, so out...go on." I turned him back toward the door with a gentle shove. "Go keep Mama company while I find Marline's music."

It only took a matter of minutes before I found the *Viva Las Vegas* album, and Marline dropped it onto Dad's old record player in the living room. We began our performance to the driving beat as Elvis and Ann sang Ray Charles' *Tell Me, What'd I Say*. I guess what really ticked Mama off was, when I danced up to where Don was sitting during one of the *aah...aah...ooh...ooh* parts, doing the shimmy like Ann Margaret. Then, I ran my hand up the back of my neck and flipped my hair forward, giving him the eye, while singing *it feels so good...baby, it feels so good.*

"Oh well," I said, closing the album with a snap. It might not have been quite appropriate in front of a minister like Mama said. But it was what Marline and I had done on stage, and we had a blast. Besides, Donald Ray Gardner was more than my pastor, and the look on his face when I flipped my hair was worth Mama's wrath.

I smiled as I took the record back toward the bedroom, and paused to poke my head through the kitchen doorway.

"Sorry, it won't happen again," I said.

"I certainly hope not," Mama said, measuring sugar for a pineapple upside-down cake.

"Don't worry, it won't." *At least not in front of you.* I hummed *Tell Me What'd I Say* as I dropped the record back into its proper slot in my collection.

Chapter 16

"She is a pretty horse. Here, let me help you with that," Don said, as I hoisted the saddle. He had agreed to drive me and Mama to the stables while Dad was working, so I could groom and care for Cupcake.

"Yes, we were a little surprised when Margie bought this horse. She had been saving to buy a car, but when Mable told her the owner wanted to sell this mare, she rushed to the bank and withdrew her money," Mama said.

"I'll get a car, eventually," I said, giving the cinch a tug. "I've almost got enough saved right now to buy a pretty good one. But you don't get a chance to buy a horse like Cupcake every day."

"Didn't you already have a horse," Don asked, rubbing Cupcake's muzzle.

"Yes. I had a little gelding named Roscoe. That's him over in that pen," I said, pointing toward the black and white munching hay. "Roscoe's a nice horse, but he was getting old, and wasn't fast enough to compete. So, I sold him to Chuck and Mable. They use him as a rental, for people who want to go trail-riding."

"You use Cupcake to compete on? She doesn't buck, does she," Don asked as I hoisted Donnie into the saddle.

"No," I sniggered, "not that I know of. Why?"

"Why? You have my son on her back, that's why. You said you compete on her, and you ride broncs..." Don's eyes bounced from his son toward me and back again.

"Oh, I'm sorry. He's safe. Really," I said.

"Margie doesn't just ride broncs, Pastor. Didn't she tell you," Mama said with a giggle.

"No. What else do you do?"

"I've done some barrel-racing, and a little tiedown roping. I've been leaning toward calf-roping. I'm actually pretty good at it, but they won't let me compete in the PRCA circuit, because I'm a girl, and people like Marline and Angela don't want to rope. They say it's too rough."

"It isn't actually safe, you know," Mama said. "People get broken fingers, and actually lose them once in awhile."

I glanced at Don, who was staring wide-eyed.

"That only happens if you get your finger caught in the rope," I said.

"You've got to be joking. You'd do something that might cause you to lose your fingers?" Don gave a nervous laugh.

"Only if you happen to get your finger caught in the rope when the calf hits the end. Yeah, you might break it," I said.

"Or tear it off," Mama added.

"Yeah, but I've still got all mine. See?" I wiggled my fingers in the air.

"But for how long," Mama said.

"Ma! I'm careful. Besides, I don't rope very often. You know that."

"I'm sorry," she turned toward Don, "but am I wrong to worry about my daughter?"

"No, I don't think so. I know I worry about my children all the time. Just like I am this very minute. Are you sure this horse isn't going to buck them off," he said as I hoisted Caroline into the saddle behind her brother.

"Donald Ray Gardner! Do you actually believe I would do anything to hurt either of these babies? Cupcake is the gentlest horse in the stable."

I held the reins and started leading the quarter horse around the arena, limping against my stiff knee.

"Here, let me do that," Don said, taking the reins from

my hand. "You go sit beside your mother, and rest."

"Thanks." I climbed up on the railing to watch as he led Cupcake and the giggling children in a big circle.

"You almost caused another war, by telling him I could lose some fingers roping. You know that, don't you?" I gave Mama a sideways glance.

She laughed and gave me a swat on the behind. "That was my intention."

"Why?"

"How do you think it makes me feel, knowing my child is doing something dangerous, and seeing her hurt and banged-up? You'll learn. Someday, when you're in the hospital, watching your own child being wheeled into the emergency room, you'll know how it feels."

"I'd feel that way about one of them," I said, nodding toward Donnie and Carol.

"Good. I hope so. You think they might become yours one of these days," she added after a minute.

"I don't know. I'm kind of hoping they might." I gave Mama a grin. "What do you think?"

"I'm hoping so," she said with a nod. "I think that would be real nice."

Chapter 17

"I didn't mean to cause such an uproar. I'm sorry. I just wanted to play volleyball."

"I know. Don't worry about it." Don gave me a sideways grin and raised his eyebrows with a shrug. "They'll just have to get over it."

It had been almost three months since I rode Irish, and the stiffness in my knee was completely gone. So, when Marline asked if I wanted to join the volleyball game the church was having on youth night, I said, "Sure, wouldn't miss it." Well, thinking volleyball was the same for everyone, I slipped into the same spandex shorts and halter top I'd worn in high school, then pulled on a pair of sweats. Everything was fine, until we'd finished choosing teams, and I removed the sweats. Some of the older ladies, sitting and watching on the sidelines, who I guessed to be youth sponsors, began making comments like, "Oh, my word, who let her come dressed like that?" Someone else said, "Isn't that the same young woman Pastor Gardner has been seeing? Someone needs to have a talk with him."

Well me being who I am, I simply blew their comments off, and went on with the game. We were doing pretty good, too. At least the team I was on was ahead. That was when Don called me into one of the side rooms and closed the door.

"Better put these back on," he said, handing me the sweats.

"Why?"

"Because, some of the youth sponsors and a few of the

young people think your outfit is too revealing."

"And, what do you think," I asked.

"Now, that's a loaded question." He gave a nervous laugh and turned red. "I'll have to admit I've rather enjoyed watching you jump around dressed like that. But, some of the others don't feel the same as I do. Well, I take that back. Maybe they do, and that's their problem. Look, just put the sweats on. Okay?"

"Okay, Pastor Don," I said, pulling on the sweatpants. "But I've worn this outfit in front of hundreds...maybe thousands of people, running in track meets and playing volleyball across the San Joaquin Valley, and this is the first time anyone has ever said anything about it."

"Yes, I know. And I've actually seen more revealing uniforms in college."

"How about Olympic Beach Volleyball?" I finished pulling the top over my head and gave him a grin.

"Now, let's don't even go there. I know exactly what you mean." He grinned and kissed my nose.

"You said some of the young people were upset? Which ones?"

"You don't need to know," he said with a stern look.

"Why not? Was it girls, or some of the guys? I'd like to know."

"Mostly girls, but I'm not going to say who."

"Figures," I said, giving him a quick kiss. "Sorry I caused such a fuss."

I overheard one of the ladies say, "Much better," as I returned to the game. My position had rotated me to the front and center of the net. A frumpy-looking girl with mouse-brown hair glared at me through the net and sneered. "It's about time you put on something decent. We're here to play volleyball, not have a fashion show."

"Really? I'm sorry I didn't catch on sooner." I smiled sweetly before spiking the next ball against her big mouth.

Chapter 18

"Please sit down. It's good to see you, Margie. How is the knee doing?" Norm Mendenhall was president of the Oakdale Saddle Club, and had responded graciously to my request to meet with the members of the board.

"Thank you," I said as Harold Swaim held a chair for me to sit at a long table. "My knee has healed up nicely, and I'm ready to start riding again. That is why I've asked to meet with the Saddle Club."

"I noticed you're limping. I hope that isn't caused by some permanent damage to you knee." Lenny Ferguson said.

"No," I said with a laugh. "I twisted my ankle jumping from the back of Mable's pickup after unloading some bales of hay. But I'm almost healed from that one also."

"I've read your letter, and I believe everyone knows why you've asked to meet with us. But, why don't you tell us in your own words why you're here," Norm said.

"I know some of you will probably think I'm crazy," I said, "and perhaps I am. But I would like to see if there isn't some way of changing the rules, so women who feel like I do can compete with men in rodeo events."

"Women competing with men in a rodeo? Doesn't Kaila Mussell already do that? I don't see that there'd be any problem, as long as you can get PRCA backing," Lenny Ferguson said.

"Well, yeah, but she's the only one that I'm aware of, unless you go to Australia. The Warick Rodeo has what they call the *Ladies Buckjump*, where women ride saddle broncs. They don't actually compete against the men, but they perform in the same rodeo, in the same events as the men." I said. "But in actuality, I wouldn't be competing *against* the men in the first place. I would be competing *with* the men."

"Excuse me," Doreen Dumlao cleared her throat and said, "I believe I know what you mean, but why don't you explain the difference, Margie?"

"As I'm sure you are aware, rodeo is perhaps the only sport where sex, size and strength doesn't matter. I can see why a girl would have problems competing with guys in something like football beyond the junior high, or high school level. They would be too small physically, and would be getting constantly knocked around and hurt. The same goes for even tennis or track. The size and physical strength of the men would simply over-power most women.

"But rodeo is different in that, it is the rider competing *with the animal* to achieve a score, and not competing *against* another rider. It doesn't really matter how big and how strong another rider is, or how well any other rider might do. It is based on how well a particular rider, male or female, does on a given animal."

"That may be true, but physical strength and conditioning does play into it," one of the other members said.

"Sure, but not like you'd think. Emma Ott was only five-feet tall, and Jane Burnett wasn't much bigger. And don't forget, Ted Nuce wasn't any Arnold Schwarzenegger, but you couldn't find a better bull-rider when he was competing."

"No, I don't suppose you could," Lenny said with a chuckle. "And some of what you've said is certainly true. I've watched several WPRCA events, and the women competing in those events certainly know what they are doing, and handle themselves well. Why is it you want to compete in the PRCA, and not with the women?"

"I don't mind competing in WPRCA events. In fact, I'm a member, and I compete regularly in bareback, breakaway roping, and I do a little barrel-racing every now and then. But I don't think there should be any distinction or difference between us. I feel PRCA and the WPRCA should be considered the same, and hold their events together."

"I've known Margie and her family a long time," Harold Swaim said with a chuckle. "Her, and that group of friends she hangs around with have always felt this way. Margie's been on a quest to change the world since the day she was born."

"Well, Margie, I don't know if what you're asking is possible, even if we happened to agree with you...and I'm sure not everyone does," Norm Mendenhall said.

"I know Mr. Swaim doesn't," I said with a laugh.

"I wouldn't be too sure about that. Harold's been your biggest supporter," Norm said. I turned to stare at Harold open-mouthed as Norm continued.

"The problem is, you're asking the Oakdale Saddle Club to change or abolish PRCA rules, and that isn't possible. To get the PRCA to change their rules, you'd have to send your request to them, and lots of luck. Then, you'd have to get both organizations, the PRCA and the WPRCA to agree to shorten their programs, in order to compete together at the same time. That means fewer men and women competing in each rodeo, and knowing some cowboys and women it would effect, I think you'd have a tough time getting either side to agree with the changes.

"In the meantime, we'll consider your request to continue riding exhibition. But, after seeing you get hurt last April, not everyone is in full agreement with that, either."

"That wasn't really my fault. It was caused by the horse slipping on the wet arena, and the stirrup-hobble. I wasn't able to jerk my leg out of the way when Irish fell," I said.

"Yes, Harold has explained that to us, and happens to agree with you. We'll let you know our decision, and thank you for coming in, Margie. It was good to see you, and I hope your ankle gets better soon," Norm said, standing to shake my hand.

"Thank you, I'm sure it will. And, thank all of you for taking time to listen. I appreciate it very much," I said, mustering the biggest smile I could.

They offered their *thank yous* and best wishes as I was

leaving. The Saddle Club members were some of the nicest people ever, and I knew Norm was right. I had come to the wrong place trying to get the rules changed. There was no way they were going to risk losing their PRCA standing by bending the rules. Besides, even if they did allow me to compete in Oakdale, the PRCA would not accept my score as official, or allow me to compete in other arenas unless I joined their organization. Without going higher, or becoming a PRCA member, I was stuck doing exhibition riding or competing in the WPRCA with Marline.

"Okay, I can do that," I said out loud.

"You can do what," Don said as I joined him in the Country Club lobby.

"They told me I needed to take my request higher, so that's what I'm going to do." I stood on my tiptoes and gave him a quick kiss, then grabbed Donnie and Caroline's hands as we walked toward the parking lot.

"So, how did it go in there," Don asked as we reached the car.

"Both good and bad. They're all a bunch of nice people who listened, but they told me I would have to go higher if I wanted to change the rules."

"What about exhibition riding? Wasn't that one of your requests," he asked, slipping Donnie into the car seat.

"They said they would let me know. They didn't like seeing me get hurt." I buckled Carol in and gave her a kiss.

"I didn't either," he said.

"That's good, because I didn't like getting hurt," I said with a laugh. "Let's stop at K Mart. I need to get some paper and envelopes. I've got a few letters to write."

"Okay..." He drug the word out with a grin and started the car forward.

So, Harold Swaim's been on my side all the time and I didn't know it. How about that old coot?

Chapter 19

"That's nice," Don said, studying the silver-plated buckle.

"Thanks. Here, take a better look." I pulled the belt from around my waist. He rocked the shiny piece back and forth in the sunlight and smiled.

"Very pretty. You won this Sunday afternoon?"

"Yeah, in Salinas. They had some pretty good competition, but I drew a real good horse."

"You didn't get hurt or anything," he said as Caroline ran up, begging to see the buckle.

"Here, you can hold it," I said, handing her the belt. "Just be careful and don't drop it on the pavement. Okay?" She ran to stand over their front lawn as Donnie looked on, begging for a chance to touch the new treasure. "It's alright, honey. He can hold it, as long as he stays over the grass."

"I'm sorry, what were you saying?" I turned back to Don.

"I was asking if you had gotten hurt?"

"No," I shook my head. "Oh, I got a little black-and-blue mark on my hip from dismounting, but no…I didn't get hurt."

"Getting a bruised hip isn't getting hurt," he said with a grin.

"Do college quarterbacks ever get bruised?" I grinned right back.

"Quit changing the subject on me." He laughed.

"I'm not changing the subject. They are both rough

sports, aren't they?"

"Yes, but I gave mine up when I graduated, and decided to have a family," he said.

"Don't I recall you saying that Caroline was on her way *before* you graduated from college?" I drew up close and cocked my head to one side.

"Yes, Linda was pregnant, but I had given up football long before she was born. Now, what about you, my dear? When are you going to give up getting thrown from horses?"

"I'll consider it when I decide to start a family. Fair enough" I asked with a nod.

"I guess that's fair enough," he said with a nod of his own. Our kiss was broken by two squealing children fighting over the belt and buckle.

Chapter 20

I was up before daybreak Saturday morning and put coffee on to brew, then climbed into the shower. I bathed and did my make up, then grabbed the second prettiest dress I had, which wasn't hard, considering I mostly wore jeans and boots. I drank my coffee as I drove Dad's pickup to the post office to mail a protest letter to the PRCA, telling them what I thought about their stupid rules, then headed toward Don's house. I was using the arm-load of papers I'd picked up at the printers the day before as an excuse for going so early. Don had been relying on me to do little chores for him and, of course, I was happy to do most anything he asked, because it made me feel more a part of him. There wasn't a minute of the day I wasn't thinking about him, or wishing he were there. It was real scary, because I hadn't felt this way about anyone, not even when I thought I was in love with Barry.

I stopped in the middle of the street to stare at the red Mercury in his driveway before parking the truck. I gathered the papers and rang the doorbell, thinking it was probably some preacher-friend who had dropped by, when the door opened to reveal a pretty dark-eyed girl, dressed in a bathrobe. We stared at each other for a long minute, before she cleared her throat and spoke politely.

"May I help you?"

"Yes, I guess so. Is Don, I mean, Reverend Gardner in?"

Her dark eyes sparkled as her perfectly shaped mouth broke into a grin. She was too pretty to be hanging around my boyfriend, especially dressed, or not dressed, the way she was.

"Oh, yes he is. Would you care to come in?" The grin grew to a smile that made her freckled nose crinkle.

"Yes, I would. Thank you." I placed the stack of papers on the end table next to the sofa. Her dark brown hair, which hung just below her shoulders, bounced lively as she whirled and yelled.

"Hey Preach, there's someone here to see you."

"Be out in a minute," his muffled voice said from the bedroom.

"Get you some coffee?"

I shook my head and waited while she poured herself a cup and sat on the sofa opposite from where I sat and crossed her legs. The robe parted, revealing a set of tanned, shapely limbs that most women would kill for. God, I hated every inch of her.

"So, how long have you known Donnie?" She sipped her coffee.

"A little over four months." There was another pregnant moment of silence. Finally, I just couldn't stand it any longer.

"Excuse me, but who the hell are you, and what are you doing in my boyfriend's house? And I hope to God you don't say you spent the night here."

"I guess Donnie's never told you about me?" She smiled sweetly. "I've known him a lot longer than you have. And yes, I did spend last night here, but I've spent many evenings with him."

I bolted from the chair, but she held out a hand and shook her head as I stood at the edge of the coffee table glaring with clenched fists.

"Before you lose your temper, you have to understand Donnie and the way he is."

"I don't have to do anything of..." Don came out of the bedroom humming a tune and stopped when he saw me.

"Oh, it's you, Margie. You're out early, aren't you? I see you two have already met." He leaned to kiss me, but I pushed him away.

"Don't you kiss me." He took a step backward as I

squared to face him. "Who is she and what's she doing here? And if I find out you've been sleeping with her, you're both dead."

The brunette laughed hysterically as Don's mouth fell.

"Why..." he choked back a laugh, "would I want to sleep with my sister?"

"Sister?" I glanced at the girl who wiped the corner of her eyes on the sleeve of the bathrobe as she tried composing herself.

"This is Peggy, my kid sister. She arrived late last night. Remember, I told you about her?"

"No. All you said was you had a sister who was younger than you. You've never shown me a picture. The way you talked, I thought she was some little kid.

"Look, all I know is, I come here this morning and meet this pretty girl, woman, actually, dressed in a bathrobe. And she calls you *Donnie* and say's she has spent a lot of nights with you. What *should* I think?"

"I see my sister has been up to her old games. You've got to watch her or she'll give you ulcers."

She got off the sofa and hugged me.

"I'm so glad to finally meet you. Donnie's told me everything about you. Well, everything I could worm out of him." She held me at arm's length. "But he didn't tell me that you look like...I mean, what you look like. He described you as being a young cowgirl, that's all."

"That's how he described you, also, only not the cowgirl part. I thought you were gonna be a little kid, maybe twelve or thirteen."

"Donnie!" She glared at him. "You need to communicate better. We're both grown women. Look at us."

"I can see that in Margie. That's what interests me about her. But you're still my kid sister and will be when you reach a hundred years old."

He grinned as she hit at him.

"Now, can I have my good-morning kiss?" His arms felt good around me and the smell of his spiced after-shave turned me on, so I kissed him twice.

"Peggy, can you watch the children for me? I have an early meeting that I'm gonna be late for if I don't hurry."

"I don't understand how men can be so romantic one minute and turn it off the next."

"Yeah." Peggy nodded her agreement as he kissed the top of her head. Picking up the stack of papers I'd placed on the table, he said "bye" and gave me a quick peck on the lips before bounding out the door.

"Well, so much for my plans of a romantic morning, looking at each other across the table through steaming cups of freshly-brewed coffee." I shrugged my shoulders.

"That only happens in movies. Here, sit at the table and we'll look at each other through that steam and get acquainted." She set a cup of coffee on the kitchen table and poured herself a second.

"You don't know how close you came to getting your eyes scratched out," I said as she sat down. "I had no idea who you were, and I thought that...well, it's possible."

"I had an idea you were close to bashing me, and was trying to decide which way I was going to run if you came around the table. But the look you had on your face when I opened the door was priceless. I wish I'd had a camera. I used to play that sort of game when we were teenagers. I'd answer the phone and try to sound sexy. It didn't work on Linda, because she knew me. But none of the rest knew I existed. As you just found out, my brother doesn't talk much about his family. Don never seemed to mind, and even played along. Except for one time. He and Linda had this huge fight during their junior year of high school, and split for about a month. He started seeing this other girl, mostly out of spite.

"Becky Johnson," she glanced upward thoughtfully. "I'll never forget her. Anyway, I put the act on so well that Becky burst through our front door and slapped his face. He called me from my bedroom where I was doing homework, and ordered me to tell her the truth. Instead, I threw my arms around him, yelling for her to leave my boyfriend alone. So, she slapped him again. He was angry for a week that time."

"I thought he and Linda had gone steady though high school."

"They did, except for that short time. But you know how it is when a guy looks like my brother, and is a big star on the football team. There were always girls calling, hanging on him, and trying to take him away from her. There's one thing I can say about my brother, he stuck with Linda the whole time, so I didn't mind running the others off." She grinned.

"That was a mean trick to play on Becky Johnson, but I would have given anything to see it." I laughed. "You looked surprised to see me this morning."

"I was. I asked my brother a lot of questions when he told me he was seeing a girl named Marjorie Green. But all I got out of him was that you were young, pretty and loved horses. That's all. He didn't tell me that you looked exactly like...you do." Her eyes watered and she blinked several times. "You're beautiful."

"Thanks, so are you. What else did he tell you about me?"

"Nothing, except your personality and where you came from."

"Oh? That I've got horse manure on my boots, or something like that?" I took a sip of coffee.

"Something like that." She paused to take a sip of her own. "He kind of talks between the lines, but I know my brother, and he more than likes you. And so do I."

I smiled. "How can you? You don't even know me."

"I know enough to know I like you. What did he tell you about us? His family?"

"That he had this kid sister. Oh, you're supposed to be playing with Barbie Dolls, by the way. And you live with your mother in Bakersfield. Your father was a minister who passed away some time ago. I don't know what from. That's about all. I didn't ask a lot of questions. Maybe I should have."

"Sounds funny to sum up someone's life in a couple of sentences, doesn't it? What did he tell you about Linda?"

"Nothing. Only that she died of cancer. God, now that you asked, I suddenly feel strange, knowing so little about the man I claim to love. I don't really know him at all, do I? He could be an ax-murderer for all I know. He hasn't volunteered any information at all."

"Did he ever show you a picture of her?"

I shook my head no.

"That's Don. Abbreviates everything except the Bible. Ask him a question about Moses and you'll get a two-hour sermon."

"I know, I did." We both laughed.

"The point is, you're going to have to ask him pointed questions to get answers. He's a great guy. You're right to love him. I would fall in love with him too, if he wasn't my brother. But he's got his faults."

"Don't they all?"

"Yeah," she giggled, "that's why they need us. But one of my brother's is being closed and private. After Linda died, he shut the door on himself and couldn't let anyone in. Oh, he might share little bits here and there, if they don't get too close and personal. Your job is to chisel and pry at that beautiful facade of his. That is, unless you want to marry a stranger."

I felt my heart jump. "Marry? He hasn't asked me."

"No?" She raised her eyebrows.

"No, he hasn't. What did he tell you?" She shook her head, and I reached across the table to grab her wrist. "Come on, Peggy, what did he say?"

"Look, all you need to know is that he's in love with you, and he's going to ask when he thinks the timing is right. Okay?"

"Ugh, you are evil," I said, and she laughed.

"What do you know about our mother? She'll be here next Saturday for Donnie's birthday party."

"Only that she's in her early fifties, has gotten remarried to a nice man who has a lot of money, and is a little overbearing."

"That's an understatement." Peggy leaned back in her chair laughing.

"Why, what's wrong?"

"Well, let's just say she absorbs all the oxygen when she enters the room. But, you'll find out soon enough." She slid away from the table with a chuckle. "I think the kids are awake. I can hear Donnie pestering his sister in the bedroom. Would you mind watching them while I get dressed?"

"No," I said, shaking my head.

"Thanks, I'll only be a minute."

She half-skipped and ran toward the guest bedroom as I downed the last of my coffee in one gulp. I was even more confused than when I arrived. I had a boyfriend with two children who had closed himself to the rest of the world when their mother died. He had a sister who enjoyed playing jokes, and a mother who sucked the air out the room. But worse yet, my boyfriend had told every one but me we were getting married when the timing was right...whatever that meant. But I wasn't supposed to worry, because, according to his sister, Peggy, I was gonna find the answers soon enough.

I placed the dirty mug in the sink and hurried down the hall to rescue Caroline from her brother, wondering what I'd gotten myself into.

Chapter 21

I helped clean the stalls and feed the animals before catching a ride with Marline, who had stayed to practice her barrel-racing with Buster. Unlike most people, I love the smell of fresh hay and animals, but working in that environment on a hot day can make you quite unacceptable to others you might happen to meet.

Marline parked her blue pickup in front of my house, and I sat staring at the green Mustang sitting behind Dad's truck in the driveway. Peggy's car was parked across the street.

"I wish he would've waited until I had a shower before coming over."

"Why? He's seen you after you've been riding," Marline said.

"Not like this. Look at me, Marline. I'm all sweaty and dirty. And I smell like…"

"Yes, I know what you smell like. I've been smelling you for the last five miles. Go on, he'll still love you, even if you smell like a wet horse. Remember? Sweat is sexy." She laughed.

"Wanna come in," I said, opening the door.

"No, I'm going to go jump in the shower myself. I've got a date."

"Anyone I know?"

"Yeah." She grinned.

"Who?"

"You'll find out soon enough. Now, go on," she put the truck in gear, "and give him a kiss for me."

"Not on your life," I yelled as she drove away.

I unlatched the gate of our small picket fence, when Peggy exploded through the front door, followed by Donnie and Carol.

"God, I can't believe she did this!" she said, grabbing me by the shoulders.

"Who?"

"Mama. I just can't...I never thought she had it in her!"

"Calm down," I said, pulling loose long enough the give the kids a hug and kiss. They didn't seem to mind my smell.

"I can't. She arrived a couple of hours ago and insisted on coming right over to meet you. And she had the gall to bring Helen Fisher with her."

"Helen Fisher," I said, staring at the front door.

"Yes. She's a real bitch who's had a crush on Don since grade school. She did her best to break up his relationship with Linda, and she's in there right now trying to worm her way between you and Don."

"Really," I said, closing the gate. "And what's he think about it?"

"He's never liked her that I know of, but she's rich and sneaky. I wouldn't trust her as far as I could throw her," Peggy said in a hushed tone as we reached the porch.

"Trust another woman around your brother?" I laughed. "Not on your life."

I held the door open for Donnie and Carol then, bracing myself as I stepped inside.

"Gama's here," Donnie said, jumping onto the sofa beside a slightly overweight woman. I wanted to meet his mother, but not like this, with sweat dripping from every pore.

"Hi," Don said, rising to kiss me. I took it to be some sort of statement for his mother, and the woman she'd brought with her.

"Sorry we're here so early," he continued, "but they insisted on meeting your family before checking into the motel."

I'll just bet they did. My eyes were adjusting to the light inside the room, and I got my first good look at the well-dressed woman staring my way. She stood, and my spurs clinked as I took a couple of strides to meet her with an out-stretched hand. Her handshake felt like half-cooked noodles.

"Hello. You must be Marjorie. I'm Donald's mother, Joanne Carlton."

"Pleased to meet you," I said with a nod.

"Why Donald, she's only a child," she said, and I decided she could go to the Devil. She was probably kin to him anyway.

"Margie, this is Helen Fisher, an old friend of mine," Don said as a tall, thin brunette rose from Dad's easy chair.

I took the hand she extended, and it felt exactly like his old lady's, and I knew right then why they liked each other so much. They were exactly alike. This girl couldn't have been more than three or four years older than me, but the way she did her hair and clothes made her look older. We both smiled at each other like enemies do, and I gave her credit that at least her brain worked.

"Why Don," I said, "she's so much older than you." That brought an icy-glare from Helen Fisher, and the declaration of war was complete. I was stoked! She was gonna be sorry she ever set foot in Oakdale. I excused myself and went into the bedroom to put on my battle gear.

It only took a matter of minutes for me to shower and slip into the one and only sundress I had. Marline was always amazed at how quickly I could get ready to go some place when I really wanted to. But when you don't have that many outfits to choose from, it doesn't take long to make up your mind what you're gonna wear. I pulled my hair loose and brushed through it quickly, then put on some make-up. After one last look in the mirror, I opened the door. They were standing, as though they were preparing to leave.

"Sorry for the way I looked earlier. I do want to have a chance to get better acquainted real soon." I offered my hand to his mother. She stared at me with an open-mouthed expression, kind of like Peggy when we first met. I started wondering if I had forgotten something, like buttoning my front, but I had checked everything before opening the door.

"Oh, you will, believe me, you will," she said, glancing at Don and back to me several times. "Yes. Yes, I can see why Donald would fall in love with you."

I offered my hand to Helen Fisher who didn't say anything, but looked kinda pale like she was about to throw up. They left and I ran to double-check myself in the hall mirror. Everything was fine.

"What was that all about," I asked Mama.

"I'd say she's frightened because you're prettier than she is, and she knows she doesn't stand a chance."

Chapter 22

"Whoa, he's yummy!" Peggy gushed, as Barry Swaim drove away in his four-wheeler. We had gone shopping at K Mart to pick up the decorations and whatnots for Donnie's birthday party, when we bumped into Barry in the parking lot. He, of course, asked about Peggy, and she almost wet herself meeting him.

"Yeah, Barry's that alright," Marline said with a snigger.

"He's Margie's old boyfriend," Angela said.

"Don't remind me, Angela," I said.

"No, really?" Peggy grabbed my by the arm. "Tell me about him."

"Well, there's not much to tell. He's handsome, rich, and a lot of fun to be around. And he does rodeo like the rest of us," I said matter-of-factly.

"Yeah, he's that alright, if you don't mind sharing him with dozens of other girls," Marline said.

"You ought to know. It was your fault I got mixed up with him in the first place," I said, grabbing a shopping cart.

"Why? Did you date Barry also," Peggy asked Marline.

"I was dating Barry when he decided he liked Margie better," she said.

"We've all dated Barry," Angela said. "Every girl from here to Merced's dated Barry Swaim."

"Didn't it make you mad when he dumped you for Margie," Peggy said.

"Make me angry? Yeah…it hurt my feelings, if that's

what you mean. But, like Angela said, it would have happened sooner or later, because that's the way Barry is. Besides, it was kind of my own fault. Marge and I used to trade dates once in awhile for fun, like we swap clothes. We were out on this double-date one night, and I was with Barry. She was with this good-looking exchange student from England...."

"Sean William," I interrupted. "He was dreamy."

"Yeah, well, I kind of had my eye on him most of the night, and I knew Barry had had the hots for Marge for quite awhile. So, I talked them into switching partners halfway through the movie, just for kicks. Well, I was planning on switching back after that date, but it turned out to be almost a year before she was willing to give him up. You rat!" Marline said with a friendly scowl.

"Yeah, Margie holds the record for being with Barry the longest, doesn't she," Angela said.

"Probably, but I haven't kept track," Marline said.

"The thing about dating Barry is," I stopped in the middle of the aisle to face Peggy, "you'll have a lot of fun. He's funny, and lots of laughs. He's got the money to take you to restaurants, concerts, amusement parks and places you normally wouldn't be able to go. But he'll be doing the same thing with another girl, when he's supposedly going steady with you. You can't trust him." I started the cart forward.

"I was under the impression he had broken it off with Marline, but found out he was still trying to see her, and a couple of other girls, several weeks into our relationship. It was Marline who first spilled the beans and told me what was happening."

"And you didn't break up with him?" Peggy gasped.

"No. Stupid me. I believed him when he said he was sorry, and wouldn't do it again. Besides, Barry was the best thing to come along, in my book," I said. "How about those?" I pointed toward some Sponge Bob paper plates and cups.

"They'll work," Marline said, and tossed them into the cart.

"And, I couldn't be angry with Marline, because she was his girlfriend before I came onto the scene. Besides, Marline's been my friend as long as I can remember," I said.

"Same here. I'd never let anyone hurt her, not even Barry Swaim," Marline said.

"What they're trying to say, girl," Angela took Peggy by the shoulders, "is Barry's okay…if you don't mind sharing him. Just realize before you start, that he's going to have more than one girlfriend, and they might even be one of your friends."

"And you can't let it bother you, or you'll go around hating every girl in the San Joaquin Valley," Marline said, as she dug into the cooler-section for several bottles of fruit punch.

"Now that he's seen you, he'll probably be calling to ask you out. Just know the rules before you start, because none of us want to see you hurt," I said. "It won't make us angry if you decide to date him, but do it for fun and not love. Because Barry is going to be Barry, and I don't think he'll ever change."

"He might if he met the right person," Peggy said.

I looked at the other two and shrugged before saying, "Okay, whatever."

"How about some nice lilies," Marline said.

"For Donnie's party," Peggy asked.

"No, for you, Dodo-brain, after Barry gets through with you."

Chapter 23

Donnie's third birthday party was about as exciting as a party for two, three and four-year-olds could possibly be. There were about a dozen kids and their families from the church, along with Marline, Angela and my parents, who joined us at the park to celebrate the affair. Each kid got balloons, hotdogs, punch, ice cream and their very own cupcake to destroy, not including the birthday cake with three candles. I'd been involved in enough kid parties at the stables to think of bringing plenty of wipes to clean dirty hands and faces as the day progressed. Each child also got a little present of their own to open, while Donnie ripped the wrapping off of his.

Angela brought a piñata that Don had to finally break after the kids had exhausted and bored themselves swinging the small Louisville Slugger in vain. The candy hidden inside was the final blow for Avery Williams, who puked down the front of his blue shirt after consuming four pieces. I helped his mother clean and change him to the *ugh* and *agh* gagging-sounds made by other children.

Changing Avery Williams was the only thing that Helen Fisher did not try to horn in on. She was making a convenient pest of herself, and I wasn't the only one feeling ticked-off. I was rummaging through the ice chest for a fresh coke, when Angela joined me.

"If that new friend of yours keeps it up, someone's gonna stuff her inside a piñata and beat the crap out of her."

"What friend?"

"Helen what's-'er-name," Angela said, with a motion of her head.

"She's no friend of mine," I said, popping open the coke.

"You won't mind if I drag her behind Zorro for a couple of miles then?"

"No, have at it," I said shaking my head. "What'd she do this time?"

"Oh, it's just that every time one of us starts a game, she takes over and makes it look like her idea."

"You noticed that too?" I handed Angela a cold soda.

"Thanks. It's hard not to notice. And the way she's playing up to Pastor Don, I don't know why you just don't punch that smug face of hers in."

"That's something you would have done in high school," Marline said, taking a seat on top of the picnic table.

"Yeah, like that'd really make me look good. The pastor's girlfriend beating the crap out of one of his old girlfriends in the middle of the park. Some of these kids mothers are the wives of deacons, you know," I said, before taking a long swig of my drink.

"So, you're just going to stand by and let her take over," Peggy said.

"There's nothing I can do about it. I'm already in enough trouble for cussing in church and wearing my track outfit to play volleyball. Besides, it should be up to your brother to do something. Shouldn't it? And why are all of you over here, and not helping with the children?" I glanced at Helen scrambling and trying to re-gather the children who'd just rebelled against the game of kick-the-ball she had commandeered from Angela.

"She wanted to take over, I say let her have at it," Angela sneered.

"Wasn't my turn to help anyway," Marline said.

"I wouldn't bother to spit on her if she caught fire," Peggy said.

"Well, what about the kids?" I stared at each of them, and got a *so what* look in return.

"Oh, alright! Here, you can have my coke," I shoved the

can at Peggy.

"Thanks, I was kinda thirsty. Have fun rescuing Helen," she added as I stomped away.

There wasn't much rescuing to do, as Mama and several of the mothers were already corralling the little monsters. I got them involved in a game of tag before discovering that Helen had disappeared. One glance toward the picnic table told me why. The giggling slug was busy sharing a plate of cake and ice cream with Don, while I attended to the children. His mother was seated at the same table watching my way.

"I wonder just how fast and how far Zorro could drag her?"

"Did you say something, Honey," Mama asked.

"Huh? Oh, nothing." I shook my head. "I was just watching Helen Fisher play up to Don, and thinking about something Angela said."

Chapter 24

Don's mother and Helen Fisher decided to extend their visit another week, which cut into my time with Don. Not that I wasn't invited to join the family activities he had planned to keep them entertained. I did go out to dinner with them on Tuesday evening, and bowling in Modesto Thursday night, but work kept me tied up during the day. The actual truth was, I didn't really want to be anywhere near Helen Fisher. My dog, Hobo, was better company, and a whole lot smarter. But Saturday was a day I'd been looking forward to for months, and I wasn't going to let her or anyone else keep me from rafting down the Stanislaus River.

"You and your big mouth," I hissed at Marline, as we lined up at the Knights Ferry water park to be assigned rafts.

"It isn't my fault. Your boyfriend and my pastor must have said something. Helen just sort of invited herself. What was I supposed to say…no?"

I glared at the long-legged brunette in the black French-cut one-piece crowding next to Don. The only bathing suit I owned was a red bikini. But after my experience at the volleyball game, I'd slipped a white, thigh-length Minnie Mouse tee shirt over the bikini. I didn't consider myself a prude by any stretch of the imagination, but Helen's one-piece was showing almost as much skin as my bikini did without the tee shirt.

"Look at her, trying to make sure she gets assigned to his raft," Angela hissed.

"Well, Margie needs to get over there and take her

place!" Marline laughed and gave me a shove that caused me to stumble over a life vest and bump into Don.

"Whoa, what's going on," he said catching me in his arms.

"Sorry," I giggled, "Marline pushed me."

"Careful, guys, no horsing around! Someone's going to get hurt," he yelled. "It was nice of you to drop in anyway," he added with a grin. "I've missed you."

"Really?" I could see Helen glaring at me as I smiled at the man I loved.

"Yes, more than you know."

We were rudely interrupted by one of the men from the Sunshine River Rafting yelling, "Okay, Pastor Gardner's group! Your rafts are ready! This way please. Twelve to a raft. Careful now. Remember the rules. Everyone wears a life jacket, and those who have never rafted before, go with experienced rafters."

I was about to climb into Don's raft when Helen started whining. "I've never done anything like this before. Please, Donald, may I ride with you? I'd feel much safer."

"Neither have I," he said with a chuckle. "I'm going to be following the advice of these young people."

"Oh, but you're such a good swimmer. Please...I'd feel safer."

He looked at me and shrugged. "I'm sorry, Margie. There's only room for one more person. Would you mind riding with Marline and Peggy?"

"Yeah, sure I'd mind. But go ahead." I let go of his hand and turned away.

"Marge!" he yelled as I stormed back into the line.

I didn't answer as the guy from the rafting company yelled, "Step lively and hurry it up, folks. There's a lot of people waiting."

"What's going on?" Peggy raised her voice to be heard.

"He's taking Helen instead of me."

"He's taking Helen, and you let him," she yelled.

"Bunch up, folks. Twelve to a raft." A different guy

began hurrying us into little groups. Don's raft was filled and they were getting their final instructions as we crowded into a raft next to them. I glanced over my shoulder to see who was in our group, and the girl with the mouse-brown hair was glaring at the back of my neck. *Geeze, can it get any worse than this?* I turned to smile and stuck out my hand.

"Hi, I'm Margie."

"I know who you are." She continued glaring.

"Well, yeah. I know we didn't get off on the right foot. But seeing as we're about to be stuck in the same raft for the next five hours, don't you think we ought to call a truce and become more friendly?" I continued smiling.

She grudgingly took my hand. "I'm Julia Semmens."

"Okay ladies, I guess you're the all female raft," the man said, urging our group forward. I studied my partner's faces for the first time and they were girls, mostly junior high age, except for Marline, Peggy, Angela, Mouse-hair and myself.

"Ooh, it's cold," one of the girls said, sticking her hand in the water.

"Well, duh! It's coming from the snow in the mountains," one of the other girls said.

"Okay, let's all work together," Marline ordered, as we pushed into the current. I'd guessed she had appointed herself captain of our river craft. "We're the girl-power raft, and we're gonna rule the river! Right, girls?"

"Yeah!" They waved their paddles in the air and screamed.

"We'd better work together," Mouse-hair said. "I called yesterday to see how the river was running, and they're letting extra water out of the dam today." I glanced at the river's edge and realized she was right. I'd been rafting several times, but never with the river running this high.

"So, what does that mean," one of the younger girls asked.

"That means we're gonna have lots of fun," Angela said.

"Yeah, girl fun!" Marline yelled.

"Yeah!" they yelled and waved their paddles high. They

suddenly grew quiet as the roaring of the rapids and screams coming from Don's raft drew nearer.

"Left side, paddle hard! Right side, back-paddle, quick!" Marline yelled. "Keep it in the center!"

The roar grew deafening as we neared the rapids. Helen Fisher's screams could be heard above the rest as Don's raft disappeared from view.

"Right side forward, hard! Left side, back-paddle. Quick! Straighten it up, girls! Keep it straight!" Marline was in her full-command mode. I heard Mouse-hair utter an expletive as our raft nosed downward over the rapid.

Chapter 25

The current catapulted us forward, where our raft flipped in mid-air, causing me to land in a river of screaming girls. We were wearing life vests and bobbed like orange and yellow corks as the current carried us away from the next screaming raft being catapulted over the rapid.

"Hurry girls, let's flip our raft back over," Marline yelled as I dogpaddled her way. Peggy and I got to the raft at the same time, and began shoving it toward the shallow where we could turn it right-side-up as Marline barked orders.

"Sarah, you and Julia grab the ice chest before it gets away. The rest of you collect all our paddles. There should be twelve of them."

"I'm freezing!" one of them yelled.

"The sooner you get the paddles and we get back into the raft, the sooner you'll feel warmer. Hurry now!"

We got the raft righted, paddles and ice chest collected, and pushed back into the current.

"Look at her making a fool of herself," Peggy said as we eased past Don's beached raft. The teenagers were waiting patiently as he carried a squealing Helen, with her arms latched around his neck, out of the current and toward their raft.

We all turned as Mouse-hair said, "She's making more of a fool out of him."

"You said it, Sister," Peggy affirmed.

"Who the heck is she, anyway," Mouse said. I quietly worked my paddle against the current as Peggy expounded the history, mostly bad, about Helen Fisher and why she should be exterminated. It was about fifteen minutes later, when Don's raft drew closer, that Mouse came totally unglued.

"Look at her! Holy crap, does she think she's something, or what?"

Helen had herself perched without a life jacked on the edge of Don's raft allowing everyone to paddle, while she posed with her breasts poked outward and her head tilted back, trying to look like a Sports Illustrated model.

"She is," I said.

"Yeah, you can say that again," Peggy said with a snigger.

"No, I meant it," I added. "Take a good look at her. She is pretty and has a great body. Her acting like a slug hasn't kept her from collecting the guys." I shrugged. "At least it seems to be working on mine."

"How can you say that?" Peggy stopped paddling to scowl. "You can't really believe my brother likes her, do you?"

"She's in his raft, and she's been with him the entire week. What do you think?" Everyone grew quiet and eyed the raft floating twenty yards to our right.

"Now, I know I hate her," Mouse said. "The way she's exposing herself in front of Pastor Don is disgusting!"

"Is that why you were upset when I wore my running outfit to play volleyball," I asked.

"No, you made me feel like a blob." She glanced at her chubby legs.

"She does that to a lot of people," Angela laughed.

"I'm sorry. I didn't mean to. I wanted to play, and it was the only clean outfit I had." I gave her a crooked grin. "Besides, there's no reason for you to feel like that. You're a pretty girl."

"Not even!" Mouse snorted.

"Yes, even," Marline said. "With a little make up and the right hair, you'd hold your own with most of us."

"Yeah, you've got the right bones. We could make you over in one afternoon," Angela said.

"Really? You'd do that for me?" Mouse held her paddle

across her lap to study each face turned her way.

"Really. We'll do it next Saturday. But right now, we've got a bigger problem. What are we going to do about her," Peggy asked.

"Allow me ladies," I said. I unbuckled my life vest and pulled the Minnie Mouse tee over my head. There were a few whistles and cat-calls from the raft of teenage boys tailing ours. I rolled over the side and into the water.

"What are you going to do," Angela said as I clung to the side.

"Helen Fisher seems to be my problem, doesn't she? Just be prepared to battle after I declare war." I kicked away and swam to the raft of boys, who turned out to be a group from our church.

"Hey guys, we're going to be stopping midway to eat lunch. Want to join us?"

"Yeah, we kind of planned on it," the boy closest to me said. "Why?"

"Some of the girls in my raft were hoping you would." I cocked my head and smiled.

"Yeah, sure, if Marline's willing to share my sandwich," one of the guys on the other side said.

"Sure like that's gonna happen," another sniggered.

"She might. I'll ask her. What's your name?"

"Dave. Tell her Dave Decker wants to eat with her," he hollered. I pulled halfway up onto the side to spy a pimple-faced kid who looked about fourteen grinning hopefully.

"Okay, I'll ask her. But there's something I need you guys to do first."

"Uh-oh, here comes the catch," the one closest to me said. "What is it?"

"Nothing big. In fact, it's something you were already planning to do. See, Pastor Don's raft?"

They nodded. "Yeah, the one with the Porcelain Goddess," Dave said.

"Yeah, that one. All I want you to do is, paddle up close…maybe slightly ahead…and keep them busy."

"Why?"

"I'm going to baptize the Porcelain Goddess."

"Whoa, yeah! I've gotta see this!" the one close to me said. "Let's go!"

I slipped to the back of their raft and motioned for the girls to follow as we neared the Porcelain Goddess. I ducked underwater as we drew alongside and came up behind Don's raft, then waited until the boys were completely ahead. They were already flipping water with their paddles and taunting those on Don's raft as Marline guided our raft close. No one on Don's raft had seen me, and it was easy to work my way to where he was straddling the edge behind Helen Fisher. Gripping the edge of the raft, I latched onto his tee-shirt and gave a tug.

"Aguh!" he gasped as he tumbled into the water.

"Donald!" Helen turned and yelled. I planted both feet against the side of the raft as I latched onto her wrist and kicked away. Her scream could have been heard in downtown Modesto as she hit the water.

"Yeah, war!" Peggy yelled and both rafts began splashing and drenching those who remained in Don's raft. I had almost reached our raft, when Don's hand grabbed onto my ankle.

"Come here, you little devil." He pulled me into his arms with a laugh. "Dunk your pastor, will you?"

"Ahhhh!" I squealed as he hoisted me over his head and tossed me into the middle of the river. Then he swam to meet me, where he gave me a kiss.

"Thanks. It was getting kind of dull and stuffy over there."

"You're welcome." I kissed him back before returning to the girls.

"You witch!" Helen was standing in the middle of their raft screaming. "You did that on purpose! You, horrible, horrible..."

"Calm down, Helen," Don said pulling himself into the raft. "They're only having fun."

"Not her!" She waved a bony finger at me. She didn't

seem to notice the dozens of people in different rafts laughing. "She pulled me in the river on purpose!"

"Why Helen, I'm surprised at you," I said real loud. "I didn't know anyone actually believed they could go rafting with a group of teenagers and not get wet."

~   ~   ~

The rest of the afternoon was much of the same, with all three rafts attacking, splashing, and pulling one another into the river. The only one not enjoying herself was Helen Fisher, who complained and cried all day. At one point, one of the boys in her own raft shoved her overboard. It was late in the afternoon when the Orange Blossom Road bridge came into view, signaling the end of our ride. I watched as a group of rafts a hundred yards ahead beached themselves at the county park. Peggy began paddling furiously and yelling.

"Come on, guys, let's cut them off!"

"Peggy, what are you doing," Marline said. "We're at the end of our ride."

"No, not until we're out of the water. Come on and help me. Let's cut them off!"

Those with Don had allowed their raft to drift toward the middle of the river, and in a matter of seconds, we had slipped between them and the landing on the north bank.

"Hey, what are you guys doing," Don said as our rafts bumped.

"The war's not over," Peggy shouted and gave their raft a shove toward the opposite bank. She kept yelling and urging us to crowd them, while giving their raft an occasional push with her oar.

"Agh! Duck!" the boy at the front yelled as their raft passed under some low-hanging branches. Everyone, except Helen, lay flat as the limbs scraped against the raft. Instead of ducking, Helen chose to scream and grab onto one of the branches, which caused the raft to slip from under her, leaving her to dangle in the water screaming.

"Why doesn't she let go," Mouse asked.

"'Cause she's brain-dead," one of the younger girls said.

"Come on, let's get out of this thing," Marline said, and steered us toward the docking area. We climbed out as Don's raft pulled in next to ours. Helen was still clinging to the limb screaming. People were lining the bank, laughing and urging her to let go, but she clung to the branch as though it were made of gold.

"Better go rescue her, Pastor," Angela said.

"Na, if she's that dumb, let her stay," Peggy said.

Since there were few places in the river deeper than my chest, Don simply leaned into the current and walked toward the screaming banshee, who clung to his neck, making him carry her back across the river. I was beginning to think the whole day had backfired when she planted a big kiss on his lips as they neared the docking area. Don, on the other hand, jerked free and tossed her back into the river. Then, he slipped an arm around my shoulders, and we crossed the grassy area toward the busses waiting to take us to our cars, leaving her to throw a fit in the water.

Chapter 26

"Go! Go! Go!" I jumped up and screamed, as Marline rounded the last barrel and turned Buster toward the gate. She'd handled the brown quarter horse magnificently, holding him tight through each turn.

"Yeah!" I waved my Stetson as the official time of 17.505 seconds was posted, moving her into first place above Gloria Rodriquez's 18.506 run.

Don's mother had returned home Monday following the rafting trip, taking an angry Helen Fisher with her. Everyone, especially me, heaved a sigh of relief. It was now the following weekend, and we were in Turlock for the Women's Professional Rodeo Association event. The stands were packed, and I was glad I had insisted on arriving early enough to grab seats up front, where Donnie and Caroline could see without having to be held. Carol seemed content with the arrangement, and proudly displayed the red boots I bought to match the small Stetson I'd given her. Her brother, on the other hand, became restless and wanted to be held a mere thirty minutes into the program.

"Wow! That'll be hard to beat." Gary raised his voice over the noisy crowd.

The crowd erupted again as Angela Vasquez burst through the gate on her black quarter horse named Zorro. My heart stopped as she charged the course like the pro she was, rounding each barrel tighter than the last. I loved Angela like a sister, and it was hard not to root for her, but Marline and I had been connected at the hip since kindergarten. That was the first time the school had to call my parents in for a conference, because I'd punched Billy Owens in the nose for throwing sand in Marline's eyes. There wasn't a day following that we hadn't swapped lunch goodies, or even the clothes we'd worn to school. As I said earlier, we even swapped a few dates as teenagers. It had been only the last few years that we had gotten close to Gloria and Angela, and that mostly because of our rodeo connection. The four of us spent quite a bit of time eating fries and drinking cherry cokes at McDonalds, and talking about guys. But nothing, excluding death, could have separated Marline and me, and I wasn't too sure it could.

It was on the last turn that Zorro knocked over the barrel, and a five-second penalty caused Angela to settle for a score of 18.486.

"It doesn't take much to make you into a loser, does it," Don said over the roar of the crowd.

"Not when you're counting hundredths of a second," I yelled back, then lowered my voice as they quieted down. "But no one here is really a loser, unless you wind up in last place. They might've put up a $75.00 entry fee, but the top finishers all get a chunk of the $1,200.00 purse, and they get points added to their overall score. Marline will probably get 400 points, Angela something like 350, and Gloria will wind up with around 300 points."

"Just for being here?"

"No, the points are based on their performance. And you get more points for each rodeo. They're collected throughout the year, and whoever racks-up the most points during the season, is crowned the national champion. They get the big cash prize and a nice buckle," I said with a grin.

"Nearly all these girls are in the running. Last year's barrel racing champion was ranked twentieth about midway through the season, then had a run of good luck that put her into first place."

"Why aren't you out there," Don asked, adjusting Donnie on his lap.

"Barrel racing's too tame for Margie. In fact, she thinks

the entire women's circuit is too tame for her," Gary said with a snigger.

"That's not true," I said as they began announcing the next event. "I'm not taking anything away from them. I do it once in awhile, but barrel racing is all Marline, Angela and Gloria do."

"They have other events you could compete in," Don said.

"Yeah, they've got bareback and bull riding like the men. And they've got team and tiedown roping and breakaway roping. But the men seem to get the bigger and stronger animals as a whole, and they draw bigger crowds," I said sulkily.

"So, what you are saying is, you don't want to compete against your friends, you'd rather compete against men. Getting even with Barry Swaim wouldn't have anything to do with it, would it?" Don gave me a crooked grin.

"Na-uh," I shook my head, "you ought to know me better than that by now. The Women's Circuit is fine, and it's what I mostly do. It's all I *can* do. I don't know, it's hard for me to explain.

"Look," I said, shifting to stare him in the eye, "if I beat Marline, or any of these women at anything…let's say I by some chance won the Women's National Finals at bull riding. Then, I'd become just another women's champion bull rider. Everyone would tell me how great I am, pat me on the head and go on about their business. Oh, I might get a nice paycheck and a buckle and my picture might be plastered on the cover of a few magazines, but after a few months, nobody would know, or even care who I am. But, if I can compete against the men, even if I never become national champion…if I can just ride with them and compete at their level, then they'll have to recognize me for more than just another pretty girl with a nice body.

"What Marline and Angela are doing is fine, I just don't think its fair they won't allow women to compete alongside of the men. But, I've always felt I needed something a little more exciting than barrel-racing anyway."

"Like getting bucked off Irish and banged-up," Don said.

"Yeah, something like that." I nodded.

"Well, why aren't you competing today in the bareback bronc riding?"

He was studying me, so I thought about my answer before shifting to smile and give him a quick kiss.

"I thought about it, but I've got other interests right now."

Chapter 27

"Whadda ya think? Is this one okay," I asked, spinning in a circle.

"Yeah, it's very pretty. It's just a different look on you than what I'm used to seeing," Marline said thoughtfully.

"Well, does it make me look dorky, or what?"

"No, you look nice...really," she said studying me up and down. "I'm just used to seeing Marjorie Green in jeans and boots, and this is a different look on you. Why are you so interested in a change all of a sudden?"

"Well, duh, why do you think," I snorted.

"You're in love with Pastor Gardner, is that it?"

"I thought that was obvious. Now, tell me the truth...does this dress make me look like a lady or what," I asked.

"Yeah, yes it does make you look like a lady, although I don't think it's necessary. Now, are you satisfied," Marline said.

"Good, and yes I'm satisfied. Let me get back into my own things. And it is so necessary," I added loudly from the changing room.

"No it's not. He fell for the cowgirl Margie, not the lady," she yelled back.

"Don't you think a pastor's wife should look like a lady?"

"Whoa, has it gone that far? I haven't heard."

"No, not yet...but I'm trying," I said, poking my head out the door.

"Oh, thought you had some real news to tell me. Just don't over-do it, okay?"

"I won't. He's real important to me, Marline."

"Well, hurry it up. I've got to get home and make myself presentable. I've got a date." Marline raised her voice for me to hear inside the changing room.

"Really? Who with," I yelled back.

"Yes, really. And why does it sound unusual for me to have a date on a Saturday night?"

"I didn't mean it like that," I said, poking my head over the stall door. "I just meant, you didn't say anything about having a date until now. Who with?"

"You don't want to know," she said.

"Why? Is he ugly," I yelled, pulling my boots on.

"No, he's quite the opposite. He's handsome, rich, has a good personality and a lot of fun to be with."

I stopped in the middle of buckling my belt to shove the door open and glare. "You're going out with Barry Swaim, aren't you?"

"Yes, as a matter of fact, I am." She smiled and raised her eyebrows.

"Why, Marline? For the love of God, why are you going on a date with Barry Swaim?"

"Because, he asked me, and I happen to like him. That's why."

"Geeze, Marline! Didn't he hurt you enough the first time? Why do you want to go back for seconds?" I grabbed the three dresses I'd chosen and stormed out of the changing room.

"Here, give me those," Marline said snatching them by the hanger. "You're going to wrinkle them before you even wear them. And," she added as we approached the checkout counter, "I am well aware he might let me down and hurt me a second time. But the simple fact is I still haven't gotten over him from the first time."

"Really," I said, taking her by the arm.

"Yes, really." Marline handed the dresses to the girl behind the counter. "And whatever Barry does, or does not do, can't hurt me anymore than watching him with you."

"Oh, Jesus, Marline! I didn't know, I'm sorry." I grabbed her in a hug.

"I know you didn't, silly. Now, quit worrying. It's only one little date with one of the best looking guys in Oakdale. How bad can that be? Besides," she said, pushing me away to smile, "he's taking me to *The Red Lobster*. So, no matter what happens, I'm getting a great meal, and he's spending a lot of money."

"Your total comes to $219.86. Will there be anything else," the girl behind the counter said.

"Ah, no...that's all," I said digging into my belly pack for the checkbook. I waited until we'd reached the parking lot before saying anything else.

"We'd better hurry, if you're coming back to Modesto. You should have said something earlier, and I wouldn't have drug you all the way over here."

"That'd be stupid. We always spend Saturdays together. Besides," Marline paused to grin as she unlocked her truck door, "There was no way I was going to miss seeing Marjorie Green pick out pretty dresses, now was there?"

Chapter 28

"Oh, wow!" I said, opening the present from Don.

"Well, what is it, Dear," Mama asked as I stared into the box.

"A Bible."

"A Bible?" Dad looked up from his cup of coffee.

"Yeah, and it's beautiful."

"Well, let us see," Marline said. Our tiny living room was packed with people Mama had invited to help celebrate my twentieth birthday. It probably wasn't much of a party, as parties go, but we had plenty of junk food to go with the cake and ice cream, and soft drinks and coffee to wash it down with.

"Thank you," I said to Don, as I passed the Bible around. "It is beautiful, and I love it."

"You're welcome. I didn't quite know what to get you, but I noticed the one you've been bringing to church looks kind of beat up."

"Yes, Margie's had that one for years. I got it for her when she was six years old," Mama said.

"Yeah, but it didn't get beat up by her reading it. She used to throw it once in awhile when she got mad," the old man said with a snigger.

"Dad!"

"Well, its true, isn't it?"

"Sounds like her," Marline said.

"Well, I won't be throwing this one, because it came from you," I said, giving Don a quick peck on the lips. "Would you like another cup of coffee?"

"Yes, I'd love another cup, and I'm glad you like it. It isn't easy for a minister to choose the proper gift for a parishioner," he continued, as I grabbed both of our cups and headed toward the kitchen," especially one that is special to him. Some of the things I considered seemed impersonal, but something like lingerie would have been way too personal."

"Oh, I don't know about that. It all depends on what type of message you're trying to send," Angela said with a crooked grin.

"Angela!" I paused at the kitchen door to glare. "He's not like that. He's a minister."

"Ha! He's a man, and all men think alike when it comes to women," Gloria said with her thick Spanish accent.

"Come on, Marge. Who're you trying to kid? Don't you think of him as more than your minister? Didn't I just see you kiss him?" Angela said, as all four girls crowded into the kitchen behind me. I folded my arms across my chest, trying to look serious as they laughed.

"I don't believe you guys! I mean, especially since most of you attend our church. To think that…you'd believe your own pastor would look at me that way."

"Mother of God!" Gloria burst out laughing. "You don't believe he does?"

"No, I don't," I snapped, and turned to fill the empty cups.

"Come on, Margie," Marline leaned close to my ear, "you've had some dreams about you and Pastor Don. Haven't you? Be honest now."

"I told you that in the closest confidence, Marline Dickerson!" I spun in anger, but froze as I spied Donald standing in the kitchen doorway with my parents. "Oh God, I can't believe I just said that!"

"I rest my case." She glanced around the crowded room and smiled.

"Okay, okay!" I waved my hands while they laughed. "I'm guilty! I do think…wonder…dream, whatever you want to call it, about us every once in awhile." I covered my face. "I can't believe I'm admitting this in front of my parents. I'm so embarrassed!" I jerked up as Don started laughing.

"You're not helping, you know. You could tell them!"

"Tell them what?"

"Tell them you don't think of me that way."

"Well, I have been married and have two children. And to be perfectly frank, Margie, yeah," he nodded, "I have thought about it…you…that way a few times." His face turned red as he continued laughing.

"Ah!"

"Here, you can give me a refill while you're feeling embarrassed," Dad said as he handed me his cup. "And to be frank, I for one am glad you're thinking that way."

"Dad!"

"Why does that surprise you?" He paused as I handed him the steaming mug of coffee. "I want to have grandkids some day."

"How can you…? We're not married… He hasn't even asked me!"

"I think I can trust you two to wait and do the right thing. But if you ever do get together, and keep thinking God might strike Don dead for touching his wife, I'd be waiting a long time for you two to have any children. Wouldn't I?"

"Well, I have no idea how we got from discussing the Bible to this. Let's change the subject, shall we," Mama said. "How about some cake and ice cream?"

Chapter 29

"You don't really think of me like that, do you?" We were standing by his car saying goodbye. Most everyone, except Marline, had already gone, and she was busy helping Mama clean and straighten the house. Donnie and Caroline were buckled into the back seat, and would be asleep long before he reached home.

"What way?"

"Like they were saying earlier. In the house."

"Well, yeah. I admitted as much in front of your parents, didn't I? I mean it's hard not to. You are a beautiful woman, who I find hard to resist."

"Thanks, I feel the same. I mean about you being hard to resist... I mean, you're a man, and I find..."

"I know what you mean, and thank you." He took my hands and kissed my fingers.

"I hope you don't mind." I took my time studying the curve of his lips.

"Mind what?"

"My thinking of you that way, about us being together like that, every once in awhile," I said.

"No, not at all. I'm guilty of thinking that way about you myself, every now and again."

"I don't know much about these things, but I've heard its sin...to think like that."

"It all depends on how far you allow your thoughts to carry you. If you tried to fulfill your dreams in an inappropriate manner, then yeah, I guess it would be sinful. But to have urges, or a natural desire to be with someone you care about? No, I don't believe that's sinful. But," he added, kissing my nose, "I don't think you have anything to worry about."

"Good," I said, hugging him real tight, "because I love you so much it's scary."

"The feeling's mutual." He kissed me. "I've discovered that thinking about you is beginning to interfere with my ministry."

"Oh, no, don't say that!" I held onto him real tight.

"There's nothing to worry about. If I find it's too much to handle, we'll simply have to do something about it. Won't we?"

"Like what?"

"Mmmmm, I'd rather not say right now. But I believe that, between the two of us, we can figure something out. What do you think?"

He kissed me again, long and tender this time.

Chapter 30

"So, it's more than just a casual date now and then, isn't it?"

"Um-hum," Marline said with a grin.

"What's it been, something like three weeks now?"

"Four this Saturday."

"You've done it, haven't you? You've let your guard down and fallen for Barry Swaim!" I snapped at her. "Geeze, Marline! I thought you knew better from the last time."

"Come on, Marge, I thought you'd at least give him a chance. Besides, it's my life. Why can't you try being happy for me...like I am for you and Pastor Don?"

"Because Don's different. I can trust him around other women, and you know what Barry's like," I said.

"Maybe that's true, but it's different this time," she said "Really?"

"Yes, really," she said with a nod.

"How so?"

"I don't quite know yet, but believe me...it's different. I can tell."

"Okay, Marline, I'll try being happy because you're my friend. And I'll pray that he doesn't hurt you, like I think he will," I said, giving her a hug.

"Thanks, Marge. I love you," she said, hugging back.

"I love you too. But you'd better be right about Barry, because if he hurts you again, I'm gonna kill him."

"It's a deal," she laughed. "I might even help you."

Chapter 31

I was having trouble cornering Barry Swaim. He had been hitting the PRCA circuit hot and heavy, and the fact that he had taken Marline, Angela and Gloria with him had me kind of worried. He was also starting to make a name for himself both riding saddle broncs and team roping with Terry Walker, all of which made me jealous, seeing as I had opted to sit out most of the season to solidify my relationship with Don. Marline showed up on my doorstep the day they arrived back in town to show off the buckle she'd won in San Jacinto.

"You should've come, Marge. We had tons of fun!"

"Yeah, I thought about it, but I don't know. I thought I'd kinda sit this one out," I said with a shrug.

"Well, too bad, 'cause it was a blast. Angela's aunt went as a chaperone, and she's crazier than any of us."

"Good. That had me kind of worried," I said.

"What did?"

"You know. You traveling with Barry. I know how you feel about him, Marline, and I know how Barry is. And…" I shrugged, "well, I was kind of worried, that's all."

"Marjorie Ann Green! You thought Barry and I would be…? I ought to slap your face!" She laughed. "I thought you knew me better than that."

"I do. It's just that I know Barry, and he was forever trying to get me in the backseat of that Camaro he used to own."

"Well, for your information, he's never tried that with me, and he had plenty of opportunity on this trip. We were alone on several occasions, and he had his own hotel room. Absolutely nothing happened."

"Really?" I asked.

"Really," she said with a nod.

"Wow! That's not like Barry," I said. "Wonder what's got into him?"

"Like I said, it's different this time. He even said he loved me," Marline said, giving me a crooked grin.

Barry in love? That was a scary thought. I kept wondering what the snake was up to as I watched Marline drive away.

Chapter 32

"Did your mother come?"

Peggy had called an emergency meeting at six in the morning, and the way she was crying over the phone, none of us had dared to refuse. I slid into the corner booth at The Oakdale Café next to Marline, as the rest of the gang ordered coffee. It was Marline who'd asked the question. I was too stunned upon hearing of Helen Fisher's return to even speak.

"No, she didn't come. Mom won't be here until Christmas, then again in April for Carol's birthday. Like I was saying, I'd spent the night at Angela's, and we decided to go riding this morning. Well, I ran home to get my jeans and boots and found Helen in my bed. God! I'll have to burn the mattress."

"She spent the night in Pastor Don's house alone?" Gloria asked.

"No, Donnie and Carol were there," Peggy said.

"That sounds alone to me," Angela sniggered.

"I didn't hear that," Marline said, covering her ears.

"She was in *my* bed, Marline. Not his," Peggy said.

"I still didn't hear it. My dad's one of his deacons, and it doesn't sound good."

"Well, what is she doing there?" I finally found my voice.

"What do you think she's doing here? Idiot!" Peggy said. "She's after my brother, like she's always been."

"Oh, boy! And she spent the night with him alone in the house," Gloria said.

"Nothing happened, Gloria," I snapped.

"How do you know, little girl? Were you there?" She leaned across the table and gave me an evil grin.

"No, but I trust Don," I said with a nod.

"Huh, just like you trusted Barry Scumbag Swaim? You think you would have learned something. Besides," she added, "it's not your boyfriend we're talking about. Him, I do trust. It's her you have to worry about."

"She's right," Marline said. "Like I was saying…speaking strictly from a church's point of view…if this news gets out, it isn't going to look good. I personally don't think anything happened either. But," she shook her head, "it just doesn't look good. I'm afraid some people are going to think the worst, no matter what."

"And," Gloria leaned forward to talk in a hushed tone, "knowing the type of snake she is, what's to stop her from starting the rumor?"

"Ah, I don't think so. I mean, it would make her look bad. Why would she want to say something like that," I said.

"Because, little girl, your boyfriend is a moral man. If he thinks the people of his church believe he has committed sin with this," she paused to shake her head "what they think is an innocent woman, he'll marry her just to make things right."

"Na, it would never happen," I said after a long minute.

"I agree. Never," Peggy said, shaking her head.

"Think so? Anyone care to bet on it?" Gloria leaned back and grinned smugly.

"She might be right," Marline said with raised eyebrows. "Especially if he's called before the board."

"Come on, Marline, get real. Your dad wouldn't make Donald marry Helen Fisher, no matter what he thought," I said.

"I didn't say *he* would. But he's only one member of the board. Besides, there have been several people in our congregation in the past few years, who've committed some pretty serious sins. You're not hearing me say this," she added quickly, "but it's caused the board to get pretty strict about such things. That's why you had to put on your sweats playing

130

volleyball."

"And how do you know all this? Isn't that stuff supposed to be kept confidential," Peggy said.

"My dad's a deacon, and I pick up stuff here and there, especially when he's talking on the phone. Besides, all you've got to do is listen to some of the gossip floating around the church." Marline cocked her head to one side with a shrug.

"Let me ask you this," Gloria said. "If it comes to giving up the church, or marrying this girl, which do you think he will choose?"

"Which brings us back to why I called you here. What are we going to do about Helen Fisher," Peggy asked.

"My offer to drag her behind Zorro still stands," Angela said.

Chapter 33

"That happened to be the first thing I thought of. So, I called the board this morning to explain the situation," Don said.

"Why didn't you send her to one of the motels, instead of allowing her to spend the night with you," I snapped. We were standing just inside his door having a heated discussion, while Helen sat on his sofa grinning like a Cheshire Cat.

"It was one o'clock in the morning, Margie. I'm not going to send anyone away at one in the morning, when I have an empty bed in my house."

"Okay, it's now ten-thirty. Why's she still here?"

"Because she just finished eating breakfast. I don't know why you're upset. Absolutely nothing happened. Besides," he added with a scowl, "I'll invite any friend anytime I want to share a meal at my table."

"If you'll excuse me," Helen said, rising like a queen from the sofa, "Margie's right. I should have checked into a motel instead of coming here. It didn't look good for me to spend the night without Peggy being present. I'm sorry, I had no idea she wasn't here. I'll check into the Ramada Inn this morning."

She smiled sweetly before disappearing down the hall, leaving me stunned.

Chapter 34

"Nothing like lying through her teeth. She called yesterday while he was gone asking if this might be a good weekend to come visit. I told her no, that Don was busy, and I was spending the night at Angela's. Then she shows up in the middle of the night anyway." Peggy tilted her head back to take a drink of bottled water. I had driven Dad's truck straight from Don's house to the C & M Stables, where the girls were finishing their morning ride. They had Julia Semmens, a.k.a. mouse-hair, with them. The girl did look somewhat better, with a new hairstyle and proper makeup.

"Did you tell Pastor Don about her call," Marline asked.

"Sure, first thing this morning, when I found her in my bed. I caused a big stink, and she just smiled and said she'd forgotten I said I wasn't gonna be there. My stupid egghead brother believed her, and told me to calm down. She made me feel like a fool."

"Kind of like she made me feel," I said with a nod, "real stupid for even bringing it up."

"You'd think, after her acting so stupid, and having everyone laugh at her at the river, she'd be too embarrassed to show her face," Mouse said.

"One would think," Peggy agreed.

"No, you're dealing with a real pro," Gloria sniggered. "You girls are only making fools out of yourselves fighting her like that. No matter what you say, she's gonna turn it around and make herself look good, and you bad."

"Gloria's right," Marline agreed. "I'll bet she's gotten most of her boyfriends this way. We'll have to think of something else."

"I'm still willing to drag her behind Zorro," Angela said.

Chapter 35

"Okay, Scumbag, tell me. What's the deal between you and Marline?" I'd found my chance to corner Barry when I went to Oakdale Feed And Seed to pick up a load of hay for Mable. He stared at me like I was nuts for asking such a question inside a store full of people.

"I like her," he said with a shrug. "Not that it's any of your business who I happen to like or date."

"Well, in this case it is my business. Marline's my friend."

"She's mine too. I thought you and I were kind of friends...in a weird sort of way," he said, paying for the gloves and rope he'd laid on the counter.

"We are friends, that's why I'm asking the question. I don't want anything to happen to her," I said, following him out the door.

"What makes you think anything's going to happen to Marline Dickerson if I date her?" He glared at me as he unlocked the pickup door.

"Because I know you, Barry. And I know how you were always trying to get me in the back seat of your car and do things. I don't want you treating her that way."

"Okay, look," he tossed the gloves and rope inside the cab and turned to glare, "nothing like that's happened between us. I don't know why you're not asking her all these questions instead of me."

"I did."

"And what'd she say."

"That nothing's happened."

"So? What's the big deal? Don't you believe her," he said with a grin.

"Yeah, I believe her. It's just that Marline's my best friend, Barry, and I don't want you hurting her."

"You don't get it, do you?" He climbed into the truck and studied me as he started the engine. "I'd never do anything to hurt Marline Dickerson. I like her too much. I guess I might be falling in love for the first time. I don't know," he shrugged, "maybe I always did love her. I know I'd never do anything to hurt her."

I watched as he backed out of the parking space and started forward. It wasn't until he'd reached the street that the impact of what he said hit me. I ran to the curb and yelled as he pulled into the traffic.

"Then why'd you hurt me? You slug!"

Chapter 36

I tied Cupcake's reins to a bush and sat on a rock overlooking the river to stare at the rushing water. I'd heard people talk about being depressed, but I always took it as a bunch of horse manure, because I'd never been depressed about anything in my life, ever. If something wasn't going my way, I was able to fix it so it would. I could never understand why anyone would be willing to live in misery. But I was understanding them that very moment in a way I never thought possible.

My relationship with Don Gardner, that had been going so great a few weeks ago, was out of control, and there seemed to be no way of my fixing it. Gloria had been right about Helen being a pro. She had turned into a real snake, and twice as deadly. I had never considered her as much of a threat, at least, not the whining, crying, pouting version I'd met during her first visit. But this Helen was something else…a real politician who knew how to turn anything said against her into something good, or at least, make it sound as though she had good intentions. That day's encounter had come when I had gone shopping with Mama, and we stopped at McDonalds to grab a hamburger. There they were, both of them, sitting in the green Mustang, laughing and drinking cokes like we used to do.

"I'm taking Helen to look at apartments," he said, when I confronted them at the driver's window.

"Apartments?"

"Yes, I've decided to move to Oakdale." She leaned

across the console to smile. "Isn't it exciting? Now, we can be friends!"

Yeah, right. Like that's gonna happen!

"Why? I mean, why would you move here, away from your family," I asked.

"To attend college. Turlock has a state university, and I want to get my degree," she said.

In what? How to steal someone's boyfriend?

"Okay, fine. But you've got a car. Why does Don have to help you find an apartment?"

"I'm sorry. I simply don't know the area well enough. I was hoping he could guide me to where the good areas are. I just feel so helpless on my own."

Give me a break! You're about as helpless as Bonnie Parker with a machine gun.

"I don't have to, Margie," Don said sullenly. "Helen asked, and as a friend, I'm choosing to help her find the proper apartment."

"I wish you would have discussed this with me, before carting her all over town," I snapped.

"We are not married, and I don't have to discuss everything with you prior to my doing it, any more than you need to discuss everything with me. There needs to be a little trust in our relationship, Margie."

"I do trust you, Donald…it's her I don't trust," I said.

"Now, that's enough," he said.

"I'm sorry I caused all this, Margie." Helen shook her head with a pitiful look. "Just take me back to the motel, Don. She's right to get angry. I'll find an apartment by myself."

"No you won't. This is something Margie and I need to work out separately from your finding a place to live," he said. Then, turning on me like Mable's brahma, he added, "We'll finish this later, *after* I have helped Helen find an apartment. End of subject!"

At that very moment, she was riding in Don's green Mustang while I was sitting on a rock. She had won again.

Chapter 37

Great, that's all I need! I grumbled to myself as the muddy Chevy four-wheeler pulled into our driveway. I had been sitting on our front porch with Mama, sipping a lukewarm cup of coffee and watching Dad trim the rose bushes. I still hadn't fully bounced back from my bout with the blues, and having to act civil with Barry Swaim was not high on my priority list. Barry paused long enough to offer a greeting to Dad, and received a grunt in return.

"Hello, Scumbag. What brings you here," I said, as he joined us on the porch.

"Margie!" Mama scolded.

"What?"

"You know what," she said with a sigh. "Please excuse my daughter's poor manners, Barry."

"That's what I always call him," I said with a shrug. "If I called him anything different, he'd think something was wrong."

"Yeah, I probably would," Barry said with a laugh. "How are you doing, Mrs. Green?"

"I am doing just fine, Barry. Would you care to sit down?"

"No, thank you. I can't stay very long," he said, and leaned against one of the posts. He smiled and took a sip through the straw in his *Jack In The Box* paper cup before continuing. "I just thought I'd drop by and see what's up with Margie."

"Nothing's up with me. What are you talking about?" I

snorted.

"That's just it. I haven't seen you around, and you certainly haven't been to any rodeos in three months that I know of. What's up? You hanging up your spurs, or what?"

"I've been around, you just haven't seen me," I said.

"You haven't been competing, that's for sure."

"You know why as well as anyone," I snapped. "You even came by to gloat over the fact!"

"You talking about when you bailed off Mable's horse?" Barry screwed up his face and grinned.

"Yeah, when I bailed off Comanche. Chuck and Mable both said my riding days were over. You satisfied?"

"Well...no, actually I'm not." He worked the straw up and down in his cup, poking around the ice. "There's other things to compete in. You could race like Marline, team rope, any number of events. Besides, you've ridden since. Didn't you win a buckle in Salinas?"

"Yeah, so?"

"So, why aren't you out there riding?"

"That's none of your business!"

"Yeah, I guess you're right." He popped the plastic lid off and studied the inside of his cup a long minute. "Why should I care if Margie's a quitter?" He tossed the contents of the cup in my face.

"Aguh!" I screamed and jumped to my feet as the mug holding my lukewarm coffee bounced across the wooden porch without breaking.

"Barry Swaim, have you gone insane," Mama yelled. Dad dropped the clippers and came to stare as Barry backed off the porch laughing.

"You...you...aaagh!" I yelled and bounded down the steps after him. Dad wrapping his arms around my waist was the only thing that saved Barry from a good pounding.

"Alright, now what's going on," Dad said, as I struggled against his arms.

"Barry threw his soft drink in Margie's face," Mama said

"I can see that. But why," Dad growled.

"I wanted to see if she was still alive," Barry said with a laugh. "And don't worry, Mrs. Green. It was only ice. I checked."

"What I want to know, is why," Dad said, releasing his grip.

I wound up to give Barry a good slap, but Dad caught my arm.

"She's been acting different, and me and the girls were starting to get worried, like there's something wrong with her. I just wanted to see if there was any of the old Marjorie Green fire left in her."

"That's a heck of a way to find out. Why didn't you just ask," Dad growled.

"I did and she lied like she always does when you ask her what's wrong. Isn't that right, Mrs. Green?"

"Yes, he did ask, and Margie said nothing was bothering her," Mama said.

"That's 'cause there's nothing wrong with me, you slime-bucket!" I said, brushing my dress.

"Get real!" Barry snorted. "Just look at you...right now. In the first place, the old Margie wouldn't have been caught dead in a dress, unless she was going someplace special. Certainly not around the house. You would have either been in jeans and boots or, maybe shorts. But never a dress, and it would've taken both your parents to hold you down after someone tossed ice in your face."

"I can still scratch your eyes out, if that's what you want!" I drew close to glare.

"No, I'll tell you what I want. I want the old Margie back. I want the Margie with spurs and jeans, who had a little spit in her. The one that wasn't afraid to climb back on horses and fight."

"I happen to like my daughter just the way she is," Mama said.

"Do you really, Mrs. Green?" Barry paused to grin. "Come on now. She's been wandering around like a ghost for weeks, all depressed because Helen-what's-her-face has moved in and taken some of the Reverend's attention. Meanwhile, here she sits on the front porch, in a dress, feeling sorry for herself."

"I am not feeling sorry for myself!"

"Are so!" He got close and grinned in my face, so I slapped him.

"Good! There's still a little fight left in you."

"I've got a lot more," I hissed. "Wanna see?"

"Yeah, I wanna see. Just put it into the right places."

"Okay, Barry. What is it you suggest my daughter do," Mama asked.

"Well, for one thing, get back into rodeo."

"Oh boy, here we go again," Dad moaned.

"I'm not saying she has to ride broncs, although I'd personally like to see her do that. But Margie's a cowgirl, Mr. Green. You know that as well as I do. And seeing her," he motioned toward me and screwed up his face, "like she is...just isn't her."

"What's wrong with me the way I am," I snapped.

"Nothing, except it isn't you."

"Don happens to think I look nice in dresses, and he doesn't want me riding and getting hurt."

"And you really believe that?"

"Yeah, I really believe that. He's told me so many times," I said with a nod.

"Maybe, but ask yourself one question. Which Margie did the Reverend fall for? The one we see here or the one with spurs and jeans? Hummm?"

He happened to be right, and it hit me like getting kicked in the stomach. I could remember Marline saying much the same thing and I'd blown her off. But Barry's way of putting it was about as easy to ignore as Mable's brahma, Sudden Death, inside your bedroom.

"We were getting along fine until Helen Fisher came along."

"And so Margie starts dressing and acting like Helen in order to win him back, is that it?" Barry laughed and shook his head. "I don't know why I should care, except the girls and I love you too much to let you continue making a fool out of yourself."

"You want her to go back in the rodeo and get her neck broken, is that it," Dad said.

"No, I want her to be happy, Mr. Green, the same as you do. The old Margie would have spit in Helen Fisher's eye, and not cared if Reverend Gardner liked it or not. She would have continued riding horses, bucking hay and smelling like a sweaty cowhand. She certainly wouldn't have tried being something she's not, because that's only made her miserable."

"And you think that will make Reverend Gardner like her any more than he already does," Mama asked.

"That's what he started liking in the first place, wasn't it?" Barry paused to check his watch.

"I've got to run. Check on you later." He grinned and pointed at me before jogging to his truck.

"How'd an idiot like him get so smart anyway," Dad said, as Barry disappeared in a roar of exhaust with globs of dried mud flying from his tires. I didn't say anything as I went into the house and changed into my boots and jeans.

Chapter 38

"Crazy girl tried riding Comanche by herself when my back was turned," Chuck growled, as I limped toward the sofa.

"I didn't try, I did ride him!" I yelled.

"How bad is she hurt," Mama said, hovering over me while I eased down on the sofa.

"I don't think it's anything serious. But, she's a danged idiot!" Chuck yelled in my face.

"Is it your knee again," Mama asked.

"No, I twisted my ankle when I dismounted. Help me with my boot. I think my foot's swelling," I said, then yelled as Mama gave the Durango a tug.

"Here, let me help," Chuck said. "You hold her leg, and I'll pull the boot."

"Aaaagh! God! You trying to kill me," I yelled as the boot came off.

"Too bad we didn't pull your danged leg clean off." Chuck glared.

"Look at that. It's turning purple," Mama said, removing my sock. "You sure nothing's broken?"

"No, I can move my foot. See?" I wiggled my toes and foot.

"Does it hurt?"

"Well, duh…what do you think?"

"I'll get some ice." Mama hurried toward the kitchen.

"Well, it's a good thing you've still got your crutches and cane, 'cause you're gonna be needing them," Chuck said.

"And you won't be working for awhile, either."

"There's things I still can do. I'll be back out there tomorrow."

"No you won't," he pointed a bony finger in my face, "or I'll sic the dogs on you. You're gonna stay away from them horses until you learn to behave. Understand me?"

"Yes, sir." I nodded.

"Good."

Mama returned with the icepack, pain pills and a glass of water. "I'll tell you, I should have had a boy. At least I would be expecting something like this. But when I had a little girl, I expected her to be taking piano lessons, or singing, or dancing, not getting bucked off horses. You're going to be the death of me one of these days."

"I've got a rawhide whip hanging in the barn you can use, if you think it would do any good," Chuck said.

"I might be borrowing it, or a piece of rope to tie her up with. I just wish Pastor Don would talk some sense into her."

"Huh," Chuck snorted, "only trouble is, bronc busters haven't got any sense to begin with. The only thing he could do is marry her, and keep her barefoot and pregnant. But, this ornery bobcat would just ruin a good preacher, if they did get hitched."

"Don't you have something better to do back at the stables," I said.

"Yep. Speaking of which, I gotta get going. Keep an eye on her, Mrs. Green, and bonk her in the noggin if she won't behave."

"Thank you, Chuck, for everything," Mama said.

"No problem."

"Chuck," I said, as he opened the door.

"Yeah?"

"I did stay on Comanche my eight seconds."

"I know. I was watching." He winked and closed the door.

Chapter 39

"Again? So help me, I don't know about you." Don stood on the steps staring at my swollen foot and crutches.

"Maybe you can talk some sense into to her, Pastor. I certainly haven't been able to," Mama said through the screened door. I had been on my way back to the sofa from the bathroom, when I saw his car pull into our driveway behind Dad's truck, and decided to meet them on the porch.

"Come on, children," Mama opened the door, "let's leave them alone to talk. I think I still have some strawberry ice cream in the freezer." Donnie and Carol brushed by us with squeals as the door banged shut.

"What did you do this time?"

"I rode Comanche."

"I thought Chuck and Mable both said your bronc riding days were over. They let you get back on him?" Don held me by the shoulders to study my face.

"They didn't know. I sort of did it by myself."

"You did it alone?"

"Yeah." I nodded.

"You saddled that monster and rode him without them knowing?"

"Yes."

"How? How'd you get him to stand still long enough to get a saddle on him?" Don raised his voice and waved his hands as he took a step backward.

"They'll stand still long enough to be saddled and

mounted…if you put a blindfold on them."

"You blindfolded that horse?"

"Yeah, sure." I nodded.

"Then what? How did you remove the blindfold?"

"I just reached over and jerked it loose with my free hand. That's all," I said with a shrug.

"That's all," he said with a high-pitched laugh. "Then, he bucked you off and hurt you foot."

"It's nothing but a twisted ankle, and I did that myself dismounting."

"Lord have mercy," he said, shaking his head.

"I stayed on him, Don. Don't you understand?"

"No, I don't. The only thing I understand, is that you're set on getting yourself crippled."

"You're the one who gave me the pep-talk about hearing footsteps and getting back into the game. Remember?"

"Yes, but I was only trying to give you a little comfort and hope. I had no idea you would try something like this."

"Oh, so you were lying just to make me feel better."

"No, what I told you was the truth. I didn't think you'd be fool enough to really get back on animals that throw you to the ground and stomp on you. Why can't you act like a normal female, and choose something more sensible?"

"Like basket weaving, or finger painting?"

"Oh, for the love of God! I guess I'll wind up with a wife that limps like Chuck Burris," he growled.

"You'll what," I said.

"Nothing!" he yelled. "I've got to check on the children." He pulled loose as I tried grabbing his arm and opened the screened door. "Besides, I'm angry with you." He pointed with a glare.

"Don? What did you say about getting married," I yelled, but the door banged shut.

"Don?" I reached for the door, but jumped at Dad's voice on the other side of the screen.

"I knew he was fishing for my daughter the day he first showed up here."

"Geeze, Dad. Don't scare me like that."

He grinned and took a bite of strawberry ice cream. "I think there's plenty left in the freezer. It's pretty good. Ought to try some."

Chapter 40

"Noooo!" Donnie squealed and struggled against Helen's grasp. We had gathered inside the church's fellowship hall for a potluck after Sunday morning service, and Helen had taken it upon herself to sit beside the children, while I waited in line to get their plates filled with drumsticks, mashed potatoes and green beans. She was endeavoring to put on a show of affection by hugging Donnie when I returned, and he was refusing to have any part of her.

"Mommie!" he wailed and held his arms toward me as I limped toward the table on my sore ankle and set the plates on the table.

"She's not your mother," Helen hissed and struggled to tighten her grasp on the squirming boy.

"Might as well let him go, Helen. He doesn't want you holding him," said an older woman named Freda.

"Mommie! Mommie!" Donnie wailed. His father returned with paper cups filled with punch and stood at the end of the table staring.

"What's going on?"

"I was planning to feed Donnie his lunch, when he started throwing a fit." Helen continued her struggle.

"Well, evidently he doesn't want you feeding him. Quit causing a scene and let him go," Don said with a snigger, as he set the cups in front of the children.

"Yes, but…" Helen said with a scowl.

"Yes but nothing. He doesn't want you to hold him."

Helen released her hold, and he instantly dove into my arms crying, "Mommie!" I scooped him up with a kiss and whispered, "it's okay Baby," then gave Helen a shrug. She instantly gave me one of her *you can go to hell* looks.

"Well, you certainly have a way with those children," Freda said with a grin.

"She has blond hair and blue eyes like his mother did," Helen snorted.

"Oh, I'm sure that's likely true," Freda said with a nod. "But there is a little more to it than that."

"I'm sure there is," Helen agreed, and turned to give me another glare. "She's certainly had more time with them than I have."

Yeah, right. Like who was it who volunteered to baby sit while I'm working at the stables and Peggy's in school?

"It doesn't really matter who's had more time with them," Don said as he seated himself between me and Helen. Donnie and Carol instantly wormed their way into a seat on either side of me. "My son doesn't like to be held when he's eating, and there's no sense in causing a scene."

"Yes, shall we enjoy our potluck," I said with the biggest smile I could muster. The look on Helen's face caused me to burst out laughing. "I'm sorry," I said scooting away from the table, "I'm going to get a cup of coffee. Would anyone else care for one?"

Chapter 41

"Okay now, I'm going to show you how to steer, so listen real careful. Alright?"

"Uh-huh," Carol said with a nod. I had hitched one of Mable's Shetlands to a two-wheeled cart, and had Donnie and his sister strapped safely inside.

"You give the reins a gentle shake like this," I reached over to demonstrate, "and he'll start moving. See?" Both children giggled as Pedro started forward.

"Now, pull gently on the left rein," I said, walking beside the cart. Carol gave the rein a tug, and Pedro turned left. "See how easy it is?"

"Yeah," she giggled.

"Good. Now, pull gently on the right side." Pedro immediately turned right as they squealed and giggled.

"Now, see if you can guide him back to where your daddy is standing." I skipped along beside the cart as Caroline guided the pony toward her father. She took to driving the cart as naturally as breathing.

"Okay, now pull on both reins at the same time. See," I said as the cart came to a halt. "That tells Pedro you want to stop. Now, you practice, while I get horses ready for your Daddy and Helen, okay? Then, we'll all go riding together." She turned the cart away with a giggle and started Pedro into a wide circle.

"Sure she'll be alright to leave alone in the cart?" Don said as I closed the gate.

"Yep, Pedro's so lazy he'll never do more than a fast

walk if you beat him. Come on, let's pick out our horses," I said, grabbing his arm. Helen Fisher, who had again invited herself when she heard we were going riding, gave me one of her looks before pointing toward the quarter-horse staring at us over the corral fence.

"I already know which one I want. I want to ride the black one."

"Zorro? Na-uh," I said shaking my head.

"Why not," she said indignantly.

"Because that's Angela Vasquez's horse, and she'd kill us both if she knew I'd let you ride him. No one rides Zorro, unless she says it's okay, and that's not very often."

"Have you ever ridden him," Don asked.

"Yeah…once or twice…maybe more. But that was when she said I could, and I was letting her ride Cupcake. Look," I said as Helen gave a huff, "I'd let you if I could, but I can't. Zorro doesn't belong to the C&M, and Angela's pretty particular who gets to ride him, and it's mostly her. I'll let you ride Cupcake, if you want. She belongs to me."

"Which one is your horse?" Helen seemed to brighten a bit with the offer.

"Here's Cupcake," I said, petting the beige muzzle poking over the fence to greet me. "Yes, you're a pretty girl, and I love you." I gave her a kiss on the forehead.

"Okay, but it's not as pretty as the black one," Helen said, glancing back toward Zorro.

"Oh, don't listen to the old meanie," I said, covering Cupcake's ears. "You are so a pretty girl."

"I didn't mean your horse isn't pretty. I just meant I like the black one best," Helen said.

"That's okay, we'll let her ride you anyway. Won't we," I said, tossing the blanket and saddle across her back.

"Ever ridden a quarter-horse before, Helen?" I said as I tightened the cinches.

"Yes, I've been riding a lot of times. We have riding stables near my parent's house."

"That isn't what I asked. Have you ever ridden a

quarter-horse?"

"Yeah, I suppose I have. Like I said, I used to go riding quite often. Why? What difference does it make what type of a horse I've ridden?"

"Well, to answer my question, no you haven't, or you'd remember," I said, leading Cupcake out of the gate. "Let me explain a few things before you get on. Cupcake may look gentle, but she's a competition horse, like Zorro or Marline's horse, Buster. I use her for barrel-racing and roping. In fact, most of the horses used in rodeos are quarter-horses, because they're fast. They can reach speeds between thirty and forty miles an hour within the first three or four strides. It's kind of like riding in Don's Mustang when they explode out of the chute. So, what I'm saying is, be careful and don't make the mistake of thinking she's one of those stable-horses you're used to riding."

"I know how to ride a horse, and I'm not going to get hurt," she said with a disgusted sneer.

"It's not you I'm worried about. I paid about as much for Cupcake as Donald did his Mustang, and she's worth quite a bit more right now, seeing as we're getting ready to breed her.

"So, in short," I turned to give her a grin, "I'm doing you a favor by letting you ride my horse. Just stick beside us and we'll do fine. Besides," I turned away to saddle Roscoe for Don, "we'll be walking beside Donnie and Carol's cart anyway. All I'm saying is," I paused to stare at her, and knew she was fuming by the way she glared back, "if you try kicking her in the sides, or slapping her on the rump, she'll more than likely throw you. I'll get you out here some day alone without the kids and teach you how to ride a quarter-horse."

I might even let Angela drag you behind Zorro like she's been saying. I smiled and tightened Roscoe's cinches.

Chapter 42

"Okay, now ride him high. Don't let him get you to the back of the saddle," Chuck said, as I wrapped the braided rope around my gloved hand. Comanche snorted and pawed the ground nervously as I adjusted myself in the saddle.

"Ready?" Chuck asked and I nodded. "Okay, you've got him," he yelled and opened the gate.

Comanche shot across the Glenn County Sheriff's Memorial Rodeo Arena, heaving like a hurricane-tormented sea. I was vaguely aware of Marline and the two or three hundred cheering people gathered in the stands and sitting on top of pickups. I was riding without hobbled stirrups, which allowed me to spur and rock in motion with the beast trying to throw me from his back. My neck and shoulders ached, but that was normal for a bronc-buster.

"When you fork one of them babies," Chuck had warned me early on, "you'll learn to live with constant whiplash, 'cause that's what you'll get as a reward."

The ringing of a cowbell signaled I had completed my eight-second ride.

There isn't any pretty way to dismount an animal who's trying to send you into outer-space without NASA's help. During the course of a PRCA, or a WPRCA rodeo, you'll have the assistance of two or more pick-up men, who'll pull you from the saddle when you've completed your ride. Those who don't stay eight seconds wind up eating dust anyway. But, seeing as this was a small ranch-rodeo type event, consisting mostly of off-duty deputies and a few ranch hands, I only had one rider, who was having difficulty catching Comanche. I pulled both feet from the stirrups and let go of the rope. Comanche did the rest, and I landed on my butt about four feet from the bucking animal. I limped toward the gate as Chuck snagged Comanche's braided rope and steered him out of the arena.

"Wow! That was a great ride." Marline swatted me on the back.

"Are you hurt? I noticed you're limping." Mable gave me a worried look.

"Na, just trying to work out some of the kinks." I smiled real big. *Everything hurts, if you want to know the truth! Even my eyelashes.*

"Thought maybe you hurt you knee again." She eyed me from head to foot.

"No, the knee's fine. Just jarred myself landing. How'd I look?"

"Not half-bad. You need to spur a little higher, or they're going to mark you down," she said.

"Won't that make it harder for her to stay in the saddle," Mama asked.

"Yeah, it will," she said with a nod and went to care for her horse. Mama gave me a nervous laugh.

"Nothing to worry about. It's just as hard for everyone. They've all got to do the same thing," I said.

"I'm not worried about the rest, or your winning. I'm worried about getting you back in one piece," she said. This was one event that neither Mom nor Dad had planned on attending, but I was happy they'd changed their minds. Especially after getting Don's reaction to my invitation.

"I am certainly not going to drive three hours to watch you break your neck, so you can forget about it. I thought we had settled all that!" he shouted, causing me to pull the phone away from my ear.

We had been getting along a little better since our battle on my front porch, and I was a little taken aback at his reaction. I didn't think it was unreasonable to ask if he'd like to watch me ride.

"Donald, I am not going to break my neck. It's just a small rodeo to raise money for a sheriff's pension fund. It's a charity event," I said, faking a laugh.

And it wasn't much of a rodeo, compared to the Oakdale Saddle Club, or the Red Bluff Round-up, or Brawley Cattle Call. But the smaller ranch events without prize money were good practice, and closer to what rodeos were meant to be, when a bunch of cowboys were having fun during round-up and branding season. This one was especially fun, since they had allowed me to compete alongside the men bareback, then do an exhibition on Comanche using a saddle. Marline and a couple of local girls were the only barrel-racers, while Gary had teamed with a deputy for the roping. The event was to raise money for deputies and their families hurt in the line of duty. The only thing any of us would get, including Mable, who'd carted two of her prize horses six hours free of charge, was a certificate of appreciation, and maybe a brass buckle.

"It doesn't really matter if it's for a charity. You'll be getting bucked off horses, and getting hurt and you know how I feel about that. I cannot, and will not, be a part of it," Don said.

"Well, I've already given my word. They are counting on me. I wish you'd come, Don," I said.

"Go ahead. Go! You were going regardless if I went or said it was okay. Weren't you?" His shouting caused Dad to drop his paper and listen.

"Okay, fine…I think I will," I said, and slammed the receiver.

I was mostly happy I had come. It was for a good cause, and the people were really nice. But I kept feeling as though something was missing. It wasn't until I stood beside my parents, gazing at the small people-packed bleachers, that I realized what was bothering me. Donnie, Caroline and their father weren't there to cheer me on.

"You need to quit worrying about her staying in one piece," Dad was saying. "I quit worrying about her long ago. That's the main reason I bought that wheelchair at the yard sale, back when she first started acting like a dang fool. I know it's been sitting inside the garage, collecting dust. But it might come in handy some day."

"I hope not, but you might be right." Mama took me by the shoulders and grinned. "I'll never understand what it is you're trying to prove, but I love you just the same."

"I love you too, Mama," I said, giving her a kiss, "thanks for coming…both of you. You don't know how much it means to me."

They turned their attention back to the arena as Marline's name was announced. I spied Barry Swaim near the stands as I limped toward Dad's pickup and snagged a coke from the ice chest. He was busy warming his throwing arm by roping a dummy steer made of straw, with boards poking up like horns. He paused to wave, then took his time recoiling his lasso as he walked to where I was standing.

"Nice ride. I was watching."

"Thanks," I said, tossing him a cold soda. He popped the can open and took a drink.

"Mable says I need to spur a little more aggressively."

"Maybe. But what you were doing will keep you in the money. I can see if they ever do let you compete with the men, I'll have my work cut out for me." He grinned.

Chapter 43

"Why don't you like Helen, honey? She's a nice lady," Don asked with a chuckle. He had brought the children for a visit, and we were seated at the kitchen table having coffee and hot chocolate with Mom and Dad, when Caroline informed us she didn't like Helen Fisher.

"Because, Dad!" she said real loud.

Don glanced at me as though I was somehow to blame.

"Hey, don't look at me," I said, shrugging my shoulders. "I don't know why she doesn't like her. Donnie doesn't either, for that matter."

"It's not that my son doesn't like her. He, for some reason or other, thinks of you as his mother." He turned back toward Caroline and asked again, "Why don't you like Helen? Don't be afraid, you can tell me."

"Because, Dad, she…she's mean and has squinty eyes." She made a face, trying to copy one of Helen Fisher's *go to hell* looks, and Dad burst out laughing, spilling his coffee.

"That about nails it," he said, wiping at the spill with a paper napkin. "She really does have squinty eyes," he added, as Don glared.

"Again, I don't know anything about this," I said, raising my hands.

"You shouldn't say things like that about people. They can't help how they look," Don said to Carol.

"Ah, excuse me for saying so, Pastor," Mama began quietly, "but you just asked your daughter to tell you why she didn't like Helen, and promised not to be angry. Now, you're breaking that promise and scolding her for doing what you asked. You should be thanking her for being honest. Children can't help how they feel."

"Yes, you're right," he said, and took Carol's hands. "I'm sorry, Baby. I'm not angry with you. I was just wondering why you didn't like Helen. Forgive me?"

"Uh-huh," she said with a nod, and he kissed her. He looked at me and I grinned.

"It's true, you know," I said with a shrug, "her eyes do get squinty when she's ticked-off about something."

Chapter 44

"Oh, hello," I said, answering the phone.

"You sound distracted. Did I catch you at a bad time?" Don's voice sounded kind of nervous on the other end.

"No, I was reading another rejection from the PRCA."

"Oh? How many does that make?"

"An even dozen and this one's kind of straight-forward, more or less telling me to stick it. The fact that I'm a woman who got hurt during one of their rodeos makes them leery of giving me a PRCA card. I've gotta prove somehow, that I'm okay to ride and capable of earning at least $1,000.00 a year, but how do I do that without riding? I guess it'd be alright if I was a guy who'd gotten his neck busted...but I've got long hair and breasts, and that makes a difference. It doesn't look like they're gonna let me ride saddle-broncs in their stupid rodeos, no matter how much I beg," I said with a sigh.

"Why don't you give up, then?"

"Huh?"

"I said, why don't you give up begging? Like you said, they're not going to let you compete against men, no matter what."

"Because it isn't right, that's why!"

"It might not be right, but that's the way it is going to be...at least for now," he said, and held the receiver away as Donnie began whining. "Not now son, I'm talking to Margie on the phone. I'll be with you in a minute. I'm sorry about that," he added, coming back to me.

"That's okay. What did you call for, anyway? I'm sure it wasn't to discuss my letters to the PRCA."

"No, not really," he said with a chuckle. "Actually, I called to break our date for tonight."

"Break our date? Why? We've been planning this for weeks now."

"Well, Helen's parents arrived rather unexpectedly, and they're only going to be in town one evening. They were hoping to spend some time visiting."

"Donald, Helen knew we had planned on going out this evening. She could have invited them to visit next weekend."

"I'm sure Helen didn't have anything to do with their decision, Margie. You don't know her parents. They are just spur-of-the-moment people. They've been friends with my mother for years, and I feel sort of obligated to visit with them. I was hoping you'd understand."

"Oh, I understand alright...more than you care to know."

"Margie!"

"It's alright, Donald. Really it is. Go have your visit with precious Helen and her parents. I'll sit at home and watch television with my parents."

"I'm sorry you're taking it this way, Margie."

"How did you expect me to take it, Don? Between your work at the church, and doing little favors for everyone, we spend so little time together as it is. Tonight was supposed to be special."

"I'll make it up to you. I promise." There was a long pause when I listened to his breathing.

"Okay, I'll hold you to it. I did notice, though, I wasn't invited. She seems to invite herself most everywhere we go, but Margie's not invited to meet her parents?"

"I'm sorry. Of course you're welcome. We're just going to be sitting around discussing old times and people you're not acquainted with. I didn't think you'd care to meet them."

"No, that's alright, Don. You go ahead and visit with Helen and her parents, and have fun."

"I'm sorry, Margie."

"I know you are."

I hung up the phone fuming. Helen Fisher was really getting to be a pain. Angela Vasquez might have to fight me in order to drag her down the streets of Oakdale.

Chapter 45

"Na-uh," I said, making my face a moving target. "Not one goodnight kiss, until I get some straight answers." It was three days later, and he had taken me to The Garlic House for a romantic kiss-and-make-up dinner, and we were standing on my front porch in the moonlight saying goodnight.

"Answers to what?"

"You know. What you said the day we were right here and you were angry because I rode Comanche. Remember?"

"I'm still upset about that. You could have re-injured your knee, or been seriously hurt." He held onto both of my hands and stared into my eyes.

"Would that have bothered you?"

"Now what kind of a question is that? Yes it would have bothered me. I love you, Marjorie Ann Green, although I'll never know why."

"Because you think I'm gorgeous, you want to kiss me, hug me and marry me..." I said, giving my best Sandra Bullock imitation.

"Yes, that's all true, but you also drive me crazy." He grinned. "Now, it's getting late, and I have to give the neighbor's daughter her freedom from babysitting." He leaned to kiss me, but I jerked away.

"Not until you tell me what you meant about marrying someone who limps like Chuck Burris."

"Well, I think that Chuck Burris would make a perfectly horrible wife."

"Don," I said, punching his shoulder. "Come on, tell me!"

"Okay," he sighed and took me by the shoulders, "I have been thinking about proposing, but there are a lot of things to consider." My heart suddenly sank.

"Like what?"

"Like, for starters, your jealousy over my friendship with Helen Fisher."

"Donald, that woman is after you, and will get you any way she can. You're the only person on this planet that fails to see it," I said.

"Margie," he heaved a big sigh, "I really don't want to argue about this...not tonight."

"Okay, Don...okay." I held my hands in surrender. "I promise not to say anything. I'll do my best to bite my tongue and turn the other way, no matter what she says or does."

"I doubt you can do that," he said, laughing.

"I promise to try. What else?"

"Like I already have two children."

"No problem. I love them like my own."

"I know, but you would be starting with an instant family, just the same. Third, there's the age difference. I'll be twenty-seven next month."

"Seven years? No biggie. Marline's dad is ten years older than her mom, and they're happy. What else have you got," I said with a grin.

"Okay, and here's the *biggie*, as you call it. The dedication issue."

"The what?"

"The issue of what each of us considers important."

"Getting married and living happily ever-after," I said, and he laughed.

"That my dear, is exactly what I'm driving at," he said, touching my nose with the tip of his finger.

"Explain."

"To you, everything is a rodeo. The horses, bulls and clowns. The excitement of a roaring crowd. And you still haven't given up the idea of being able to compete with men."

"Well I should be allowed to. There's absolutely no reason women should be banned from competing in the same rodeos and events men do," I said.

"Perhaps, but that is not the issue we are discussing." He grabbed my shoulders and studied me before continuing.

"I don't think you're going to give those things up easily. And I've got a suspicion that getting married is just another event in your big rodeo of life."

"No, that's not true, Don. I know getting married is serious business, and it scares me something fierce. But I have changed a lot these past few months. You've got to admit that."

"I know you have. You've quit smoking and drinking, as far as I know. I never asked you to give any of those things up. You did it on your own, and I appreciate it. You came forward in front of the whole church to dedicate your life, and I baptized you myself. That took real courage. I've never questioned your commitment to Jesus."

"Then, what," I said.

"Being a minister happens to be a full time job. I have a congregation to care for. That means being there whenever they need me. It means getting calls in the middle of the night, when someone is seriously ill, or has been in an accident. It means putting your own plans on hold to conduct a funeral or wedding. It means being the last one to leave the church on Sunday, when most families are enjoying their Sunday dinner. But most of all, it means being here with the congregation on weekends, instead of traveling across country to compete in a rodeo.

"The ministry is my life, Margie. It's all I've ever wanted to be, the way you've always wanted to compete in the rodeo. I haven't asked you to give up the rodeo, and it wouldn't be fair." He shrugged. "I'm sorry I got you into this, Margie. I really am."

"Was Linda as dedicated as you are saying?" I blinked hard against the tears welling in my eyes.

"Yes, as a matter of fact, she was."

"What about Helen? Is she that dedicated?"

"Let's not go there."

"I'd like to know. Do you think Helen is that dedicated?"

"I really don't know. I've never asked, but then she isn't involved in rodeo, or anything I can think of, the way you are. She just might be that dedicated." He heaved a sigh.

"I'm sorry, Margie. I really am. I really do love you." I didn't move as he gave me a quick kiss on the lips.

"I know," I said, and waited until he had driven away before going inside and locking the door.

Chapter 46

"Oh, Don, isn't it beautiful! Where are we?" I twirled and danced around him and the small fawn he was petting.

"Don? What's the matter with you Eve? My name is Adam, not Don." He stared at me like I was completely nuts.

"Adam?" I whirled once more, taking in the beautiful lake and trees. "Adam and Eve," I squealed. "Then this must be the Garden of Eden?"

"Certainly, you know that. Eve, what's the matter with you? Have you been down by the lake eating from that tree again? You know that you're not supposed to do that." He scrunched his face like he was ticked-off.

"No, no! I wouldn't do that. It's just that, everything's so beautiful. I've never seen anything so pretty in my entire life."

"That's very understandable, since you're only three days old. But it is rather beautiful, at that." He put an arm around me.

"Oh, do you know how much I love you? It's as though we were made for each other." I threw my arms around his waist and squeezed.

"We were, Eve. We were made for each other. There isn't any one else in the entire world." He kissed me, and I knew for certain he was telling the truth. I leaned my head against his chest, absorbing every ounce of love seeping from his pores, when I heard a noise in the grass at my feet. I screamed, as a big, ugly snake rubbed against my leg.

"Kill it Don! Kill it! Don't let it get me!"

"My name is not Don, its Adam. I'll swear, I don't know what's gotten into you." He didn't seem to notice the serpent.

Then, in a huge puff of smoke, the snake turned into this sexy brunette, who looked like Helen Fisher. She had on a French-cut two piece made of leaves, showing way more skin than the black one she had at the river. She slithered up to drape her arms and a bare leg around Don, then laughed at me.

"I don't want you, stupid. I want him."

"Come on, Adam," she said, tugging one of his hands. "Helen's come to rescue you." They walked away hand in hand, leaving me alone. My heart exploded into a million pieces.

"Don," I cried, "don't leave me. I love you, Don. I'll change. I'll be like her. I love you!"

She glanced at me over one shoulder and sniggered. "You didn't really think that you could keep him, did you?"

I jerked upward in bed, sweating and shaking all over. I closed my Bible and put it back on the nightstand, deciding the creation story wasn't what I should have been reading that particular evening.

I checked the clock, and it was only one-thirty. I knew I wasn't going to sleep at all, not after that dream. I washed my face and got a glass of milk from the kitchen. The old man had a western novel lying on the floor next to his chair, so I snagged it, along with the milk, and headed toward the bedroom. I drank the milk and read three or four chapters of Louis L'Amour's *Ride The River*, before falling asleep cross-ways on my bed with the light on.

Chapter 47

"Well, I didn't think it was a laughing matter at the time," I said, as Marline wiped her eyes. She had come to take me shopping, when I decided to share my dream with everyone over Saturday morning coffee. Even the old man, who isn't much on humor, had split a gut laughing.

"No, but you'll have to admit, it is funny," Mama said.

"Maybe this morning, but not the stuff he said on the front porch, about rodeo and my not being able to commit. How does he know I wouldn't make a good pastor's wife? I'll bet Helen Fisher had something to do with his sudden change of mind."

"It wouldn't surprise me in the least," Marline said.

"You've got to admit, it's a big job, Margie. Sure you love him that much?" the old man said, raising his eyebrows.

"He's all I've been thinking about for months." I stared into my favorite mug.

"Not really," Marline said, as she refilled her cup. "You weren't thinking about him when you rode Comanche, or when you were talking to the Saddle Club, or writing those letters to the PRCA, were you?"

"That's not fair. Besides, what does my riding a horse, or trying to get a bunch of hard-heads to change their minds, have to do with him asking me to get married?"

"Everything," Mama said, "just like your father said, it is a big job. And Pastor Don is not sure you would be willing to give up rodeo in order to stay home and be a wife and mother. I don't know if you can answer that question yourself, can you?"

"I don't know. I think I can. I believe I'd like to give it a try," I said, and Dad chuckled.

"No, that's not going to work either, not with a man like the reverend. He's going to need more than *giving it a try* out of you. What's more, those children deserve more. If you can't do it and make it work, then don't even try."

"How'd you get so smart?" I scowled.

"I got a lot of bumps and bruises learning what I just told you. The thing is, none of us around this table can tell you what to do. You've got to decide for yourself," he said, toasting me with his cup. "Good luck."

"Maybe we can't tell her what to do, Mr. Green. But we can certainly speed things along," Marline said. "Pastor Gardner needs to make up his mind also."

"About what," the old man asked.

"About how much he loves your daughter, and we can help him make up his mind about that." She scooted away from the table and placed her cup in the sink.

"How's that," I asked.

"He likes fishing right?"

I nodded.

"Well, come on," she grinned, "you said you needed to get him a birthday present. How about shopping for some man-bait while we're at it?"

Chapter 48

"Good morning, Jerk," I said, sliding into the pew next to Barry. "Where's Marline?"

"Freda called her early this morning, and asked her to take her place in the nursery. I guess she caught the flu or something."

"That's too bad. She's a nice old lady."

"Yeah. Kind of tries mothering me and telling me what to do every now and then," he said with a snigger.

"Good. Why don't you listen to her?"

"I listen. I just don't do what she says."

"Maybe you should."

"Maybe." We sat for a long minute listening to the piano play funeral music.

"Don't get any ideas, just because I'm sitting next to you. You're still on my list of favorite people to hate."

"Well, that kinda hurts," he said with a pouty-face.

"Why's that? My hating you never seemed to bother you before."

"You've never looked like this before."

"Now, that hurts *my* feelings. Gee, think of all the time we dated. I was under the impression you might've liked my looks just a little," I said with a crooked grin. Barry's parents stopped in the aisle to stare, before taking seats in front of us. Harold twisted around to shake my hand.

"Good morning, Margie. That's a mighty pretty outfit you have on."

"Thank you," I said, smiling back. I was wearing the new red business suit and white blouse Marline had helped pick out. Although the outfit was totally modest, it fit snug in just the right places, and made me look older. My hair was piled neatly on top of my head in order to reveal my neck, and topped off with a small matching hat, which I had cocked slightly to one side.

"Yes, very lovely. Don't you think so, Barry," Mrs. Swaim said. The old lady had been heartbroken when Barry and I had stopped seeing each other, although I'd never known why. I thought she would have been just as ecstatic to have him dating Marline.

"Yes, and that was what I was trying to tell her," Barry said, "but she took it as an insult."

"No, what you said was, I never looked this good before. It came across as though I had been ugly or frumpy, while we were dating, and suddenly turned into something attractive."

"See," he said to his mother. "This is why we broke up. She's always twisting things I say into something else."

"Now, let's not go into why we broke up. Not here, anyway," I said with a laugh.

"What I meant to say was," he began as the song leader took the stand, "that you've always been beautiful, but now, you're gorgeous. It's like turning a pearl into a diamond."

"Why, thank you, Barry. That's the second time you've complimented me these past few weeks. You'd better watch out. It might become habit-forming."

"Shhhhh!" The lady seated next to Barry gave us a glare, so I turned my attention toward the front.

It was positively the worst sermon Don had given during the time I had been attending church, but I loved every second. He stuttered and stammered, and lost his place several times. We were seated close enough for me to watch the beads of sweat roll down his cheeks as his gaze continually drifted my way. I smiled sweetly and, may God forgive me, actually pursed my lips as though I were sending him a long-distance kiss during one of those glances. He totally lost it that time, and had to repeat himself in order to regroup. I took my time chatting and shaking hands after the closing prayer, then clung onto Barry's arm as we were leaving. Helen Fisher had parked herself beside Donald as he stood at the door shaking hands and chatting with people as they left the building. I made it a point of stopping.

"Good morning, Helen. How are you," I said, extending my hand.

"I am just fine, Margie. How are you?" Her weak handshake matched her icy glare.

"I am just wonderful, thank you. Nice dress," I said, trailing my fingers across the ruffled sleeve of her blue-print. I had seen the same dress in Macy's, and knew she had spent a lot of time and money picking it out. Marline had considered buying one just like it, but decided it paled in comparison to my red suit. I turned toward Don with a grin as Helen continued glaring.

"Good morning, Pastor. Lovely morning isn't it? And oh," I said, brushing his arm lightly with my fingers, "I really enjoyed your sermon."

"I'm glad someone liked it. You look nice, Margie."

"Thank you. So do you, Pastor," I said, and turned away. The glare he gave Barry could have peeled the paint off Dad's old truck. I allowed Barry to escort me to where the old man had parked and glanced back at the church. Don had disappeared, abandoning Helen with those who were busy socializing on the lawn.

"Well, I'd say your little plan worked," Barry said with a grin.

"What plan?"

"Getting under the pastor's skin. I don't know what happened between you two, but whatever it was, I'd say you got even."

"You don't mind…sort of being used as bait?" I raised my eyebrows.

"Mind? Heck no! I'm glad you still think of me as being good enough. Besides, it's kind of fun knowing a preacher can sin the same as we do."

"Sin? Now wait a minute. We didn't do anything like that," I said.

"Quit jumping to conclusions, Margie. What I meant was, your preacher boyfriend could've killed me several times this morning, especially when he saw us leaving together. My Dad and the rest of the old-fart board members had better install some metal detectors, or frisk him next Sunday. He might be packing, and I'd hate to get shot during one of his sermons."

"I don't think he'll go that far," I said with a snicker. "Thanks, Barry. I actually enjoy being friendly-enemies."

"Yeah, me too. Let's do it again." He laughed. "Next Sunday?"

"Maybe. We'd better fill Marline in first. I'll give you a call."

Barry left as Mom and Dad joined us. I waited as Dad unlocked the truck and Mom slid inside.

"What," I said as the old coot glared over the top of the truck at me.

"What? You know what!"

"No, I don't. What'd I do this time?"

"Oh, just get in, you dunder-head!" he said, slamming the door.

Chapter 49

I could tell they were fuming, and we were almost home before I broke the silence.

"So, do you think gloating is a sin?"

"What," Mama said with a curt laugh.

"Gloating. Is it a sin to gloat?"

"Well, yes…I guess it probably is. Why?"

"Then I guess I'd better do some repenting, because I'm gloating right now," I said, as Dad parked in the driveway. They both stared, so I continued.

"Don hurt me real bad the other day, so I'm feeling pretty good about getting under his skin today. So, if that's gloating, then I guess I'm a sinner."

"I would think you should feel pretty bad about using Barry Swaim to get back at Pastor Don. Don't you? Using him that way might hurt him," Mama said.

"Barry? Na, you couldn't hurt him with an ax handle. He's alright. Besides, we've already had that discussion, and he's okay with it. In fact, he said he had fun playing along."

"Then you weren't hitting on Barry Swaim just to get back at Don," Dad asked.

"Dad! We were sitting together in church, not on a date. Besides, none of it was planned, it just happened. I saw him there alone, and sat beside him. I didn't realize that my sitting beside Barry Swaim would have any effect on him, until Don started stumbling and falling all over himself behind the pulpit. But I'll tell you what," I said, twisting to face them, "I enjoyed every second, and I'll do it again."

"Now, that's a double whammy," Dad said with a grin. "That's vengeful-gloating. Two sins combined, and I *do* think God would frown on it. But," he waved his index finger in the air, "I'll admit to feeling the same way several times myself."

"Well, shame on the both of you," Mama said. "And I hope you don't plan on carrying this ruse too long, dear. Too many people stand a chance of getting hurt. Don't forget about Marline. She's your best friend and, if I'm not mistaken, still likes Barry Swaim. How would you feel if your little game hurt her?"

"Barry and I have already talked about Marline, and I plan on telling her this afternoon. I promise not to do it again if she says no, but some of us have already been hurt, Mama. I don't plan on carrying it any longer than I have to," I said, squeezing her arm. "I'm hungry. Let's go find something to eat."

Chapter 50

"Well, hello, Pastor. It's nice of you to call." I had answered the phone on the third ring. I heard Mama's fork drop to her plate with a loud clink as she paused to listen. Don cleared his voice several times before continuing.

"I...I'm wondering if I might come over to visit this afternoon?"

"Certainly, you may visit any time you wish. It would be nice seeing you." I glanced at the old man and old lady and grinned. "And please bring the children. We miss seeing them too."

"Carol and Donnie?"

"Yes, those are they're names, aren't they?"

"Yes. I guess I can bring them. I was hoping to get some time alone with you. We need to talk, Margie."

"Talk? I suppose that is possible. What is it you would like to discuss, Pastor?"

"Would you please knock off the *Pastor* bit? I'm trying to be serious." I raised my eyebrows toward Mama.

"Alright, Donald. I'll see you when you get here, and you can believe our talk will be as serious as my Aunt Dorothy's heart attack."

Chapter 51

I was watching, and met them on the front porch when they arrived. Don waited while I scooped Donnie into my arms and hugged and kissed Carol. I listened patiently, and "ooohed and aaahed" as they proudly displayed what they had made in Sunday School. Then Mama politely stole them away with the promise of bowls of ice cream.

"I guess I should start this off by asking about Barry Swaim," Don said, after Dad had completely shut the door.

"Let's leave Barry out of this. What took place between us doesn't concern him."

"I saw you two sitting next to each other in church today, and…"

"And we were worshiping God," I said, cutting him off. "Is there some rule that says I can't sit beside an old boyfriend and worship God inside your church?"

"I thought you said he used to hurt you," he stammered.

"No worse than you hurt me."

"I know you're angry with me," he said, coming closer.

"Furious, is more like it! God, I can't believe it's that hard for you to understand. Your wife must have been a saint to put up with you!" I yelled.

"Just let me explain," he said.

"There's nothing to explain, Don. I understood what you were saying about my being committed to rodeo, and you to the church. And I realize there are a lot of things I don't know about your ministry, and what our getting married would entail. But the thing that really, really hurts is," I paused as my lip trembled, "that you didn't even give me a chance. You made up both our minds and blew me off. You don't know how far, or even what, I was willing to give up for you. You just said *Margie's not good enough*, and walked away."

He stared a long minute before saying, "That's not true."

"Not true? How can you say such a thing?"

"I thought long and hard about our relationship. I'd never do anything to hurt you, Margie."

"It's too late...you already have."

"I know and believe me, I'm terribly sorry."

"So am I," I said fighting my trembling chin.

"Well," he sighed after a minute, "where does that leave us?"

"I don't know. You tell me, Pastor."

"Let's be serious about this, Margie."

"I am serious. You seem to be the one making the rules. You tell me where I stand, and I'll do my best to play the game." We stared at each other for what seemed an eternity before he spoke.

"I'd still like to be friends."

"I don't know if that's possible, but I'll try."

"Okay, I will too," he said, and gave me a quick kiss on the lips before disappearing inside the house. I waited awhile before bounding down the steps and through the gate. I wasn't heading anywhere in particular...just walking. It was gonna be hard hiding how much he'd hurt me, with tears running down both cheeks.

Chapter 52

"I can guess where he got those ideas," Peggy said sullenly. The gang and I were squeezed into a corner booth at Denny's having coffee when I explained what had been happening between me and Don, and what had transpired on my front porch.

"Helen Fisher," Marline asked.

"You bet. I walked in on them when they were talking in the kitchen the other day. Helen got real quiet when she saw me, but I'd already heard enough to know she was hinting that Margie was too dedicated to her rodeo to be a pastor's wife." Peggy added cream and stirred her coffee while she talked.

"What'd you say," Angela asked.

"Me? Nothing. What could I say?"

"Well, what was she doing there inside your house, Marline said.

"She's there all the time, even when she's supposed to be at school. And that's not all. She follows him around and even pops into the church office in the middle of the day, with some lame excuse like she just happened to be passing by and thought he'd like a little company," Peggy said.

"Well, he must like her company," I said, and took a sip of coffee as everyone stared. "He'd run her off, if he didn't. Wouldn't he?"

"Maybe not," Gloria said with a shrug. "My Rafael had this girl hanging around him once. She was trying to steal him, same as this Helen. But my man was too nice to run her off.

Besides, he kept thinking this girl and I were friends."

"There's no danger in Don thinking Helen Fisher and I are friends," I said with a snort.

"Yes, but your man is nice, isn't he," Gloria asked.

"What'd you do," Angela asked.

"Me? I kicked her butt and told her not to come around my Rafael again," Gloria said.

"Yeah, I've considered that one too, but that'd just make things worse. Besides, like I said, he must like her company, or he wouldn't be letting her hang around. And, I suppose, that kinda leaves me up the creek," I said.

"Maybe not." Peggy made a slurping sound as she sipped her coffee.

"How's that," Angela asked.

"I don't know, but I'd like to see Margie play Helen's little game against her." Peggy smiled as we took turns staring at each other.

"Well, for instance," she continued, "let's say she starts treating Helen kind of friendly like…"

"Like that'd ever happen," Angela said with a snigger.

"No, I mean it," Peggy said. "You know, if Margie quits talking crap about her to my brother, and treats her all nice and polite-like."

"Yeah, like you did Sunday, when you complimented her on her dress," Marline said. "Barry said that pissed her off something fierce."

"Either way," Peggy continued, "it would give Helen less ammunition to use, and Margie could go about winning the people of the church onto her side, by acting like…I don't know…Barbara Bush, or Princess Diana."

"I thought she'd already done that…I mean, most of the church already likes her. Don't they," Marline said.

"Yeah, they like her, but I mean really win them over to her side. They're mostly seeing Helen's good side now, but wait until Margie starts treating her all nice, and she flings it back into her face, and talks crap behind her back."

"What makes you think she'll do that," Angela said.

"Because I've known Helen Fisher and her family all my life and they're like that...all of them. Helen would explode if she couldn't talk about someone behind their back."

"Now, that's someone who'd make a good wife for your preacher-brother," Gloria said with a laugh.

"Yeah, like don't I know it," Peggy agreed.

"Okay, so Margie turns all nice..." Marline started.

"I thought I already was," I said with a shrug.

"Okay," she said with a snigger, "but nicer...much nicer. Now, what do the rest of us do?"

"You? Why should any of you get involved?"

"Because, we're all friends and friends stick together," Gloria said, leaning across the table.

"It's simple," Peggy said with a grin. "Margie's nice, and we submarine Helen Fisher."

"Barry said I ought to forget trying to compete with Helen, and go back to being a cowgirl," I said after a long minute.

"That too," Angela said with a nod. "You should be who you are, but what Peggy's saying makes a lot of sense. Go back to being who you are, *Margie the bronc rider.* Only this time, you're gonna act more like Dale Evans, instead of Calamity Jane."

Chapter 53

"I hope you like it. It was the best I could think of," I said as Don tore the ribbon and paper from the birthday present I had given him. His twenty-seventh birthday party consisted of a few friends and people from the church, gathered in his living room for cake and ice cream.

"Oh, wow!" he said, staring at the picture. I had taken a color photograph of me riding Cupcake during a barrel-racing event in Turlock, and had it enlarged and framed. The Modesto Bee photographer who had taken the picture had completely captured the spirit of barrel-racing, and I was thrilled when it appeared in the sports section of their paper. I called his office, thanking him, and asked for a copy, which he was only too eager to supply. His camera had caught Cupcake stretched in a full run, with me leaning forward and hair trailing in the wind.

"Do you really like it," I asked.

"Like it? I love it," he said, giving me a peck on the lips. Helen glared from where she was seated next to Marline on the sofa. All Don had given her was a "thanks" after opening the leather-bound desk organizer she had given. That, on top of the fact that I'd been treating her with nothing but respect, especially in front of Don and the members of the church, was driving her crazy.

"Better hang on to that one, Pastor," Marline said. "There aren't many pictures of Marge barrel-racing, and it's going to become a collector's item one of these days."

"I am. I'll hang it in my bedroom, where it will be the

first thing I look at in the morning," he said, holding the picture for everyone to see.

"Well," I said, acting offended, "I was hoping you might want to wake up to the real thing in the morning."

"Margie!" Mama said with a gasp.

"It's true!" I said.

"That's possible." He leaned to kiss me and added, "We'll see."

Chapter 54

"What?" I stopped in the middle of the aisle as he started laughing.

"Do you have to wear those things everywhere we go?"

"What things?"

"Spurs," Don pointed toward my boots, "you're still wearing them."

"So?" I took Caroline's hand and continued clinking toward the booth.

"In case you haven't noticed, The Nutcracker is a rather nice restaurant." He slid into the booth opposite me, and hoisted Donnie into a booster chair.

"Get real. This is Oakdale you're talking about, Donald. Half the folks in here are cowboys."

"I just took it for granted that you might be willing to remove them before coming in here," he said with a crooked grin.

"You called me at work, saying you wanted to grab a bite to eat. I thought it would be okay to wear boots and jeans. You never said anything about dressing up, or even coming here. Besides, most everyone in here is wearing boots and jeans, for your information. See," I added as a couple of lanky cowboys clinked their way past our booth and sat at a table.

"Okay, I stand corrected. The boots and jeans are fine. And it isn't that I haven't noticed a few people wearing spurs inside a supermarket or convenience store since arriving here. But since I had planned on us going out to eat and take in a movie, I can't see the need for spurs."

"You never said anything about a movie, Pastor Gardner," I said, glaring across the table.

"I didn't?"

"No, you didn't." I shook my head.

"Okay, I'm sorry. But can you at least remove them before going into the theater," he asked with a crooked grin.

"What for? I'd just have to strap them on again tomorrow morning." I leaned across the table and grinned back.

"Don't you have to every morning you go to work?"

"Not this morning, I didn't."

"You didn't what?"

"I didn't strap them on, because I never unstrapped them in the first place." I glanced up and added a "thanks" as the waitress handed me a menu.

"You don't remove your spurs when you take your boots off at night?"

"No, why should I?"

"No reason. I just thought that was something people did…remove their spurs before taking their boots off and going to bed." He shrugged as he studied the menu.

"Get real, Don. This *is* Oakdale we're talking about. *The Cowboy Capital Of The World?* More professional rodeo cowboys and cowgirls come from here than anyplace on the planet. Quit acting like a greenhorn Yankee!"

The waitress slid a glass of water in front of each of us and pulled a pad from her pocket. "May I take your order, please?"

"Yeah, Carol here," I motioned with my head, "wants a hamburger and fries from the children's menu. What about Donnie?"

"He'll take the same," Donald said with a nod.

"I'll have steak, baked potato with gravy and a diet coke. The man across from me will have an old boot," I said with a glare.

"I beg your pardon?" The waitress giggled.

"Don't pay any attention to her. We were just having a

discussion about cowboys and spurs. I'll have grilled cod with rice."

"Half the people attending our church are ranchers," I continued.

"Yes, I am well aware of that."

"It's a wonder they've put up with you this long. Get a little manure under your fingernails, pastor." I grinned and toasted him with my water.

Chapter 55

"You're sure about wanting to buy the truck, now?" Dad leaned against the fender and folded his arms.

"Well, yeah. That's why I asked. I've got the money," I added after a pause. The old coot had bought Harold Swaim's used Chevy pickup, and was planning on placing an ad in the paper to sell the Ford, when I made my offer.

"I believe you. Money was the last thing on my mind. I thought you hated this truck. Why the change of heart all of a sudden?"

"I don't know. I need transportation, and you need to sell the truck. Besides, it's not such a bad truck. What's the problem?"

"There's no problem. I just thought you would buy a nice car with your money, instead of an old beat-up pickup," he said.

"Well, yeah. I've thought about it, and I think driving a nice car to the stables everyday might not be such a good thing. It gets kinda rough in the winter, and dusty in the summer. Besides, I've gotta run into town and pick up extra feed or hay every once in awhile, and this truck would be perfect."

"Makes sense," he said with a nod. "But you know how old it is, and it has a lot of miles under the hood."

"Yeah, but it runs good."

"Sure, but I'm not guaranteeing for how long. You're sure you want it?"

"Yeah, I'm sure."

"Okay, it's yours." He turned and headed toward the house.

"How much?"

"Five dollars."

"What? Come on, Dad! I'm serious. How much do you want for the truck?"

"Five dollars." He paused as he opened the door and grinned. "You give me five dollars and pay for the insurance, registration and any repairs in the future, and the truck's yours."

"Why? You can get a lot more than five dollars. Look, I'm willing to pay whatever you planned on asking, Dad."

"I know I can get more." He held me by the shoulders. "But I'd rather give it to my daughter. Give me five dollars, and I'll sign the pink slip."

"Okay."

I sat up in bed that night thinking I might have some tall repenting to do, considering all the bad things I'd said about the old coot over the years. Maybe Mom was right. He did have a soft spot hidden under that rough exterior of his. Anyway, I sort of got back at him by giving him a big kiss goodnight before going off to bed. It actually made the old man cry. Me too.

Chapter 56

"Why are we stopping here," Don asked, as I pulled into the Bucksworth Western Wear parking lot. I had asked Peggy to watch the kids, while I took him for a ride in my new/old pickup.

"You'll see. Come inside."

"I've never been inside a western clothing store, and was just wondering what we were doing here."

"Quit asking so many questions and come on," I said, grabbing his hand.

"Wow! This is quite a place," he said, allowing the doors to swing shut. "Is this where you buy your clothes?"

"Some of them. I get a lot of my stuff from Oakdale Feed and Seed, 'cause I go there for work. They sell everything from boots to saddles, and keep a lot of hay and feed in the warehouse. Come on," I gave his arm a tug, "what size of shoe do you wear?"

"Size twelve, why?"

"Because, my dear, you are getting a pair of boots."

"I've never worn a pair of cowboy boots in my life." He hesitated as we reached the boot racks.

"You're going to be wearing them now. Sit down. Brown? Or do you prefer black?" He gave me a blank stare. "Okay, brown Durangos it is. Pull your shoes off and try these."

I discovered it was much easier to shop for a man who can't make up his own mind, than it is for a woman. The man will simply stand there, looking like a calf staring at a new gate, while we women will try every blouse or shirt on the rack. We had picked the boots, two pairs of jeans and three shirts in a matter of minutes. Then came the hat.

"Eighty-five dollars for a hat," he gasped.

"Want a better one? They've got one over there for four-hundred. Wanna try it on?"

"Hah?!! I'm not paying four-hundred dollars for a hat. I don't care how good it is."

"Well, I'm not asking you to. This Stetson is on sale for half price. Now, I happen to think it makes you look rather sexy, myself," I said, slipping the dark brown hat onto his head.

"Really?"

"Yes, really. But if you don't like it, you can simply go on looking like a greenhorn. Is that what you want?"

"Well, I don't know how the church would like having a sexy pastor," he said, studying his image in the mirror.

"It's too late, they already have one. But you don't really have to wear the hat while preaching. It's okay to wear just it for me," I said, giving him a quick kiss on the shoulder.

"Alright. I'll have to see if I have enough in my account to pay for all this," he said, digging a checkbook from his pocket.

"You don't have to pay for it. It's my gift to you."

"No, you don't have to…"

"I know I don't have to, but I want to. Besides, I've got the money, since Dad wouldn't let me pay for the truck. I'm simply passing it on to you."

"But…"

"Ah-ah," I held a finger to his lips, "you know better than to argue with me when my mind's made up. I'm buying clothes for the man I love. Besides," I said, laying an armload on the checkout counter, "someday, I hope it'll be *our money* we're spending…not just mine."

Chapter 57

"I fail to see what your problem is, young lady. We have you registered to compete in the lady's barrel-racing." The woman's voice had a condescending tone that made me want to spit in her face. I might have, if it were possible to spit long distance over the phone. I took a deep breath, and tried again in my sweetest voice.

"I understand, and that is why I am calling. There has been a mistake, because I applied to compete in the saddle-bronc division."

"But, you *are* a woman, am I correct?"

"Yes, the last time I checked, I was still a female." I chuckled.

"I'm afraid that all we have is men competing in that division. Women usually ask to compete in the barrel-racing. That is why we placed you in that category."

"Yeah, I know. But I want to ride saddle-broncs with the men. That's what I asked for."

"I can't seem to find you listed as a PRCA member. Are you a new member?"

"No, I've been planning to join, but right now I'm a WPRCA member.

"Then, I'm afraid what you're asking is impossible. May I ask, why do you wish to compete against the men?"

"Because I find it more exciting."

"Well," she laughed, "I'm sure that assumption is correct. Let me check and see what we can do. Could you hold, please?"

"Yes, Ma'am." She pushed a button, and I was listening to George Jones cry, *If the drinking don't kill me...her memory will.* He finished, and Waylon Jennings had almost finished singing about a girl named Amanda before a man's voice came on the line.

"Miss Green?"

"Yes, Sir."

"I'm George Bennett, and we've had quite a discussion around here about your request to compete in the saddle bronc division. I'm sorry about the mix-up, but you'll have to stay with the women for the present. That is, if you still want to compete here in Laughlin."

"May I ask why? I've already competed against men here in Oakdale, and several other rodeos in our area," I said.

"Yes, I understand, and if there was any way of putting you into the men's program, believe me, I would do it. But the saddle bronc program is reserved strictly for PRCA members, as you well know, and it's already been filled. We simply don't have any more slots available, even if it were possible to place you in the event."

"Okay, what about letting me ride exhibition? I wouldn't be going against any men, and my score wouldn't really count for anything."

"Mmmm, we've never had a request like that before, and frankly, I don't know what the ramifications would be."

"I'd either ride for eight seconds, or get thrown. How hard is that?"

"It isn't quite as simple as that," he said with a laugh. "I wish it were. I'll tell you what, why don't you compete with the women this year, and I'll see what I can do for next year? Maybe by then, you'll have your PRCA card and there won't be any question of your competing.

"Look," he added after a long pause, "I'll check with our insurance agency, to see what needs to be changed. And we don't even know how the men would react to having a girl ride in one of their events. Some of these guys would probably feel we were trying to ruin rodeo altogether. Then, even if I could get their okay, there's still the board of directors to consider. We'll have to get them to agree, and believe me, getting them to agree on anything's not that easy. The rodeo's only a few weeks away, and there's just not enough time to get it all done, even if I could find a slot for you."

"I didn't know it was that much of a hassle," I said. "When I told them I wanted to ride with the guys around here, they just did it."

"Yes, well for your information, I called Oakdale while you were on hold…"

"Harold Swaim?"

"Yes, Harold and I have been friends longer than you've been alive. Anyway, he informed me that quite a few strings were pulled, and favors were called in, simply because you are a local girl, and fairly popular. He also said you are nice and quite lovely to look at."

"Really?"

"Yes, really. Now, all of those things put together make me want to see you ride here in Laughlin. I think it would be a great crowd-pleaser. But I don't have enough time to put it together right now. I promise I'll do my best for next season."

"Okay, thank you for all your help, Mr. Bennett. I hope to meet you when we get there."

"That's it?" he said with a chuckle.

"Ah, yeah. Was there supposed to be something else," I asked.

"No, except Harold told me to get prepared to be reamed out when I turned you down."

"Oh," I laughed, "I guess I have been kinda rough on Mr. Swaim. But that was mostly before I started going to church and became a Christian. I'm trying to act more like Jesus now."

"That's good to hear. I'm a Baptist myself, but I'm not so sure I always act like Jesus. Could you hold on a minute?"

"Sure." There was a long pause when I heard him say something to somebody with his hand over the receiver.

"Miss Green?"

"Yeah?"

"I might be getting myself in some sort of trouble here, but I'll guarantee you'll be riding an exhibition sometime between events. How does that sound?"

"Great!" I thanked him, hung up the phone, then sat staring at a blank television screen.

Huh, who would've thought saying I was a Christian would've opened any doors? I guess I ought to say that a little more often. George Bennett seems like a pretty nice man. But, of course, I'm sill not getting scored or paid. I guess I might as well go back with the girls. Even that smarmy female thought that's where I belonged. What's the matter with me...or any girl, competing with the guys? Are they scared we're gonna beat them, or something?

I stomped to the cupboard and grabbed a glass, then jerked the freezer door open and filled it with ice.

So Harold Swaim thinks I'm lovely to look at? How about that old coot? Holy crud, maybe Barry comes by his skankiness naturally. I wonder if his wife knows he looks at the girls that way? Gloria's got some huge boobs that she has to bind to keep from bouncing when she rides. I wonder what he thinks about her?

I opened the refrigerator and rummaged around in the back until I found a coke and cracked it open.

Don likes to watch barrel-racing. God Almighty! Maybe he likes watching Gloria bounce and jiggle! Stop it! Stop it! You idiot! I opened one of the drawers pulled a couple of slices of cheese from a pack, then rummaged for what else I might find.

Well anyway, I'm sure George Bennett will try, and he might even see if he can't get them to allow me to compete with the men next season...that is, if I play my cards right. Besides, they've got a pretty good purse in the women's division in Laughlin, so maybe it's not all lost. It'll be fun, and maybe Don will come watch.

"Geeze, how'd I get back to him?" I jerked up and whacked my head against the open freezer door.

"Oh, God! I can't believe I did that!" I dropped into a

chair holding the cold can against my head.

"What, Dear," Mama said, poking her head through the laundry room door.

"I hit my head."

"Oh, where does it hurt?" She pulled the can away for a look. "I see. What did you bang it on, a cabinet?"

"No, the refrigerator."

"The refrigerator? How in the world did you do that?" She laughed.

"I left the freezer door open while I got a coke."

"Then you hit your head on the door when you raised up," Mama said with a nod.

"Yeah, something like that."

"How many times have I told you to close the door when you're finished?"

"About a million. I don't listen too good, do I?"

"Not always. Sometimes you seem like you're a million miles away, in some little world of your own."

"Mostly the other side of town," I said with a grin.

"Where?"

"With Donald Ray Gardner, where else? Every time I turn around, I'm thinking about him. I can't seem to focus on anything. It's Don this, and Don that. Just now, I was thinking about the rodeo in Laughlin, Nevada, and he pops into my head. That's when I raised up and hit the door. Dang, that hurts!" I rolled the cold can against the spot. "I don't know what's wrong with me lately."

"I have a sneaking suspicion my little girl is in love."

"Yeah, so? I thought love was supposed to make you happy...not miserable."

"Sometimes it does both." She kissed the swelling on my forehead and smiled. "I hope you can find something better to bang your head against than my refrigerator. You realize it will dent, don't you?"

Chapter 58

I decided to go back into the WPRCA circuit and quit fighting the men at every turn. It was taking too much of my time, and my bank account was extremely low, not to mention my spirits. I was able to hit Yuma, Laughlin, Lake Elsinore, Phoenix and Las Vegas, competing in the women's bareback division. The competition was tougher than I'd imagined, causing me to have added respect for women like Kelly Kaminski, Paula Seay and Liz Pinkston. Every one of the women were good cowhands who knew what they were doing, and I'd wager my last dollar they could hold their own against most men. They were not doing too bad in the money department, either. Kelly had raked in $179,000 in prize money over the year, and the others weren't too far behind.

As for me, I don't guess I had done too badly, after getting a late start. I held my own as far as riding, and took home a couple of buckles. But the deposits in my bank account only totaled a little over $20,000 for the entire season. Now, here I was, just a few days before Christmas, stuck inside the house because it was raining like Noah's flood, and feeling bluer than frozen lake water.

"Things haven't been going too well for you, have they?" I glanced up from my mug of coffee as Mama took a seat across from me at the kitchen table.

"Oh, not that bad. Just feeling kinda moody, I guess." I took a sip, and it burnt my tongue.

"Want to talk about it?"

"Nothing to really talk about. I was just thinking about the season, and how everyone did so much better than I did."

"You didn't do so bad, honey. You won several events and brought home some beautiful prizes," she said.

"Yeah, buckles and ribbons. But Marline made more money barrel racing." I paused to take another sip. "I don't know. I'm thinking about giving it all up, and working full time at the stables."

"That's your decision, honey. No one is trying to force you into quitting."

"Huh! Little do you know. Don would love for me to get out of rodeo," I said with a snigger.

"Why, has he been asking you to?"

"No, he hasn't said anything out loud, but I can tell." She raised her eyebrows and grinned as she sipped her coffee, so I continued.

"Well, you know when the old man's got something on his mind, don't you?'

"Yes, I am well aware when something is bothering your father. Go on."

"It's hard to explain, but things just haven't been the same between us when we're together. He treats me different. Kind of distant…almost like I am a stranger. I don't know if he even likes me anymore." Mama scooted away from the table and pulled a pack of English muffins from the cupboard.

"Have you asked him about it?" She paused with a muffin halfway in the toaster. "Oh, I'm sorry, would you like a toasted muffin with your coffee?"

"Yeah, thanks. That would be nice. And yes, I've asked, and he says there's nothing wrong. He just laughs and gives me a little kiss and says he still loves me and tells me not to worry about it."

"But you think there is."

"Well, yeah. I don't know how to explain it…but something's different."

"Then, perhaps it's you."

"Huh?"

"Would you like your muffin buttered," she asked as the toaster popped up.

"Yeah, thanks. What about me?"

"Well, for instance," she paused with the butter knife and grinned, "how have you been treating him?"

"I treat him nice enough. We aren't arguing or fighting, if that's what you're driving at. I've even been nice to Helen Fisher."

"I know you have, but that's not what I mean. Here's your muffin." She slid the plate in front of me and popped another one into the toaster. "What I mean is, do you treat him the same as you did before Helen Fisher returned and started vying for his attention?"

"She isn't just *vying* for his attention. The lying snake's trying to steal him. And yes, I treat him the same. At least I try to."

"Really?" Mama paused to butter her own muffin, then resumed her position at the table. I had to wait until she had taken a bite for her to continue.

"As I understand it, after that last big fight you two had, you said you wanted to start over, as if you two had just met. That's what you told me, anyway. Is that correct?"

I nodded.

"That means you are setting the ground rules for your relationship, and Donald feels he must follow those rules, or risk losing you. I've watched you closely these past few months while you're together, and you've been treating him more like a friend than a lover."

"Mother! What do you think we've been doing? He's a minister!"

"I didn't mean lover as in you're having sex with him. Although I guess that might be possible. He does have two children, and more than likely got them the old fashioned way. I meant lover as when two people really care about one another. They do show some amount of affection, and I don't believe you're doing that...not like you did before you thought he might be falling for Helen."

"Well, I guess it might be a little different. I wanted to go slow, and not get hurt again."

"What do you want out of him, Margie? Tell me that," she said, reaching across the table to grip my hand.

"I've thought about it, and I want him to adore me. I want him to love me more than Helen, or anyone else…including his dead wife."

"That's not going to happen, and I would never ask him to, if I were you."

"Why not?"

"Because it is impossible. I don't mean about Helen Fisher," she said with a grin as I got all huffy, "I meant about his wife, Linda. He might love you as much as Linda, but never more. His love for Linda will remain with him the rest of his life. It will change over the years, into something like a precious memory, but never completely go away. On the other hand, his love for you stands the chance of growing into something living and vital. But I'm afraid if you ask him to love you more than her," she paused to take a sip of coffee, "he will feel you are asking him to cast aside her memory, which is impossible, and it will kill your relationship."

"It's probably dead already. I don't know what he wants from me." I tossed my half-eaten muffin back on the plate.

"Men aren't much different from us when it comes to love." She grinned and munched a mouthful of muffin. "You said you wanted to be adored? Then, adore him, and see what happens."

"I do. I've spent a lot of money…"

"I'm not talking about money. And very frankly, I think your spending money on him and the children has made him rather uncomfortable. I'm talking about adoring him with your heart."

"But what if he doesn't love me in return? That'll kill me, Mama. You don't know how I felt when I saw them together in his car at McDonalds that day. And it almost killed me when he rejected me on the front porch like he did."

"No, I don't know how you felt. But your father and I

200

had only been married six months when they took him away and put a gun into his hands, and stuck him in the middle of that jungle. I died a little every day he was gone. I was afraid to answer the door, thinking it might be someone telling me my husband had been killed. I was afraid to check the mail, knowing it might be the last letter I would ever receive from him. I prayed and begged God every minute of every single day to bring him back safely. And, when he did, your father had changed. He wasn't the same man they had taken. The war had changed him. It's not like in the movies, where everything is make-believe. He discovered there were people who were actually trying to kill him. He watched many of his friends die, and had to live with the fact that he had killed other humans himself.

"You father was a religious man when he left. The Harvey I got in return didn't want anything to do with God. He was an angry, bitter, cold man. He drank and used drugs. Oh, he still loved his country, and would fight anyone who said anything against it. And as far as we were concerned, he said he loved me, but I believe he had actually forgotten how to love."

"Why didn't you just leave him, if he was that bad," I said, refilling both our cups.

"Because I loved him."

"It's a nice story, but I don't know what this has to do with me and Don."

"I'll tell you, if you will listen."

I nodded.

"I thought hard on how I wanted him to be, and how I wanted him to treat me. Then I began treating him that same way."

"That's all? You think it's that simple?"

"It is that simple. Oh, it took years to bring him around, and he's still not the old Harvey that went off to war, and probably never will be. But he's a whole lot better than the one I met at the bus station when he returned. And treating Donald the way you would like him to treat you will give you the same results."

"I don't know. What if it doesn't?"

201

"What if it doesn't give you the exact same results? It can't make you any more miserable than you are making yourself."

"You wanna bet?" I laughed.

"Look, you're afraid of being hurt again."

I nodded.

"Well, my dear, so is he. The difference is, he has two children that adore you...and that, I might add, is your fault. They also stand being hurt if your relationship with their father fails. And, as things stand, it just might.

"You set the rules to this silly game you're playing," she added after a long minute. "It is going to be up to you to end it. And if you haven't noticed, the vultures are starting to circle."

"Huh? What's that supposed to mean?"

"You're an intelligent girl. Figure it out for yourself."

I sat staring into my empty mug long after Mama had disappeared into her bedroom to wrap Christmas presents. I had no idea what she'd gone through with Dad going off to war. I'd known about his being in Vietnam, but not the rest. The old gal was a lot smarter than I'd thought. The trouble was, treating Donald Ray Gardner the way I wanted him to treat me might cost me more that I was willing to pay. But vultures circling? She was right, that wasn't too hard of a puzzle to solve. But what if the vultures turned out to be my own friends? I suddenly had a vision of Marline Dickerson floating in the air, circling above Don's head. She was joined by several others, floating in a lazy circle, grinning and drooling. Geez, this was gonna take some *cogitating* on my part, as Chuck would say.

Chapter 59

"Well, what do you think? Does the word *duh* mean anything to you," Angela said. I glanced at Gloria and Marline as they laughed. The four of us had crowded inside a McDonalds booth for hot chocolate, when I mentioned Mama's vultures.

"Honey," Gloria said in a thick Spanish accent as she gripped my hand, "when I came here five years ago from Mexico, my grandfather, he told me, 'Gloria, baby, America is the land of opportunity. You can become anything you wish, and I find that that is so. Sooner or later, these others will discover the same. You give them the opportunity, and they will steal your man."

"But not you guys. You're supposed to be my friends. She wasn't talking about you guys, was she?" Everyone of them allowed their gazes to drift everywhere except my direction.

"Come on, guys, he's my boyfriend!"

"So, what do you think? That we are blind? He's a beautiful man, and you're not happy together," Gloria said with a laugh.

"But, he's a Baptist, and you're Catholic."

"So? For such a man, I would become protestant."

"God, I can't believe you guys."

"Don't look at me," Angela said. "Sure, I've noticed him, and I'll gladly take him off your hands, if that's what you want. But, I plan to keep circling until you three kill each other, then take over."

"You too," I asked Marline.

"Hey, I warned you a long time ago, I had a crush on him. Remember?"

"What about Barry?"

"What about him?"

"I thought you two were an item."

"They were, until she caught him kissing Debbie Risner in the K Mart parking lot," Angela said.

"That slug! He promised he wasn't gonna hurt you. I'll kill him!"

"Marline already did. She decked him in front of God and everyone," Gloria said with a snigger.

"Really? How come I'm just hearing about it?" I stared at Marline who shrugged.

"It just happened a couple of hours ago, and I didn't actually *deck* him. I...sort of slapped him silly."

"Okay, good! But Don's still my boyfriend and you guys are supposed to be my friends."

"Honey," Gloria squeezed my arm, "we *are* your friends, and we never touched him. But the others? Hey, they could care less. They'll cut your throat to get at your man."

"They've already started," Marline said.

"What do you mean by that?"

"Oh, that someone, and we all know who, started a rumor about you and Barry Swaim going at it pretty hot and heavy when you were together."

"That's not true!"

"I never said it was, and it wouldn't make any difference in our friendship either way. And Barry, bless his evil two-timing heart, has been denying every word. But some of the others around that church are aware of his reputation, and take the rumor as gospel. It won't be long before it reaches Pastor Don's ears, if it hasn't already." She toasted me with her chocolate.

"What can I do?"

"Follow your mother's advice. What have you got to lose," Angela said with a grin.

Chapter 60

"You slug! You double-barreled creep!" I screamed and swung my lariat as he retreated against the tack-room wall.

"Ow! Geeze, Marge! Watch it with that thing. That hurts!" Barry rubbed his arm where the end of the rope had caught him.

"Not as much as you hurt Marline. You promised!" I drew the rope back for another attack.

"It's not like you think. Believe me!" He cowered toward Cupcake's stall.

"Whadda ya mean, *not like I think*? When they catch you kissing someone in the K Mart parking lot, what is everyone supposed to think? You creep!" The rope whistled and cracked against the wall as he ducked away. I quickly snapped it back in an arch and caught him across the leg before he had a chance to recover.

"Oh, God! Cut that out!" He leaped over the gate and landed in the straw near Cupcake's feet, causing her to whinny and dance away. "Dammit, that hurts," he said, rubbing his leg.

"Good. And if you think hiding behind Cupcake is going to protect you, you'd better think again. I'll have her stomp you to death if you don't give me the right answers. Now, explain yourself, and it'd better be good, because you promised not to hurt her."

"Okay, yeah…maybe I was kissing Debbie, but it wasn't like everyone thought."

"Really," I said, coiling the rope for another attack.

"Then what was everyone supposed to think? It's not like you were kissing your sister or mother...at least I hope you don't kiss 'em that way."

"No, but me and Debbie used to be pretty tight. Remember?"

"Yeah, I remember, Barry. She was the one you threw me over for. Right?"

"Yeah, well. Anyway, I ran into her in the parking lot and showed her the ring I got for Marline, and..."

"What ring? No one mentioned any ring."

"Well, they didn't know. No one did."

"You expect me to believe you bought Marline a ring and didn't tell her about it?"

"I was going to take her to The River's Edge at Knights Ferry for dinner and give it to her, but she broke our date."

"No kidding? Well, I guess that was pretty rotten of her, wasn't it? She should've just turned the other way when she saw you kissing another girl, huh? Is that what you think?" I shook my head and laughed.

"No...no," he looked down as he dug inside his pocket, "that was pretty stupid. But when I told Debbie I was planning to ask Marline if she'd marry me, she got all excited and gave me a kiss. Well, I sort of got carried away and kissed her back. That was when Marline and Gloria showed up."

"You were gonna propose? You were kissing Debbie Risner and planning on proposing to my best friend? Barry, you are about as dumb as one of those piles inside Cupcake's stall."

"I know. Wanna see the ring?" He held out the tiny box.

"Yeah, this I've gotta see." He snapped the top back to reveal the white gold solitaire.

"Well, that's very pretty, Barry. At least you've got good taste. Did you buy it in K Mart?"

"This? Na, I was in there getting socks. I got this at a store in Modesto."

"So, what are you planning to do now? Take it back?"

"No, I was hoping you'd help me out. You know," he shrugged, "maybe talk to her. Kinda smooth things out a little?

That's why I came here to see you."

"Na," I said shaking my head, "you got yourself into this one, Barry. You can get yourself out. Then, maybe you'll learn when you're supposed to be with one particular girl, to keep your grubby hands and lips off everyone else. Besides, my own love life is so screwed-up, you certainly don't need my help."

Chapter 61

"I don't know what to tell you, Don. It isn't true." I stared at the paper cup as I worked my straw in the ice. It was about a week following the rodeo, and the rumors about me and Barry Swaim had grown to iceberg proportions. We had stopped at McDonalds for cokes, when he finally decided to bring it up.

"Maybe you should ask Barry himself," I said with a weak smile.

"I did," he said moving his own straw in the ice.

"What'd he say?"

"Pretty much the same as you. He said you guys spent more time fighting than you did kissing."

"That's true."

"Why'd you date him, if you two didn't like each other?"

"Oh, we liked each other's company," I said with a snigger. "At least I liked hanging around with him. He's funny and likes to do crazy things. But I couldn't trust him around another girl ten seconds. That's why I was so scared he was going to hurt Marline...and he did," I added with a nod.

"Yeah, that's what he said about you."

"That he couldn't trust me?" I snapped upward.

"No, he admitted he couldn't be trusted, if you'd like to know," Don said with a chuckle. "He said he liked your company, because you were fun and enjoyed doing crazy things, like dying your hair pink. But he also said he enjoyed arguing and fighting with you."

"Yeah, he must've, 'cause that's about all we did."

"He said your relationship was more like brother and sister, than boyfriend and girlfriend." Don stared at me as I thought.

"Yeah, now that you mention it. I never thought of it like that before, but I guess Barry is like the brother I never had. Kind of hurts to think of it that way."

"Hurts? Why? Do you still love him?" Don creased his forehead.

"No, nothing like that. But we dated a long time and I took it for granted that he might've thought a little more…I don't know. How would you feel if you suddenly discovered Linda loved you like a brother instead of a husband?"

"Pretty weird," he laughed, "I mean, we did have children together."

"Well, you get the general idea," I said and returned to torturing the ice with my straw.

"So, what are we going to do about the rumors?"

"Nothing, right now. I've already talked to a couple of members of the board, and they agree that it would only make things worse if we try fighting the rumors right now. Besides, Barry has taken it on himself to tell the truth where and whenever he has the chance. Other than trying to find out who it was, and why the rumors started, I don't know what else anyone can do."

Huh, you don't need Magnum PI to solve that case. I took a long sip through the straw and grinned.

Chapter 62

"Dad, can I ask you for some advice?"

The old man stared from the top of the stepladder with a string of Christmas lights in his hand.

"Well," he said after a pregnant minute, "this is a first. What is it you want to know?"

"Things haven't been going too well between Don and me, and…"

"I thought you two were getting along pretty good. At least that's what you let on in front of everyone. What seems to be the problem?" He allowed the string of half-hung lights to dangle as he climbed off the ladder and sat on the porch. "Here," he patted a spot next to him, "have a seat."

"Thanks."

"Okay, tell me about it."

"I don't really know how. There's just something different. Like he's kind of distant when we're together. I talked to Mama, and she says I need to commit myself to him."

"And you don't think you need to?"

"Yeah, but I'm kind of scared. What if he doesn't commit back? Know what I mean?"

"Yes, I think I do," Dad said with a slow nod. "But love's like that, Margie. There are no real guarantees. I wish there were, then there wouldn't be so many divorces. Love's a gamble at best, and you can't hold back, expecting the other person to commit without any assurance of getting something in return, because it won't happen."

"I was afraid you'd tell me that," I said, burying my face in my hands.

"Why? Did you expect me to give you some magical formula, and tell you how to make Pastor Gardner love you first? If I could do that, I'd write a book and appear on Oprah and make a zillion bucks. But you can't expect a guy who's been married and has a couple of small children to commit to a relationship he's not really sure about. He needs some sort of guarantee that you're willing to do the same. It doesn't work that way."

"I do love him, Dad. That's the trouble. I don't know why he doesn't seem to know it."

"I think he does. He just doesn't know how much. What makes you think different?"

"Well, he acts like he's scared or uncomfortable around me. I don't know. It's kind of like…" I tried grabbing the words with my hands, but couldn't find the right ones.

"Okay, let's see if I can help," Dad said, patting my leg. "What is really important to him?"

"Don?"

"Yes, that's who we're discussing, isn't it?"

"Well, his church. God, most certainly. People…he likes people. That car of his. He washes and waxes it all the time."

"Yeah, those are general things. But, you've been so busy trying to win him, and worrying about Helen Fisher, you've missed a couple of key items about the man. And, until you discover what they are, and focus on them, I don't think you'll ever reach him the way you want." He climbed back onto the ladder and began hanging the lights.

"Hey, wait a minute. What are the points I've missed," I yelled.

"Na-uh," he shook his head, "that's not my department. If you want to be his wife, that's something you'll have to figure out on your own. I can't be running over to your house every day, trying to patch up your relationship between you and your husband."

"Well, how do I go about finding out?"

"You're supposed to be a smart girl. Focus on the man and figure it out. Look," he paused to stare down at me, "right now, all you're seeing is the relationship. Try looking at the man for once, and discover what he's really like. I don't think you really know."

He turned back to the lights and added, "Let's just hope Helen Fisher doesn't figure it out before you do."

Chapter 63

"Ow, you got me," Don said, and rolled on our living room floor as two giggling children pounced on top. Caroline squealed as he tickled her ribs, then he grabbed Donnie and blew a raspberry against his neck.

My God! It's so simple. How could I have ever missed it? I allowed my gaze to drift from the spectacle on the floor to Dad and back again. It was the very evening of our discussion on the porch, and I could feel the old man studying me from across the room. He nodded and gave me a toast with his coffee cup as my gaze turned toward him.

And why wouldn't his children have been the key? I had taken it for granted that he loved and cared for them, the same as most parents. But they happened to be the most precious gift Linda had given, and were his only connection to her. It made total sense. I crossed the room and kissed Dad on the cheek.

"Thank you."

"You're most welcome." He smiled and returned the favor.

Chapter 64

Don's mother and stepfather had decided to spend Christmas in Oakdale. Peggy had become a permanent fixture at Don's house, allowing him more time for his ministry. I liked her being there, because outside of our becoming friends and allies, her watching after the kids meant I got to spend more time alone with Don. Mama invited the whole family to spend Christmas day at our house, and fixed a huge turkey with all the trimmings. The only downer was that Mama had taken it upon herself to invite Helen Fisher.

"She'll be spending Christmas by herself, Margie. You ought to be a little more understanding," she scolded, when I got in her face.

"Oh, I understand, alright. There is no earthly reason she couldn't have spent Christmas in Bakersfield with her own family, if she really wanted to. That snake just wants to worm her way into our Christmas to be with Don."

"Perhaps, but do you really think Jesus would want you to turn her away on His birthday?"

I didn't know what Jesus would want me to do with Helen Fisher, but I doubted it involved allowing her to spend Christmas with my boyfriend. Besides, I wasn't feeling any too hospitable toward her, but decided to make a show out of being nice for Mama's sake. I also decided, if Helen could ruin my holiday, I would return the favor.

"Okay, I'll admit it, I am a snake," I said as Peggy snickered. "But she's asking for it."

"You don't have to apologize to me. I think it's a great idea. What do you want me to do?"

"Just keep an eye open, and let me know what she's getting them for Christmas. I'll do the rest."

Chapter 65

We had gathered in the living room before dinner to hand out presents and take pictures, which happened to be one of Dad's little holiday rituals. I waited until Helen had given her presents before making my move.

"Oh, wow! Look, Durangos, just like Margie's!" Don said as Carol ripped open the present I'd given her. I could see Helen's expression drop from the corner of my eye as the electronic game she had given got cast aside as Carol tried on her new boots.

"Not exactly alike," I giggled, "but I knew she had outgrown the others I'd given her to go with her birthday hat."

"And a new hat," Joanne said, passing the hat to her husband to examine.

"A real Stetson," Phil Carlton said. "You have good taste, Margie."

"Thanks, I think so. That's why I picked Don." Peggy laughed as her brother turned red.

"A rocking horse," Don said, as his son ripped away the wrapping paper. "Margie, you spent a lot of money on my children. You shouldn't have."

"Why not? They're mine also." I paused to let the thought sink in as everyone glanced at each other, then stared at the thunder-struck pastor. The expression on Helen's face was worth a million. You could've driven a team of horses into that trap of hers the way her jaw dropped open.

"Here's your present." I shoved the tiny package toward

Don. "Open it."

Peggy leaned over his shoulder as Don took his time removing the ribbon and bow.

"Oh my God!" she said before uttering a profane word and covering her mouth. "Sorry," she laughed, "it's just...oh my gosh."

"What is it, Don? Please show us," Joanne said, as he continued to stare into the box.

"An application for a marriage license, with Margie's information and signature already filled in. The other half is blank." He held the paper high.

Joanne spilled her coffee, and Phil ran to the kitchen for paper towels as Mama burst out crying. The old man gave me a *you've finally gone nuts* look and shook his head.

"Well?" I said as Don continued staring at the paper.

"I...I...didn't expect anything like this. I..."

"I wanted to give you something real special, because I think you deserve it," I said, slipping into his lap. "I love you so much, the best present I could think of was me. I'm giving you me, if you'll have me."

"I can't believe this! What kind of a joke is this? You can't... Don!! Tell her no!" Helen shouted.

"Oh, hush," Joanne snapped. "She's not asking you to get married. She's proposing to my son."

"But...!"

"I said hush! I want to hear what my son has to say."

"I don't know what to say. This is...really a surprise. I..."

"You don't have to answer right now," I said, kissing him on the lips. "Think about it, and let me know. I just want you to know I'm yours, no matter what."

"Yes," Peggy squealed as he threw his arms around me. I don't recall him ever saying "yes, I'll marry you." But the fact he kissed me a dozen times was plenty good enough that minute.

217

Chapter 66

"I've been meaning to ask you about that. What in heaven's name is *mutton busting*?" Don hovered over me as I wrapped Caroline's hair into a ponytail.

"It's not *mutton busting*, its *mutton bustin'*," I said, slipping the hair scrunchy into place. "You've got to say it right. Get a little cowboy in your veins, Pastor. *Mutton bustin'*."

"Okay, *mutton bustin'*. Now, what is it?"

"Just hang on, you'll see." I strapped the protective helmet on Carol's head.

"Wait, this isn't going to be dangerous, is it?" He grabbed my arm.

"No more dangerous than riding a bike and she does that all the time. Look," I added, after he continued gripping my arm, "do you think I'd actually do something that's going to hurt this baby? Trust me a little, Donald."

"Well, you've got to admit that sounds strange, coming from someone who loves being thrown from horses," he said with a laugh. "You're serious about riding another exhibition during the rodeo?"

"Yes, but there's no way I'd let either one of those kids get hurt, if I could help it. But, to answer your first question, mutton bustin' is an idea we picked up from the Rodeo Of The Ozarks. The Saddle Club's going to try it here in Oakdale this year, to see how it goes over. I've watched them do it, and it's a real kick-in-the-head. Not literally speaking," I added with a grin. "There'll be around twelve children, between four and six years old competing once a day, and since they can't weigh more than fifty-five pounds, Carol's perfect."

"Okay, what is it you want my daughter to do?"

"She's going to be my daughter also, just as soon as you get over being scared and say you'll marry me," I said, giving him a quick kiss.

"Maybe in June."

"June?" My heart leaped and I jerked around to stare at him.

"Yes, June. I'm not promising we *will* get married, there are still some things I believe we need to work out before we discuss a date. But, if we do, I think in June. That should give you enough time to heal, after getting dragged around the arena by whatever it is you're going to ride next week. Now, what about my daughter?"

"It's nothing dangerous, and she won't get hurt."

"Then why the helmet?"

"Quit being so skeptical, Don. Nothing is going to happen. They are going to be riding sheep."

"Sheep?"

"Yes, sheep. Look, all she has to do is hold on for six seconds. She doesn't even have to guide the danged thing. I don't think she could, if she tried. But, they'll judge her on her time and on riding skills. She's got to sit up straight, with no choke hold on the sheep. That's why I want her to be ready. She's going to be the best mutton buster ever, aren't you Carol?" She grinned real big and grabbed hold of my hand.

"Come on let's go show your Daddy how well you can ride."

Chapter 67

The mutton bustin' was a roaring success, with laughing, cheering parents, squealing children, and sheep running wild inside the arena. And Caroline, bless her heart, walked away with the blue ribbon, but not before giving a perfect princess-bow, and waving toward the crowd.

"You didn't have anything to do with that little girl acting so danged cute now, did you?" Terry Walker asked, as they herded the last sheep from the arena.

"Carol? Now, whatever gave you that idea?"

"Just a hunch." He grinned and propped one boot against the railing. "Heard you and her Daddy's fixing to get hitched. Any truth to that rumor?"

"Maybe, he's not asked me for sure yet. But yeah, I think so. Sometime in June." I grinned.

"Well now, I reckon congratulations are in order. But ain't you the slightest bit sorry for all the broken hearts you're gonna be leaving when you tie the knot?"

"I didn't know there would be any," I said with a laugh.

"Ya didn't?"

I shook my head.

"Only half the bronc bustin', dust eating punchers in the circuit. Most of them's gonna be crying in their beers come June. You mark my words, girl."

"That's certainly news to me. None of them has ever said a word to me, one way or the other. But it wouldn't have changed much. I'm still going to marry Don."

We stood in silence, watching a trick roping exhibition.

"I hear you drew Irish today," I said.

"Yeah. He's a good hoss."

"Yeah, I was hoping for a chance to ride him again."

"I heard they were fixing to let you ride another exhibition."

"Yeah," I said with a nod, "that's why I was hoping for Irish."

"Ain't he the same one what drug you around and stomped on you last year?"

"Yeah, one and the same. I still want him."

"Who'd they say you could ride?"

"Dakota Storm."

"Well now, that's a real hoss. He'll be plenty for you to handle out there," he said with a nod.

"Yes, I know he's a real horse...one of the best, and everyone wants to ride him. But, I want Irish. I've gotta ride that horse, Terry."

"Yeah, reckon so," he said and turned back toward the arena. "You scared?"

"Of Irish?"

He nodded.

"Maybe a little. I respect him a whole lot more than I did before getting thrown, that's for sure."

"That's good. It'll make you a better rider. All of us, who have been rodeoing for any length of time, respect the animals we're about to fork. You'd be a danged fool not to. Can't be scared, though. But ya gotta give them the proper respect, because a bull or horse is bound to do what they do best."

He stood chewing on a matchstick a minute before turning with a Texas-sized grin.

"What about that other hoss? You scared of him?"

"What other horse?"

"The marriage-hoss. The one that's about to fix you up to that feller over there." He motioned toward the stands with his head. I climbed halfway up on the gate to spy Don seating the children next to my parents in the front row.

"Yeah, a little," I said with a laugh.

"Aren't we all?"

"I thought you were married."

"I am. Most of ten years. See that filly sitting to the right of your parents…the one with three younguns? That's my Liz, and them younguns are mine."

"You happy?"

"Hope to shout! Wouldn't trade that woman for all the oil in Texas. Can't stand being without her. That's why I bring her most everywhere I go. She teaches the kids their lessons in the trailer, so they don't miss any schooling."

"I thought you said being married was a scary idea."

"No, I said I was scared when I was first fixin' to get hitched. There's a difference, you know."

I nodded, as he continued.

"But being married's no different that riding a bronc. Ya just gotta respect the person you're gonna be riding with, but you can't be afraid of them. And, you're gonna get bucked off every once-in-awhile, cause anyone who's really in love has a spat every now and then. But, the thing is, ya get up and dust yourself off, and jump right back on, because it's a heck of a lot better in the long run, than turning tail and quitting.

"I'll tell you what little girl, I look at each and every day with that woman the same as when I climb into the chute. I might get me a few bumps and bruises, but it's one heck of a ride, and a whole lot of fun."

"You've never thought of leaving, or looked at another woman then," I asked as they started announcing the first barrel racer.

"Look? Yeah, I reckon every man that's alive takes a look every now and then, same as a woman sneaks a peak once in awhile. And don't try telling me they don't. Just watching that Sam Elliott feller in a movie gets my Liz in a real romantic mood. We happen to watch a lot of westerns," he added with a wink.

"But no, I ain't never had the urge to tangle with any other filly, like some of these numb-skulls. A couple of them, and I ain't saying who, rolled in the hay with some of them gals down in Reno last year, and took a good case of VD home to their wives. I'll tell you what, they had some tall explaining to do. They're just lucky they didn't get themselves a bellyful of buckshot.

"And take old Bucky over there," he motioned toward a tall cowboy checking his grip. He's had him a young filly in every town, while his wife was sitting home tending their kids. Well, she'd planned on surprising him on his birthday a year ago last March, and shows up at his motel room with an armload of presents and a bottle of champagne. He was sure surprised alright, 'cause she caught him in bed with a local filly. Me and Liz was trying to catch some sleep in the room next door, and I'll tell you what, a wagon-load of badgers couldn't of caused more of a ruckus. Now, he's going round crying 'cause that woman of his has found herself a new man and filed for a divorce. Well, I ain't feeling the least bit sorry for him. No one was twisting his arm and forcing him to lay with that filly. Liz is the best thing that's ever happened to this old bronc buster, and I'll never do anything to hurt her."

"Wow!" I said, shaking my head. "I only hope when my time comes, it turns out half as good as yours, Terry."

"It will. Just fork that marriage-hoss the same way you're gonna fork that hoss this afternoon. Give it respect, keep your eyes glued where they should be, never consider bailing, and have yourself a heck of a lot of fun."

"Thanks."

"You're welcome."

We turned toward the arena as Gloria Rodriguez raced her quarter horse around the cloverleaf. We clapped and whistled, then Terry turned toward me with another Texas grin.

"Say, I almost forgot. Were you serious about wanting to try Irish again?"

"I've gotta ride him, Terry, or I'll never know."

"I reckon. Well, I've kinda had me a hankering to fork Dakota Storm for more than a year now. You wait here, and I'll go see what I can do."

223

I watched as he made his way to the judge's box and began an animated conversation. It wasn't but a minute, before all the judges were looking my way, and I began to wonder what I'd gotten myself into. The way Irish had bolted from the chute, and my being pinned beneath his weight, quickly flashed into my mind. Beads of sweat popped onto my forehead as the massive hooves once again swept past my face.

Stop it, Margie! Knock it off! It's exactly what you asked for, so there shouldn't be any problem. Besides, it's only eight little seconds. You can stand on your head for eight seconds, can't you? And it's nothing you haven't done a hundred times before. Climb on, focus, and ride him for eight measly seconds. You can do it.

I took a deep breath and glanced toward the man sitting beside my mother with two small children. *You can ride that horse also, just like Terry said. You've just got to focus and enjoy the ride.* The trouble was, I didn't know which horse frightened me the most.

Chapter 68

Terry Walker rode Dakota Storm like the pro he really was, collecting a score of ninety-two. Barry Swaim gave his best ride yet, proving he was on his way to becoming a great rider, although his score was somewhat lower than Terry's. We were approximately halfway through the event when they announced my name. I climbed up on the railing and stared at the black monster inside the chute.

"Come on, let's get it done, girl," Chuck said, swatting my boot.

"Yeah, make believe ya got glue stuck on yer britches," Terry yelled. There were several other shouts of encouragement as I nodded and eased my way into the saddle. Irish was already hyped by the excitement, snorting, kicking and banging against the railing, making me scamper back up the railing to keep from having my legs crushed between his massive sides and the metal pen.

"The ruckus taking place inside the Haidlen Ford chute is gonna be a real treat for you, folks," Chad Nicholson's voice boomed over the loudspeaker. "A pretty young lady you're all familiar with, Margie Green, is fixing to ride one of the biggest, meanest and orneriest critters you've ever laid eyes on. I see, by looking at the schedule, that she had originally been set to ride Dakota Storm, but she batted those big blue eyes of hers, and somehow talked everyone into letting her switch animals."

I eased back into the saddle and wrapped the braided rope tightly around my gloved hand.

"Normally, you'd think a pretty young girl like Margie would want to ride a nice gentle horse. But she insisted on riding a horse provided by the C&M Stables teaming with the Flying U Rodeo Company. This critter is called Irish, and he happens to be the same horse that drug her around this arena a year ago and put her in the hospital."

Geez! I could have gone all day without being reminded, Chad. I took a couple of deep breaths and exhaled slowly. *Okay, you can do this, girl. Let's get it done!* I jammed my Stetson down tight with my free hand and gave Chuck a nod. The gate swung open with the sound of the buzzer and Irish bolted forward with a snort, kicking his rear hooves high in the air, giving me the same feeling you get when you're at the top of a roller coaster. He spun left, kicking, and a vision of him falling and crushing my leg quickly flashed inside my head. *Stay focused. Head and neck...watch his head and neck.* He spun back to the right and all four hooves left the ground as he arched his back. The jolt caused my teeth to clack as he came down stiff-legged.

He leaped a couple of times toward the center of the arena and kicked as though he were trying to knock the noonday sun out of the sky. I allowed my spine to relax and rolled my body with the movement, as I spurred from neck to the cantle. A long strand of hair blew across my face as the Stetson shot from my head.

Let it go, Margie. Mike will get it. Watch the head and neck. Head and neck.

His snorting turned into scream-like whistles as he kicked higher, turning in a wide circle to the left, then back to the right. I suddenly became aware of the crowd as they burst into cheers at the sound of the buzzer. I had somehow stayed my eight seconds with the heaving animal.

Pick-up man Levi Rosser was having trouble getting close enough to help, so I let go of the braided rope and pulled free from the stirrups. Using the momentum of his bucking to propel me away from the flying hooves, I pushed away from the saddle and came close to hitting Mike Hayhurst, the clown, as I landed on my rear in the dust.

"How about that ride, folks!" Chad's voice crackled on the loudspeaker. I could see Don standing near the stock gate with the kids and ran to leap on the railing. Don grabbed me in a bear hug, and squeezed so hard the top rail dug into my stomach.

"You did it! I…" I cut him off by giving him a big ol' smack on the lips as the crowd hooted and whistled.

"Marg…" he said, glancing around, so I kissed him again.

"I love you!" I shouted as the hooting turned into laughter. I glanced toward the arena, and Mike Hayhurst was acting like a broken-hearted lover, faking a good cry and pointing toward us with my hat.

"Oh, you…come here," I said, dropping to the ground. I gave him a kiss on the cheek, and he acted shy, kicking dust with the toe of his boot. I grabbed my hat and climbed back up to kiss Don once more.

"Let me have Carol."

"What," Don said above the crowd.

"Caroline. Pass her over the rail to me."

"Is it alright?"

"Sure, it is." Actually, I had no idea if it was or not. But I waited with open arms until he had passed her over the railing. We ran hand in hand a little ways into the arena waving toward the crowd.

"How about that, folks," Chad boomed over the loudspeaker. "Give them a round of applause. Miss Marjorie Green and Caroline Gardner, this year's champion mutton buster. You're a lucky man, Reverend."

Chapter 69

"Oh, my God!" Mama covered her mouth and ran from the room crying. Dad let loose with the first string of cusswords I'd heard him utter since he'd started back to church. Then, he turned on me like a pit bull.

"That's disgusting! My own daughter posing...!" He motioned toward the pictures scattered on the coffee table. "I..." he took a deep breath, "you'd better leave Marline."

I was hoping she wouldn't, because the old man was about as close to hitting me as I'd ever seen. Marline had called early Monday evening, saying we had a problem, and she had to see me right away. What I hadn't expected was to see six photographs of me in the nude, doing things with Barry Swaim that I'd never dreamed of doing.

"Dad! That's not me! I never did anything like that!"

"That's your face isn't it?" He grabbed one of the pictures and shook it in my face.

"Yeah, but..."

"Then how'd it get in these pictures if that isn't you?"

"I don't know. I..."

He stomped into the kitchen and started punching numbers into the phone.

"Where'd you get these?" I could barely see Marline and had to wipe my eyes against my sleeve.

"I printed them off the internet. There's a website devoted to you and Barry."

"What? Why...how'd you...?" I felt like I was in a

tunnel.

"Find out about the website?"

I nodded.

"I got an e-mail with a link to a website, saying they had the latest pictures of *Rodeo Queen Marjorie Green and Barry Swaim.* So, I naturally wanted to see what they had, and found these. They're promising to post more in the next few days."

"Harold!" Dad's voice boomed inside the kitchen. "Get that son of yours and get over here right now. I've got something I want you to see. Yeah," he added after a long pause. "You know about 'em then. Uh-huh. I see. Yeah, I'm afraid everyone knows about it. Marline was the one to tell us. She's here now, and brought a bunch of 'em to show us. Yeah, Edith's pretty upset about it. How's Betty taking it? Yeah, I can imagine. Okay…see you then." He hung the receiver and came to tower over me, glaring at the photos on the table.

"Is Mr. Swaim coming," Marline asked.

"Yeah," Dad nodded, "he's bringing Barry with him. I want him to explain this, before everyone in town hears about it."

"I'm afraid they already have," Marline said.

"Huh?" Dad jerked around to stare at her.

"Well, as I was telling Marge, I got this e-mail with an internet link to a website, saying they had the latest rodeo pictures of Margie and Barry. I went there and found these. I'm afraid to say this…" she cringed, "but it was a mass-e-mail, sent to most everyone in the church…maybe Oakdale."

"Oh, God!" I melted into a puddle on the floor as Dad uttered another string of cusswords.

Chapter 70

"I tell you that's not me!" Barry yelled as he stomped around the room. He was about as animated as I'd ever seen him. Mama and Mrs. Swaim were crouched close to each other on the sofa sharing a box of tissues.

"Do you actually think I'm that stupid," he shouted in his father's face.

"Yeah, I've seen you do some pretty stupid things!" Harold yelled back.

"Well, what about Margie?" Barry pointed toward where I sat cross-legged on the floor. "Do you think she's stupid enough to have these taken?" He grabbed a handful of pictures and waved them in the air.

"She can be pretty stupid at times," Dad said with a nod. "If it ain't you two in those pictures, then who in the hell is it? That's what I want to know!" We were interrupted by a knock on the door.

Dad jerked the door open. "Well, I guess I shouldn't be surprised to see you, Reverend. Come in and join the circus." He made a sweeping motion with his arm, and Don and Peggy entered. Peggy's eyes were red from crying.

"Don…" I started, but he held up a hand and shook his head, cutting me off.

"Not now, Margie. I need time to sort all this out. What I want to hear from the both of you is the truth. You first," he turned toward Barry, "is that you in those photographs?"

"No. I know it looks like me and Margie, but it isn't."

"Margie?"

I shook my head.

"Okay," Don heaved a sigh, "then, maybe someone would like to explain them." He tossed another stack of the same pictures on the table.

"I can't," I said with a shrug and studied the carpet beneath my folded knees.

"Barry?"

"How am I supposed to know how those got posted on the internet? Look," he shouted, "that isn't me or Margie in those pictures! And even if we did those things while we were dating, there's no way we would have had someone taking pictures. And, what's more, there's no way either one of us would have given them to anybody to post on the world-wide-web!"

There was a long pause, and I looked up to see Don and Barry studying each other.

"You can believe what you want, Pastor, but that's the truth," Barry added after a minute. "That isn't us. I'd remember something like that. I can't explain the pictures. I don't know where they came from, and I don't know how our faces got in them."

"Okay," Don said after a long pause. "I don't know what to believe right now, but I'd like to believe you and Margie. I…just don't know." He shrugged and turned toward the door.

"What about Caroline's birthday party on Saturday," Mama asked.

"We'll still have it," he said calmly opening the door. "She's been looking forward to turning five, and it wouldn't be fair for us to cancel her party." He eyed each of us and smiled weakly. "I'd still like everyone to come…including the two in those pictures."

He closed the door and I ran into the bathroom and threw up.

Chapter 71

"I'm sorry, I can't," I said shaking my head.

"And why not? You'll have to come back to work sooner or later." Mable towered over me from where I sat eating Cheetos on the sofa.

"Not really." I popped another one into my mouth and crunched down.

"She's been like this since those pictures appeared on the internet," Mama said, handing Mable a cup of hot coffee. "Sit down, Mable." She motioned toward an empty seat. "Maybe you can talk some sense into her."

"Well, I can't blame her for feeling the way she does. I can only imagine how embarrassing something like that must be." Mable took a sip of coffee and eyed me over the cup.

"No you can't," I said, and clicked the TV off. "No one can, unless they've had it happen to them."

"But sitting here inside the house with the drapes drawn isn't the answer, Honey," Mama said.

"Tell me what is, then." I glared and crunched down on another Cheeto. "I can't go anywhere without people gawking. I tried going to Save Mart to pick up some milk and things. People stared at me like I was...was some sort of I don't know what. Women were whispering behind my back when I passed them in the aisle, and you should've heard them talking while I stood in line.

"Then, I didn't even make it to the truck before some guys in a four-wheeler whistled and asked if they could be in my next movie. Everyone in Oakdale thinks I'm some damned porn star!"

"Well, you are…at least in their minds." Mable studied me over her mug.

"You can go to…"

"No, just listen." She set her cup on the coffee table and leaned forward. "As far as they know, that *was* you in those pictures. And until you can prove them wrong, they are going to continue believing it. The thing for you to do is, go about your life as though nothing's happened."

"Easy for you to say." I rolled the top shut on the bag of Cheetos and tossed it on the table.

"Yeah, I know it's hard, but what other choice do you have?"

"I can move."

"Where to? They've got the internet in Iraq." Mable gave me a grin. "Come back to work. Irish or Comanche don't care if that's really you in those pictures or not."

"They're about the only ones. Don even thinks it's me."

"I don't think he really does, Honey," Mama said. "I think he's hurt, and doesn't know what to think."

"That's the same as believing it's me, Mama. If he doesn't know me by now, and believes I'm capable of making those kind of pictures, then it's over. I might as well join the Army and go to Iraq. They probably won't care as long as I can shoot."

"Well, just let me know what you decide," Mable said, rising from her chair. "Say," she said, patting her stomach and eyeing her slim frame, "I wonder if anyone would be interested in seeing me and Chuck posing for photos. Maybe I can make enough to pay off the ranch and retire."

Chapter 72

"What in the world," Mama said, staring out the window. The slamming of several car doors caused her to stop folding the stack of laundry and pull back the drapes.

"What is it," Dad growled from his paper.

"It seems half the church has come to visit," she said, as someone began pounding on the door.

"Tell them I'm not here," I said, bolting from the sofa.

"I'm not lying for you," Dad yelled, as Mama opened the door.

"Margie!" Gary Dickerson pushed his way past Mama to catch me closing my bedroom door.

"Not now, Gary. I don't want to see anybody."

"But ya gotta. Come look what I found." He drug me into the living room and began spreading more copies of the nude photos across the coffee table.

"No thanks, Gary. I've already seen enough of those." I glanced up as Marline and her parents, along with the Swaims and several members of the church board filed through the door. The last to enter was Don, followed by Peggy and the kids. Peggy grinned and ushered the children into the kitchen, where they began helping themselves to Mama's stash of goodies in the cupboard.

"Come here," Gary repeated.

"Na-uh," I said, shaking my head. "I already told you, I don't wanna see no part of those ever again."

"You don't have to," Harold said. "We just want to see

your back."

"Huh?"

"Turn around and pull up your shirt," Marline said.

"What the…No, I'm not lifting my shirt in front of a bunch of people. What do you take me for?" I started toward the bedroom, but Gary spun me around jerked my shirttail from my jeans.

"You…!" I balled my fist to take a swing, but he caught my wrist and jerked my shirt higher.

"See? Just like Marline and I said. Margie doesn't have any tattoos."

"What," I said staring at him over my shoulder.

"We wanted to see if you had any tattoos anywhere on your back," Harold said. "Turn around and give us a look."

"You could've just asked. And no, I don't have any tattoos," I snapped. "Anybody who's seen me in a bathing suit knows that." I jerked my shirt tail up around my waist.

"The one in the photo was lower," Duane Gilman, one of the board members said.

"Ah, would you mind showing us a little lower, Margie?" Harold asked sheepishly.

"Yeah, I'd mind. It's my body you're gawking at."

"Just do it, Margie," Marline said.

"Oh, alright," I unbuckled my belt and the first two buttons on my jeans. "I don't know why the church board is so interested in seeing me half-naked, when they've got those pictures to look at." I pulled my jeans just below my panty line and turned slowly. "Satisfied?"

"Yes, we are, and thank you Margie. You may fix yourself," Harold said.

"Alright, buster, maybe you can tell me what this is all about," Dad growled, "and it'd better be good."

"I'll allow Gary to do the explaining, seeing as how he was the one to discover it in the first place."

"Here, take a look at these." Gary knelt beside the table and began moving the pictures into neat rows.

"No, I don't want to look at nude pictures of my

daughter."

"But, they're not Margie." Gary paused to stare at those gathered in the room. "She's been telling the truth, and I can prove it. See," he held a magnifying glass for Dad to peer through. "The girl in the photo has a rose tattooed on her back, right there," he pointed with a pencil.

"You can see it better in this one," he moved the magnifying glass to another picture.

"Then, why is her face on that body if it isn't Margie?" Dad's eyes bobbed between the photo to Gary.

"That's easy to fake with computers. I can put your face on her body, if you want."

"No," Dad shook his head, "I don't think anyone would be interested in seeing *that*. Are you sure?" He stared at Gary a long minute.

"That this is a fake?"

Dad nodded.

"About ninety percent sure. Look, see how this girl's body is white, like she doesn't get much sun?" Gary moved the pencil across the picture as we craned our necks for a view. "Well we all know Margie's pretty dark from working outside. She wears tank tops most of the time during the summer. You can't find any tan lines across this girl's shoulders anywhere in any of the photos. Plus, see how tanned Margie's face and neck is?"

"So," Harold asked.

"Well, it changes real quick in the picture from being tanned to un-tanned right here." Gary pointed toward the neck in the picture.

"That could be caused by wearing cowboy shirts. I've got a neck like that. See?" Harold pulled his collar back.

"Yeah, but Margie doesn't."

"Hey!" I yelled as Gary reached for the front of my shirt.

"No, Gary's right. Show 'em," Marline said.

"I've punched guys for trying something like that." I glared at Gary as I undid the first few snaps on my shirt and pulled it off my shoulders. "I would have put on my bathing suit if I'd known I was gonna be on display."

"See? Constant tan line from wearing tank tops to work." Gary smiled at me and added a "Thanks" as I re-snapped my shirt.

"So, I guess the question is, where does that leave us," Harold asked with a sigh.

"I've already contacted a friend of mine in San Jose, who's pretty good at this sort of thing," Gary said, shuffling the pictures into a neat pile and stuffing them back into an envelope. "He's positive they're transposed images, and not very good ones. Someone put Gary and Margie's faces onto pornographic pictures. We're working with the Modesto Police, and have already traced the website builder to someone in Turlock."

"Where Stan State's located, and where Helen Fisher's attending," Peggy yelled from the kitchen.

"I'd have a hard time believing Helen's capable of doing something like this," Don said with a scowl.

"Well, whoever it was, we'll know more in a few days," Gary said.

"You'll let me know when you find out for sure, won't you," Barry said. "I wanna pay that person a visit."

"Na-uh," Harold said. "You're gonna let the law take care of it. You're already in enough trouble as it is. Besides," he pause to give me a weak smile, "Margie's the one whose taken the brunt of this in the first place."

"Yeah, but I owe them just the same. They kind of messed things up between me and Marline."

"Barry, things between us were messed up long before these pictures appeared on the web," Marline said. They continued arguing as he followed her outside.

"Wouldn't surprise me any if those two wound up getting married," Dad said with a snigger.

"That'd be a kick," Harold said. "Well, sorry to bust in on you folks this way, but the church sort of got involved in this briar patch, and us members of the board thought we'd better do some investigating in order to know which way to go. God bless, and maybe we'll see you tomorrow at that little girl's party."

"Yeah, maybe," I said as everyone started filing out the door.

Chapter 73

Leave it to the innocence of children to turn what could have been a morbid gathering into something joyous. Caroline's birthday party was turning into a smashing success. Mable and Chuck had agreed to play host, and have an outdoor party on the large grassy area next to the *C & M* arena. Nearly every member of the church who had children had shown up, and the pictures were soon forgotten, as squealing kids ran pell-mell, petting goats, sheep and Shetland ponies. Mom and I were kept busy herding a pack of the squealing midgets, while Dad and Harold Swaim roasted hotdogs and hamburgers on the large portable grill. Barry Swaim and Gary arrived late, with a couple of wannabe cowgirls, to relieve Marline and Angela, who were giving pony rides. To everyone's surprise, Barry abandoned the cowgirl he'd come with, and followed Marline across the lawn begging her to listen to his latest excuse for being a jerk. She blew him off right in front of Don's mother and Helen Fisher, who had perched themselves primly on a picnic bench in a shady area of the lawn.

"Wanna trade," I asked Gloria, as I corralled a gremlin from sticking his dirty hands into a bowl of potato salad.

"Not on your life." She grinned as she arranged potluck dishes on the picnic table.

The festivities began at eleven-thirty, and kept a pretty frantic pace that seemed to exhaust the parents quicker than their children. What I thought would have been the crowning event happened while Carol was busy unwrapping presents, and I presented her with the Shetland pony and tiny saddle I'd been hiding for weeks at the stables. Don acted almost as excited as his daughter and that really ticked Helen Fisher off. The look she gave me was one of pure hatred, which made me burst out laughing.

It was late in the afternoon when parents began dragging dirty, screaming children toward their automobiles. Marline decided to saddle Buster and give a barrel racing exhibition for the few remaining parents and children as the party wound down. She was quickly followed by Gloria and Angela on their horses. That was when I spied Helen Fisher and Don's mother admiring Irish over the corral fence.

"He's beautiful, isn't he," I said, slipping up behind them.

"Oh," Joanne jerked around, "I didn't hear you coming. Yes, he certainly is beautiful. What is his name?"

"That's Irish. And the Mustang in the next pen," I pointed, "is Comanche. They're two of Mable's favorites."

"Can I ride him?" Helen asked.

"Irish? Na-uh," I said, shaking my head. "They're rodeo horses, and no one around here has ridden them, except me and Gary, and I don't do it very often."

"She uses these animals in rodeos," Helen said.

"Yeah," I nodded, "I mean she doesn't ride them herself. She rents them out."

"That's so cruel!" she said.

"What's cruel?"

"Making them perform in rodeos, and abusing them that way." I couldn't help laughing, and she got all puffed up and indignant-like.

"I'm sorry, but you remind me of one of those animal-rights wackos, who carry signs and protest in front of the rodeo grounds," I said, composing myself.

"Well, I *am* concerned about animal's rights," she hissed.

"Good, so am I." I grinned at her before continuing.

"Does Irish or Comanche look underfed or abused to

you? How about Sudden Death, the bull glaring at you from that pen over there? You think he looks abused?"

"No, but..."

"Let me tell you something about rodeo animals. When we were in Prescott last summer, Mable was offered seventy-five-thousand dollars for Irish, and turned it down. She wouldn't part with any of her animals for any amount of money. You want to know why? Because, not only are they like her own children, she stands to make a small fortune off the colts they will sire. The better they are cared for, the better they will perform, and the more money she'll make. They get the best feed, vet care and grooming possible. They ride in custom-made trailers that make frequent rest and exercise stops. These animals are never abused. Are you, Irish," I added as I gave him a handful of grain.

"Well, I still think it's cruel for people to climb on their backs, and use whips and spurs to make them buck, and...and work them so hard." She raised her voice at me.

"Okay, you're entitled to your opinion. I won't try changing your mind, or argue with you. I just thought you might be interested in hearing the truth from someone who's been involved with rodeo all her life."

"Please continue, Margie," Joanne said. "I would like to hear what you have to say. I've always wondered about such things myself."

"Well, for starters, these animals only work about eight minutes a year."

"Eight minutes in a year?" Joanne's voice pitched with unbelief.

"Yeah." I nodded. "The ride's only eight seconds long. Eight minutes would mean sixty riders were able to complete their rides, and that never happens.

"Helen also mentioned spurs. Here, take a look at mine." I leaned against the fence and cocked my leg. "They're blunt and rounded on the tip, and roll freely." I gave the rowel a spin. "You probably wouldn't like me raking them down your back, because your skin's only one or two millimeters thick. But their hide's seven times thicker. Raking them is kind of like giving them a massage, or a back scratch.

"As far as what causes an animal to buck, we hook a flank strap like this one," I paused to dig inside a tack box, "around their flank area. It's kind of like putting a belt onto a human. I heard some idiot in Redding telling people that we tied the strap across their genitalia, causing them pain, and that was what made them buck. That's just not true. I mean," I gave them a crooked grin, "have you ever known any guy that could walk or run once he got whacked in the groin? When you tie this strap around any horse or bull's middle, and make it loose, it'll cause them to buck, because it feels more like a fly or gnat pestering them. If you strap it tight, they refuse to move, let alone buck.

"Look," I said, tossing the strap back into the box and closing the lid, "I'm not going to tell you that no animal ever gets hurt in a rodeo. But the last time I checked…and I do read the reports…less than one percent of all animals, including horses, bulls and calves, got hurt last year, and that report registers all injuries. It's not unusual to see a twenty-five year-old horse, or a fifteen year-old bull tossing riders around in a rodeo. Besides," I added as an afterthought, "the Professional Rodeo Cowboys Association would come down hard on anyone they caught mistreating any animal. And believe me, it wouldn't be pretty. There are a lot more safety rules protecting the animals, than for the people who ride them."

"Well, that's enlightening, and good to know," Joanne said with a grin. "You seem like a very knowledgeable young lady who's done her homework."

"Thanks, but horses and rodeo are kind of in my blood. I suspect that I'll still be doing some sort of riding, or breeding, when I'm sixty, like Mable. The same goes for those girls you see barrel-racing. You couldn't keep Marline off Buster if you tried."

"Oh, my word! Is that my Peggy on that horse?" I glanced back over my shoulder as Peggy raced Zorro past one barrel and turned toward the next.

"Looks like it. They'll probably let you ride one of them,

if you ask," I said to Helen.

"No, I'd rather ride this one," she said, rubbing Irish's muzzle.

"Like I said, Irish is not for riding. He's too skittish, and you'll only get thrown. You'd better let me saddle Cupcake, or ask one of the girls, if you want to ride."

"But you said you've ridden him."

"Yeah, I've ridden him a few times, mostly during a rodeo. But he's also the one who put me in the hospital. Ask anyone around here." I'd about had my fill of Helen Fisher, so I ended our conversation by giving her a big smile, then joined Don and the rest, who'd gathered to cheer the girls as they raced their horses around the arena. It wasn't but a matter of seconds before Joanne joined us, and gasped as Peggy made a second dash on Zorro. I figured the subject of Helen's wanting to ride Irish had ended. That is, until we heard her scream.

Chapter 74

I'd never figured myself to be a fast runner, but I was the first one to reach the pen, and bolted over the top rail. Helen Fisher was clinging to Irish's neck with both arms and screaming into his ear, which only made him run and pitch faster. I made a grab for his halter and missed as he darted past. Donald threw the gate open and the charging horse slammed into the metal with a loud crash. He fell, writhing in pain, as Helen bounced off the stable wall and hit the ground screaming. I tossed myself across Irish's neck as people flooded the pen.

"Shhh, shhh, it's alright, baby. Just hold still. It's okay," I said, securing my grip on his halter. I kept my weight pressed against his neck and caressed his head as he kicked and struggled to get upright.

"Someone shut that girl up," Mable yelled as Helen wailed like a stuck pig.

"Get back! Everyone, back away!" Chuck yelled and pushed at the people crowding to get a closer look. I glanced up as one of Irish's hooves brushed past Donnie's head.

"Get them away! Someone get the kids out of here," I yelled. Chuck gave Donnie a toss and Dad caught him in mid air as Mama pulled Caroline and several other children back through the gate.

"Careful, I think her arm is broken," I could hear Don saying, as he led Helen Fisher out of the pen. *Too bad her stupid neck isn't busted.* Mable closed the gate and I released my hold on Irish. He jumped upright and made an attempt to bolt to the opposite side of the pen, then stopped.

"He's hurt," I said, as the horse limped and hobbled around.

"Easy, Margie. Take it easy. He's still spooked," Chuck said. I took my time, keeping a safe distance and talking.

"It's okay. I only want to help you." It wasn't until Helen's set of lungs were out of hearing range that Irish would let me get close enough to check his injuries.

"It doesn't feel like anything's broken, but you'd better call the vet," I said to Mable, as I closed and latched the gate. "He's got some pretty big bumps and bruises."

"I've already made the call. What the hell happened, anyway? How did she get in there?"

"I have no idea. You'll have to ask her. Where is she, anyway? I'd like to stuff a sock into that mouth of hers," I said.

"I believe Pastor Don's mother and Marline are taking her to the emergency room. Don thinks her arm might be broken," Mama said.

"Did he go with them?"

"No, I think he's at the picnic table with the children."

"Good," I said, and picked my way past those crowded around the barbeque grill. I found him seated with Donnie and Carol, eating homemade ice cream. Grabbing a coke from the cooler, I slid in next to him and popped the tab.

"You just had to go to the horse, didn't you," he snapped before I had a chance to speak.

"Huh?"

"The horse. You thought more of the horse, than Helen. She was lying in the same pen with a broken arm, but you ran to the horse." He jumped up to glare down on me. "I guess we know what you consider more important, don't we? I can't believe you would think any animal is more valuable than a human! Come on children," he added, grabbing Donnie and Carol's hands, "we have to leave."

I stared in silence as they drove away, feeling lower than a lizard's belly.

"I can't believe my brother would say such a thing. You

didn't deserve to be treated that way," Peggy cried. "It wasn't you're fault that idiot tried riding that horse!"

I nodded, and she sat across from me, crying softly. Angela and Gloria squeezed in on either side to finish their soft drinks in silence. Something Texas Terry Walker had told me long ago kept running through my mind. *A good rider will always gather himself after he's been bucked off. The thing is, dust yerself off and fork another horse...the same one, if they'll let you. But one way or the other, ya gotta get right back on no matter how bad it hurts.*

Well, it sounded like good advice, but made me wonder if Terry had ever been kicked as hard as I just had.

Chapter 75

I had no more than opened a bag of Cheetos and cracked open a fresh coke when someone rang our doorbell. I turned on the television and let them ring several more times before Mama came from the kitchen and gave me an angry look before opening the door.

"Sorry to disturb you, Mrs. Green, but I need to speak to Margie," Joanne Carlton's voice drifted through the screened door.

"Certainly, she's in the living room watching TV."

Not now, Mama. Geez, that's all I need! I had gotten home feeling like Don had kicked the stuffing out of me, to find another rejection letter stuck inside our mailbox. This one was from Lancaster, telling me I couldn't compete in their rodeo alongside the men. I tossed it into the ever-growing stack, and set out to drown my sorrows with Coca Cola and Cheetos. What I really didn't want was company, especially Don's mother.

"Thank you. I would like to speak to the whole family, if I may." She stood just inside the door playing nervously with the purse in her hands. Mama just stood there a minute with raised eyebrows.

"Oh? I guess that would be alright. Please make yourself at home while I find my husband."

"Thank you."

Mama left through the back door, and I switched the television off as Joanne made her way to stand on the opposite side of our coffee table from where I was sitting.

"I thought you'd be at the church listening to your son speak," I said, crunching down on a Cheeto. "They're still having Saturday evening prayer meetings, aren't they?"

"Yes, but he isn't there. He asked Marline's father to conduct the service, so he could go to the hospital and take care of Helen."

"Figures. Better sit down. There's no telling how long it will take her to drag the old man inside. He has a history of not being sociable when people disturb him in the middle of a project," I said, and popped another Cheeto into my mouth. "As a matter of fact, I don't feel too sociable right now myself."

"That's understandable. I don't blame you for feeling that way one little bit."

"Your son's still at the hospital? I thought they would've let her out by now." I crunched down on another Cheeto as the old man and old lady appeared. They froze as Joanne exploded.

"No, he's at home. They released Helen a couple of hours ago. He started to come with me, but I told him I would be too ashamed to be seen with him in public, and ordered him to stay put!" She paused and motioned toward my parents. "Please, come in. I want you to hear this also. I owe Margie an apology."

"Why? You didn't do anything but treat me with respect. It's your idiot son and that hair-brained whatever-she-is that need to say they're sorry."

"Yes, I agree. And as I said, Donald would be here this minute, but I wanted him to contemplate his actions before seeing you again. But, after hearing from my daughter what he said to Margie, I feel I need to say I'm sorry for raising a stupid son. I was shocked and embarrassed that I hadn't taught him any better."

"Well, you can't go blaming yourself for how your children act when they're grown." Dad laughed. "Heck, I did my level-best to raise Margie as a lady, and look how she turned out."

"You raised a fine daughter, Mr. Green, and you should be proud of her," Joanne snapped. "She has more integrity and common sense in her little finger than my son could muster in a lifetime. Somehow, I seem to have missed that part when he was a child. I taught him to be honest and to love God. I instilled in him a hard-work ethic and gave him an excellent education. But I failed to give him common sense, the ability to understand something when it is taking place before his very eyes. I understood why, and how difficult and dangerous it must have been for Margie to throw her body on that animal. But it took Mr. Burris' explanation for my thick-headed son to understand how your daughter's quick action prevented a lot of people from being injured, and possibly saved my grandson's life. I am afraid Mr. Burris was very angry, and used language inside the hospital that caused quite an uproar.

"The bottom line is Margie did not deserve to be treated or spoken to that way. And I do hope she will find it in her heart to forgive us...all of us."

"Mrs. Carlton," I wiped my cheese-crusted fingers against my jeans before offering my hand, "I've never had bad feelings toward you for anything...ever."

"Thank you," she said, giving me a kiss on the cheek.

"Now, your son's a different matter. I'm pretty ticked-off with him right now," I said.

"That's understandable. I'm not here trying to patch up your relationship with my son. He's big enough to handle his own love-life. Although I'd like to ask as a favor, no matter how it turns out between you and Donald, please don't abandon my grandchildren. They think the world of you."

"Believe me I'd never do anything to hurt those babies. I might kill their father, but I'd never quit seeing them."

"I believe you mean that," she said with a smile.

"I do."

"Well," she heaved a deep sigh, "I must be going. I have a lot of packing to do. I will be leaving and taking Helen home in the morning."

"Helen? What about her apartment? I thought she was attending Cal State, in Turlock," I said.

"That's what she wanted everyone to believe. The truth is, she enrolled, but never bothered attending class. She doesn't know it yet, but she's returning to Bakersfield. I've already discussed it with her father."

"That woman needs some help," I said shaking my head.

"Yes, she does, but certainly not from my son."

I studied her a long minute before saying, "No, I agree with you on that one. How is she, anyway?"

"Her arm was broken. It is simply too bad she failed to break her neck, also." Dad and Mom burst out laughing.

"I'm sorry," she continued, "but that is the way I feel. It was her selfishness that caused the situation. She climbed onto that beast in an effort to prove she knew more about horses than Margie. She believed, somehow in her pea-sized brain, it would make my son love her more, and this girl less," she said, gripping my shoulder, "even after Margie had warned her against doing such a foolish thing.

"So," she smiled, "it was very nice meeting all of you." She glanced at Mom and Dad before giving me another peck on the cheek. "But especially you. Now, I have a lot to do, and would like to spend some time with my grandchildren before leaving.

"Oh," she paused with her hand on the door, "there is one thing more I had almost forgotten. In all this time you have been seeing Donald, has he ever shown you a picture of Linda?"

"No," I said, shaking my head.

"I didn't think so. I failed to find one displayed anywhere inside his home. Here," she fumbled inside her purse, "this might explain a lot." She handed me a wallet-sized photograph. "You may keep it, if you wish. I have another.

"Well, goodbye. Thank you for allowing me to unburden myself. I know it must have been an unpleasant experience, but it needed to be said." She waved, and closed the door. I took a glance at the photo in my hand, then stared, as a chill swept through my veins. I had been told it was a picture of Don's deceased wife, but I was looking at myself...or at least my twin. But I didn't have a twin sister that I knew of.

"What is it, honey," Mama asked, and I handed her the picture.

"Oh, my word!" she gasped and passed it toward the old man.

"Hey, where'd you get this taken?"

"That's not her, Harvey. That is Linda, Don's wife."

"Huh? Na..." he said, taking another look. "Yeah, I can see a little difference...but not much. Looks just like you." He passed the photo back to me.

"So," I said, blinking hard against the tears. "What do you think? Does he really love me, or is he using me to love the girl in this picture?"

"I don't honestly know, honey. Perhaps you should ask," Mama said.

"That's exactly what I intend to do," I said, scooping my handbag from the floor.

"Right now? Tonight?"

"Yes, right now." I dug around until I found the keys to the truck and bounced them in my hand.

"You sure you're okay enough to drive," Dad said, snatching the keys in mid-air.

"Yeah, I'm fine."

"Want me to go with you?"

"No, Dad. Honestly, I'm okay, and I need to do this by myself."

Lord, you'd better make room for your so-called servant who preaches in our church every Sunday. Because I'm planning to send him to you right now. I shoved the truck into gear and backed out of the driveway.

Chapter 76

The longer I drove, the angrier I got, and was in the throws of a full-blown grouch by the time I had parked in front of his house. I burst through the door without knocking to startle Peggy, who was drinking coffee at the kitchen table with her mother and Helen Fisher. Carol and Donnie dropped their toys and attached themselves to my legs with squeals, while their egg-head father stood in the middle of the living room floor stuttering.

"Margie! W-what a pleasant surprise."

"Where are they, Don," I yelled.

"Where are what?"

"These," I shoved the photograph in his face, "the pictures of Linda?" Carol and Donnie backed away whimpering, and Peggy ushered them into the kitchen.

"They're in the closet. I haven't gotten around to unpacking them, yet."

"After eleven months? You moved to Oakdale a year ago February, Don. You *haven't gotten around* to them in eleven months? Give me a break!" He stood there like a stump, so I continued.

"Go get them!"

"Margie, I…you don't understand…" He grabbed me by the shoulders and I gave him a shove.

"Don't you touch me! Not after lying to me all these months!"

"I've never lied to you."

"You certainly have. You never told me I was Linda's twin. Which is it, Don? Who do you really love? Me or Linda?" He turned ashen.

"Don't let her talk to you that way, Don! Throw her out of the house," Helen yelled.

"Oh, hush," Joanna said. "You're not involved in this, and it is none of your affair."

"It is so my affair! I'm in love with Donald, and I know he loves me too!"

"Don't flatter yourself. My son has never thought of you as more than a friend. He's never asked you on a date, that I'm aware of. You're a spoiled brat, and I doubt very much that he'll ever marry you. I wouldn't allow it or give my blessing, if he tried. The only reason I brought you here in the first place is, that I gave into your insistent begging, and thought your presence might somehow stir the kettle. I wanted to see if my son was indeed in love with this cowgirl as he claimed to be. I think I know the answer to that question," Joanna said with a snicker.

"I...I...I..." Helen stammered before turning on me like a snake. "Your horse broke my arm, and I'm going to sue you and those friends you work for! I'll...I'll...I'm going to shut those stables down!"

"You'll do no such thing. I will testify in court that I heard Miss Green tell you how dangerous that horse was, and forbid you to ride him. You disobeyed her orders the moment our backs were turned, and rode him anyway. You'll only be wasting your father's money, and making a bigger fool of yourself, if you try." She turned to smile at me and took a sip of her coffee.

"You may proceed, Margie. This is interesting."

"Get the pictures, Don," I hissed. "If you don't, I'll tear this house apart until I find them."

"Alright, just calm down. I'll get them for you." He gave me an angry glare and stomped to the end of the hall and jerked open a closet door. He returned a minute later with a pasteboard box. "They're all in there, except for a few of the larger ones. I have those stored in the top of my bedroom closet."

I knelt on the living room floor and was in the process of pulling dozens of photos from the box, when Helen jumped to her feet yelling.

"If you want to look at pictures, why not start with the ones of you and Barry Swaim?"

"That is quite enough!" Don spun and pointed an angry finger in her direction. "We have all seen those pictures, and whoever created them had better hope they are never found out."

"Created them? They were of her and…" Helen started.

"Yes, created. Gary Dickerson is quite a computer whiz, and believed from the beginning they were digital fakes. He contacted a friend of his in San Jose, who deals with this sort of thing, and he agrees they're fakes. Someone transposed images of Margie and Barry's faces onto bodies of porn actors, to give the impression they were doing those things. They are currently working with the police this very minute, tracing who posted them on the internet. Margie and her parents will likely turn their heads, hoping this will simply go away, but Barry is another story. He feels the photos helped destroy his engagement to Marline, and has already contacted a lawyer."

"But…but," Helen stuttered as her eyes darted like those of a caged animal.

"But nothing. Even if the pictures were real, they would have been taken long before Margie gave her heart to Jesus. I hoped someone like yourself, raised in church and claiming to be a Christian, would have been the first to forgive her. But instead, you've done nothing but attack and destroy her. I have never been so disappointed in anyone as I am in you."

"But…but Don. You don't understand," Helen stammered. "Everything I've done has been for us!"

"Us?" Don screwed up his face.

"Yes, us! I love you, Don." She ran to grab hold of his arm. "I've always loved you. I would do anything you want. I…I…moved here so we could be together. Everything I've done has been for us. Even the pictures were for you…!" She suddenly paled and backed away.

"The pictures?" Don followed the retreating woman

toward the hall.

Peggy and I stared at each other a few seconds before she burst out laughing and said, "Oh my God!"

"You were responsible for the pictures on the internet," Don continued yelling. "There is no way I would ever consider dating, let alone marrying, someone as bitter and hateful as you. I want you out of my house this instant, and I never want to see you again!"

"Agh!" Helen screamed and ran into the guest bedroom and slammed the door.

"Thank you, Donald. That was long overdue," Joanne said.

I sat for a long moment staring at the closed door before returning to the box. My hands were shaking so badly, I had trouble collecting the pictures.

They were a mixture of wedding photos, pictures of Linda playing with Caroline, and a fistful of her being big and pregnant. I stopped to wipe my eyes as I found one of her holding an infant Donnie as a grinning Caroline stood beside the bed in a delivery room. The pictures hidden inside the box told the story of a beautiful woman full of life, who loved her husband and children with every fiber of her being. I couldn't hate her, as I had first thought. I wasn't even the slightest jealous. I loved her, and wanted to know every detail of her life. I turned and motioned toward the children as tears ran freely down my cheeks.

"Carol, come here, baby. Bring Donnie with you. I want to show you your mommy."

"It's okay, honey. Go to Margie," Peggy said, urging them forward.

"See? That's your mommy," I said, handing each child a picture. "Isn't she beautiful? Oh, and look, Donnie! Here you are when you were a brand-new baby," I pointed at the hospital photograph, "and there's your sister smiling because she has a brother to play with. And here's Carol with chocolate cake all over her face. Isn't she funny-looking?

"You know what?" I hugged them in both arms. "Your

mommy loves you both very much. The only reason she isn't here today is, she had to go to heaven and be with Jesus. But, she wishes she could hold and kiss you both more than anything.

"Now, Margie's got to go home. But I'll bet your Grandma and Aunt Peggy will tell you a lot of stories about your mommy." I glanced at Peggy, and she took my place on the floor. She wiped her eyes against her knuckles, and began telling them about Linda. I wiped my own eyes against my palms and glared at their father.

"How could you?" My voice was barely above a whisper. "How dare you deprive those babies of knowing their mother! I don't know how you can live with yourself. I've never been so ashamed of anyone in my entire life!"

"You don't understand," he said shaking his head.

"I am literally heart-broken for those babies, thinking what lies ahead, having such a cruel and cold-hearted father. I never want to speak to you again!"

I stormed out of the house and slammed the door. I paused on the doorstep to dig a Kleenex from my handbag when I heard Joanne's voice through the closed door.

"Yes, I believe she will do just fine. Donald, if you let that girl slip away, I will disown you. You had better go after her and make things right."

I ran toward the truck as he opened the door.

"Margie, wait!" He grabbed at my arm through the opened window, but I jerked away screaming.

"Leave me alone! I never want to see you again, as long as I live!"

I sped away as neighbors poked their heads out their doors to stare.

Chapter 77

I had no more than pulled into our driveway, when I heard tires squealing as the Mustang slid around the corner. I bolted through the front door and locked it behind me. The old man and old lady stared as I tried to catch my breath.

"Want to talk about it," Dad said.

"No! He's coming! Don't let him in!" I said as a car door slammed.

"Why? What happened," Mama said.

"Nothing. Just don't let him in."

His weight thudded against our wooden porch and he jiggled the knob before pounding on the door. "Margie? I know you're in there. Open the door!"

"Go away!" I yelled.

"Come on Margie! We need to talk."

"I said go away! I never want to see you again...ever!"

"Open the door, Margie," Dad said as he eased himself out of his char and crossed the room.

"No, Dad! I don't want to see him!"

"Come on open the door before some neighbor calls the cops." He reached for the lock and I grabbed his wrist.

"Dad!"

"Margie!" He glared and I bolted into my bedroom and locked the door.

I could hear the deadbolt click and the door squeak open from where I leaned against the bedroom door.

"God, Dad...I can't believe you're doing this to me!" I

screamed and threw myself across the bed. I could hear their muffled voices in the next room.

I wanna die. Please, God, just let me die and get it over with. I know it's a plot. Don probably paid the old coot just so he can marry me and make my life miserable. Well, I'll show them. I'm gonna enter the Laughlin rodeo, and let myself get thrown and break my neck and wind up dead or in a wheelchair. Then, they'll both be sorry.

Chapter 78

It was only a matter of seconds before he began pounding on my door.

"Margie? Please open the door. We need to talk."

"I've already told you, I have nothing to say."

"And I don't care as long as you listen."

"I don't wanna hear anything you have to say, so go away!" He waited a bit before knocking again.

"Margie? Come on, quit playing games and open the door. You know you're going to have to face me sooner or later."

"No, I won't."

"I'll stand right here until you open this door. You'll have to come out sooner or later."

"You'll stand there a long time. Besides, I'm gonna start attending a different church. One whose pastor doesn't lie to its members."

"I never lied to you."

"You certainly did!" I jerked the door open to glare. "You never told me that I looked like Linda."

"I never said you didn't."

"No, but you hid the truth and that is as much as telling a lie. Isn't it, *Pastor Gardner?*"

"Oooh, calm down, now." He glared back.

"I don't have to calm down. How do you think that made me feel? Discovering that every time you held me and kissed me, you were actually holding and kissing Linda. I feel so used, and cheap and dirty!"

"I...I'm sorry. But I was never thinking of Linda when..."

"Don't!" I said, cutting him off. "Don't lie to me again!"

"Margie, if you'd only let me explain..."

"No," I slammed and locked the door, "I don't wanna hear another word out of you!"

"Quit acting like a child!" He yelled.

"Go to hell!"

Dad told me later that Don took one step backward before kicking the door just below the handle. All I knew was, my door flew open with a loud bang, as the brass latch plate bounced off the opposite wall and rattled across the dresser.

"Aaaugh!" I bolted like a cat, intending to scratch his eyes out, but he caught both my wrists in a vise-like grip.

"Ow! Ow! Stop...you're hurting me!" I yelled as he drug me to the living room.

"You are going to sit there and listen to what I have to say!" He shoved me toward the sofa.

"Aagh! I'm going to kill you!" I charged again, but he caught me by the arms and spun me back toward the sofa with a swift kick in the pants. "Ow! That hurt!" I landed head first and turned to glare.

"You..." he shook a finger in my face, "just listen to what I have to say!" His expression caused me to stay put.

"Okay," he heaved a deep breath as I folded my arms across my chest, "if you feel the same after I've finished, I promise to go away and never bother you again. Is it a deal?"

I nodded.

"Yes, you are right. You look almost identical to Linda. That's why I stood gawking the day we met, and why Donnie started calling you *mommy*. I wasn't staring because you were arguing with Barry Swaim."

I glanced at the old man as he snickered. "Sorry, but they fight all the time," he said.

"It felt like I was seeing Linda's ghost. Then, you explained to Marline what you and Barry had been arguing about, and pulled a pack of Camels and lit one up. Well, I knew for certain I wasn't seeing Linda."

"She didn't cuss or smoke," I said, blowing my nose.

"No, she never smoked. I'm not too sure about the cursing. She did call me a name once, while we were arguing. Anyway," he said, taking a deep breath, "I became curious about this pretty girl, who smoked Camels, cussed like a trail-hand, and rode bucking horses. It wasn't because you reminded me so much of Linda that I wanted to know you. It was to find out who you were. I found you interesting. Then, somewhere between seeing Linda's ghost, and finding out who you really are, I fell in love with Marjorie Ann Green. And that is the truth."

"Why didn't you tell me I reminded you of her?"

"Because you didn't," he said with a chuckle. "Linda was quiet. She didn't like large crowds. Oh, she was friendly enough, and everybody liked her. But, she would have rather stayed home than go out. She loved being with family. Hers and mine. And after she had Carol and Donnie…well, they were her life."

"Did you love her a lot?"

"Yes, I would have to say I loved her more than anything, or anyone. And there hasn't been a day since that I haven't thought of her in some way or other. I miss her. Her leaving hurt so much I wanted to die every time I felt her empty pillow, or sat drinking coffee and staring at her empty chair. That's why you didn't see her pictures. I found it easier to keep them hidden after the move. I didn't have to be reminded of her every time I looked at the nightstand, or lit the fireplace. I know now how stupid that was, and how harmful it must have been for my children. And, since you forced me to dig the box out of the closet, I'm surprised at how easy it's been to talk about her.

"What I'm trying to say is my love for Linda hasn't lessened my love for you. You might find this hard to believe, Margie, but it is possible to love two people equally as much at the same time."

"But, why didn't you at least tell me I looked like her, so I could prepare myself?"

"Because I didn't know how. I started to several times, but I couldn't find the words. I mean," he paused to squat at my knees and take both my hands, "how do you say to someone, *Did you know you look just like my dead wife? Perhaps we ought to get to know each other. We might hit it off.* I tried...but I simply didn't know how. I'm sorry...I really am. I'm praying you'll forgive me, and give me another chance to prove I really love you...separate from my love for Linda."

"Okay," I heaved a sigh, "I understand what you're saying, and I'll accept your reasons for not telling me, although it's still wrong and makes me mad. But that's not the first time you've hurt me, Don. I still haven't gotten over being rejected on the front porch." He paled as I brought that one up.

"And what about the pictures," I continued. "You believed I was guilty the same as everyone else."

"No, I never believed that was you or Barry. But I had members of the church and reporters calling both day and night...I simply didn't know what to think or say."

"You could have told me." I blew my nose. "Then, there's Helen. I really appreciate the way you stood up for me inside your house, but for months now...for months," I repeated with a hard glare, "I've felt like dirt, as you carted her around town. Give me one good reason why I should trust you enough to give you another chance."

"I'll give you two. Carol and Donnie."

"Aw, now that's not fair! Don't you dare use those babies to get at me!" I jerked my hands away from his.

"I'm not, but there is no way you can remove them from the equation. You'll have to consider them, the same as I do. You took it upon yourself to become a part of their lives, and now you want to take that away from them? That means they will lose the two most important women in their lives, excluding their grandmothers, in a relatively short amount of time. How do you think that will make them feel?"

"He's right, Margie. They do figure into it, like it or not," Dad said.

"Ooh, you are evil! Both of you!" I gritted my teeth as

the old man laughed. "Okay, *Reverend*, you win this round. I'll not only give you another chance, but wipe the slate clean, provided you'll do the same."

He nodded.

"We start from the beginning. When I ask you questions, I expect straight and complete answers. If I don't get them...you're gone. Got that?"

"Yes, and I'll expect the same from you."

"I've never held anything from you. I've always given you my best answer, Don, and I will continue doing so. But I wanna go slow. I don't like getting hurt, and you hurt me more than Barry, or anyone else did...ever. Is it a deal?" I stuck out my hand.

"Deal." He gave it a vigorous shake before giving me a quick peck on the lips. "I've got to go, but I'll call you later. Okay?"

"Okay," I said, fighting against an urge to complete the kiss. He paused to stare at my broken door.

"I'm sorry about the door, Mr. Green. I'll pay for the damage. Have whoever fixes it send the bill sent to me."

"Na, it was worth seeing how you were going to handle her. I'll fix it myself."

"Oh, there's one more thing," I said as he opened the front door.

"Yes?"

"Since we're starting at the beginning, I'm going back into rodeo."

"I didn't know you had quit." He glanced toward Mom and Dad.

"Neither did we," Mama said.

"Well, I did, mostly. You didn't notice I sat out most of last season?"

"Yes, but I took it for granted that was because you were healing from your injuries. You did compete in some rodeos," he said re-closing the door.

"I was over the injuries a long time ago. You said you didn't want a crippled-up wife, so I sort of made up my mind to quit. I didn't even register for the upcoming Pendleton Rodeo. Marline, Gloria and Angela are going, but I'd planned on sitting this one out for you. But I'm sending my entry fee to Laughlin tomorrow morning."

"Why?"

"Because we agreed to start from the beginning with a clean slate. I know what you said, but you've got to see if it's really Margie Ann you love, or if you're simply loving Linda through me. I've also got to find out if I can give up rodeo, and become Pastor Gardner's wife. Because if either of us discovers that we can't...I don't wanna take this any further. It hurts too much."

"That makes sense," he said with a thoughtful nod. "But rodeo? We're just not talking about barrel-racing, are we?"

I shook my head.

"I didn't think so. Alright, agreed." He heaved a sigh. "I'll call you later. Goodbye, Mrs. Green...Mr. Green. Sorry about disturbing your afternoon."

I peered through the corner of the drapes as he backed out of our driveway.

"Well, guess I'd better get my tools," Dad said with a chuckle.

"He certainly has a way of making an entrance, doesn't he," Mama said.

"Yeah, but they'll make it, if they don't kill each other first."

I glanced at them before turning back to watch the Mustang disappear with a mellow growl of exhaust. They didn't know what they were talking about. There wasn't any need of killing Donald Ray Gardner. He might've won round one...sort of...by kicking my backside. But there were better ways of handling him, and I believe I had discovered a good one.

Chapter 79

I slipped gloves onto both hands this time, making sure they were snug, and limped toward the Crossroads Feed & Ranch Supply chute. Dakota Storm had thrown me against the wall in Laughlin, and the scrapes and bruises on my left side had not healed as much as I would have liked. But it was April, and that meant rodeo in Oakdale. I wasn't about to pass up a chance of riding before my hometown crowd, in spite of making Don a little angry.

"I don't want you riding today, and that's final! Do you understand me?" We were standing in the living room when he raised his voice and got real close to my face.

"Don't you yell at me!" I set my lips into a thin line and glared back.

"I'm not yelling!"

"Yes you are."

"Margie, you haven't heard me yell...not yet, anyway. But what you're thinking of doing happens to be the stupidest thing you've come up with yet. You're not even healed from the last spill you took. What makes you think you can compete today?"

"Because I can, Don. Don't you understand?"

"No, I don't understand. And I forbid you to even try!"

"Ah! You forbid me? Just who do you think you are?"

"I am your husband," he shouted, tapping his chest. "We were married last June. Remember? Now, I've allowed you to continue your rodeo pursuits while I stayed home with the children, worrying about my wife, simply because I know how much it means to her. But not today. You're in so much pain you can hardly walk, let alone ride. I won't allow it, Margie. Not today," he said shaking his head. "I won't let you go."

"How are you planning to stop me?" I stomped out of the house and climbed into the truck.

"Margie, please. Why can't you just listen to reason once in your life?" He grabbed my arm through the window.

"Better let go, if you know what's good for you." I ground the starter and jammed the pickup into gear.

"Okay, I give up," he said, tossing his hands in the air. "I guess you do love rodeo more than us."

"Oh, don't even go there, and quit feeling sorry for yourself. I married you, didn't I? Besides, I won't be doing this forever."

"No, you'll break your neck long before you make it to the senior circuit," he said with a curt nod.

"You coming to watch?"

"I don't know."

"I hope you do."

"Why? So I can watch my wife get hurt again?"

"No, because I love you." I touched his cheek and smiled. "Bring Donnie and Carol too. They'll have fun."

"Like they did in Laughlin? They both screamed and cried when you were carried from the arena on a stretcher. Remember my telling you that?"

I nodded.

"Still won't listen to reason?"

"I did listen, Don. I'm just not doing what you said."

Now, after easing myself up on the railing, and staring at Crescent's back, I almost wished I had listened.

"You sure you're up to this, Margie," Chuck asked.

"Yeah, I think so." I nodded.

"You *think so*? Girl, you'd better do more than think so, before you crawl on this critter."

"No, I'm alright…really. I'm ready Chuck. Lets go," I said, and eased myself onto the saddle.

"Oooee, let's get it done, cowgirl!" Terry yelled.

Barry reached through the railing to stuff my left boot snug into the stirrup and pat my leg. "Do it, girl...ride him high."

I'd cornered both of them after drawing Crescent earlier that morning, and asked if there was anything I should know.

"He doesn't do anything in one single pattern, like most horses. He'll do one thing, then another...spin this way or do something entirely different than you expect. So, just be prepared to get surprised," Barry said.

"Yeah, that about sizes him up alright," Terry said with a nod. "Thing to remember is, he can be ridden. I stayed with him once, so have a couple of others. Not many, mind you. But a couple of us have. So, don't worry about what he might, or might not do. Just go out there and do your best and have some fun. The rest will take care of itself."

Do what I do best, and have fun. Okay, sounds like a plan. I wrapped the rope tightly around my right hand as Chad's voice broke over the speakers.

"Give your attention to the *Crossroads Feed & Ranch Supply* chute, ladies and gentlemen. You're fixing to see a hometown lady we're all familiar with, Marjorie Gardner. That's right, men. She's gone and gotten herself married since last time you had a chance to see her in this arena."

A collective "Aw" floated through the stands.

"On the brighter side, she's become a PRCA member and had a great season last year, proving she's one of the top bronc riders around. But she's got her work cut out for herself today. Because she's drawn a critter that's part wild Mustang and part cougar, by the name of Crescent. Now, Margie's been pesterin' everyone for two years to have a chance at this horse. She's got it today. Let's hope she's not sorry."

Like I really needed to hear that, Chad. How about some duct tape for your mouth? I jammed my hat down tight and gave Chuck a nod. The gate flew open and Crescent made several bounding leaps toward the center of the arena, where he went into the crescent shape that had given him his name. I had anticipated the move, and had experienced similar moves from Irish and other horses. What I hadn't expected was the way he jerked toward the right, then immediately back toward the left after hitting the ground. The move almost unseated me.

Head and neck...do what you do...have fun!

I've been told that horses don't have the ability to think and reason like a human, but I wasn't two seconds into the ride before I began thinking whoever had passed that bit of information was wrong. There wasn't anything conventional about the way Crescent acted. He ran toward the opposite side of the arena, then bucked like Irish, reared, then bucked some more. I allowed my mind to go completely blank, spurring and watching his head bob up and down. My own head and spine throbbed with pain and the wounds on my left side burned like fire.

He was kicking high now, almost doing a handstand on his front hooves. I leaned back, using his rump for support, then quickly sat upright as he came down. He charged forward and stopped with his nose toward the ground. The move would have propelled me into the gate, if I had not been leaning back and using my weight against the stirrups.

He bounded to the center and began bouncing into the air, using his arched back, twisting and turning, trying to dislodge me from the saddle. My hair had come loose from the scrunchie, and bounced wildly with the rhythm of the horse. I was suddenly being pulled from the saddle as someone yelled in my ear.

"Let go of the rope! Let go!" It was pick-up man Julio Moreno. "You did it! You're past eight seconds!"

I released the braided rope and suddenly became aware of the crowd as he dropped me to the ground. I collapsed, banging my nose against my knee. I took a deep breath before staggering to my feet and wiped my nose against my sleeve to discover it was bleeding. I grabbed my hat and waved to the crowd as Julio and Ryan Kiley tried desperately to corral Crescent.

"You alright?" Chuck asked as I reached the gate.

"Sure…never been better. Why?" The crowd erupted as Chad Nicholson announced my score. Ninety-one, only nine shy of a perfect hundred. I became engulfed by a crowd of fellow riders, patting me on the back and shouting in my ear. The score had placed me into first place, but no one seemed to care.

"Oh, my God, Chuck! I really did it! I rode Crescent!" I screamed as my senses returned.

"Hope to shout! And got a near perfect score to boot. Here," he said, handing me a handkerchief, "wipe some of that blood off your face."

Terry swept me off my feet in a bear hug and planted a kiss on my cheek.

"Hey, that's my wife you're kissing!" I glanced up to see Don at the edge of the crowd, holding Donnie and Caroline's hands.

"Well now, ya wouldn't deny an old busted-up cowboy one little kiss on the cheek, would you?"

"No, not in the least. She is something, isn't she? How are you doing, Terry," he added, shaking the cowboy's hand.

"Well, I was doing just fine, until this here woman came along and beat my score. Now, I reckon, even if I do come back tomorrow and take the first prize money, I'll be settling for second place in everyone's mind. I shore wish you'd keep her home. I've got me a wife and kids to support, and she's making it rough on us boys to keep our heads screwed on straight by being showed up by a girl."

"I tried, but she won't listen to me."

"Well, what's next? You got your eyes set on Red Bluff, also?" Terry shoved his hat to the back of his head and grinned.

"She'll be there, and probably hound us all the way to Las Vegas," Barry Swaim snorted. "By the way, that was a heck of a ride. I'm kinda wishing you'd go back to riding exhibition. You're going to be hard to beat."

"Thanks, but to answer your question, no. I leave the rest, including Las Vegas to you, gentlemen," I said with a bow. "I am hanging up my spurs."

"You're quitting," Chuck asked as they stared.

"For a little while. At least for now." I nodded.

"And when was this decision made? You were talking differently this morning." Don took me by the shoulders.

"Just awhile a go. I rode Crescent, and that's all I wanted...for now anyway. Besides, I really don't think they'd allow a pregnant woman to ride broncs anyway."

"What," Don yelled. "You're pregnant...and didn't tell me?"

"I didn't say that, Donald. What I meant was, I think it's time Carol and Donnie had a baby brother or sister."

"Oh," he stared a long minute before continuing, "you're not pregnant, then?"

"No," I said shaking my head. "I've decided it's time to add to our family. I'm pretty sure I'm not pregnant. I have a doctor's appointment in the morning, and I'll find out, one way or the other."

"What?" Don's shout was loud enough to cause Marline to stop showing off the engagement ring she'd finally accepted from Barry, and stare.

"Oh, boy!" Terry said with a grin.

"There's still a chance that you're pregnant, and you went ahead...against my wishes...and rode that horse today." He pointed a shaky finger toward the arena.

"Well...yeah a very slight chance. But I didn't get thrown, or anything. I'm fine. I think I want some ice cream," I said, taking Donnie and Caroline's hands. "How about you? What kind would you like?"

"She's fine, and she wants ice cream. What do you do with someone like that?" He turned toward the cowboys shaking his head.

"Well, I'd say go get yer ice cream. You knew she was half bobcat when you married her, and you oughta know by now, there's no changing her once she's got her mind set," Chuck said.

Yeah, I nodded my silent agreement as Terry and Barry laughed. I guess that did describe me in a way. I might be half bobcat, and there's little chance of anyone changing my mind once I've got it made up about something. But I actually felt good about my decision to give up rodeo...for the time being. I knew it was something Don wanted, and even though I had begun thinking of Donnie and Carol as my own, I really wanted to have a baby. I was fairly certain one might be on its way, but if not, I knew how to fix that also.

And yeah, giving up rodeo might be a little tough at first. But I'd already decided it was time Caroline had her own set of spurs. I just hadn't told her father yet, because I'd already given him enough to handle for one day.

"We're going for ice cream. Are you coming, Donald?" I cocked my head to one side and smiled.

THE END

About The Author

MAJOR MITCHELL is the author of five novels and two children's books. He lives with his wife, Judy, in Northern California. A member of The Western Writers of America and a frequent guest speaker at historical meetings and schools on the west coast, he has also written several songs, and takes the stage on rare occasions as a singer.

More about the author, his books and photo gallery may be found at www.majormitchell.net.

Correspondence for both authors should be addressed to:
Shalako Press
P.O. Box 371
Oakdale, CA 95361-0371

*For your reading pleasure, we invite you to
visit our Trading Post bookstore.*

Shalako Press

http://www.shalakopress.com

CPSIA information can be obtained at www.ICGtesting.com
Printed in the USA
LVOW10s1022031014

407138LV00003B/35/P